3.00x

To DEB
I cannot thar
there for us dur.
getting us our girls.
I could never thank you enough!!!

J. L.

MY BOYFRIEND IS A MONSTER

A HORRIFYINGLY ROMANTIC NOVEL

by J.h. Coates

Booktrope Editions
Seattle, WA 2015

COPYRIGHT 2013, 2015 JAMES COATES

This work is licensed under a Creative Commons Attribution-Noncommercial-No Derivative Works 3.0 Unported License.

Attribution — You must attribute the work in the manner specified by the author or licensor (but not in any way that suggests that they endorse you or your use of the work).

Noncommercial — You may not use this work for commercial purposes.

No Derivative Works — You may not alter, transform, or build upon this work.

Inquiries about additional permissions should be directed to: info@booktrope.com

Cover Design by James Kavanaugh
Edited by Maggie Dallen
Proofread by Laura Smith

Previously self-published 2013

This is a work of fiction. Names, characters, places, brands, media, and incidents are either the product of the author's imagination or are used fictitiously. Any resemblance to similarly named places or to persons living or deceased is unintentional.

PRINT ISBN 978-1-5137-0659-7
EPUB ISBN 978-1-5137-0760-0
Library of Congress Control Number: 2015920623

ACKNOWLEDGMENT TO THE FOLLOWING MUSIC:

Blue on Blue, Composed by: Burt Bacharach. Lyrics by: Hal David and Recorded by: Bobby Vinton

Twisted Nerve, Composed by: Bernard Herrmann

ACKNOWLEDGMENTS TO THE FOLLOWING:

Harry Potter, written by: J.K. Rowling.

Fifty Shades of Grey, written by: E.L. James.

Moby Dick, written by: Herman Melville.

A Tale of Two Cities, written by: Charles Dickens.

Treasure Island, written by: Robert Louis Stevenson.

And of course I had to throw Stephen King in to reference.

For my 3 Girls.
I am not perfect, but I promise
to be the best I can be for you.

"His excitement didn't wane, even when the shop keeper told him it was more of a book for children. In which Nathan replied, '*Sorry, a good book is just a good book, no matter what age it is intended for.*'"

My Boyfriend is a Monster

"*I do strongly believe in age appropriateness for books, but I stand firm with the above statement. A good book is simply a good book. Search them out, wherever they may be.*"

J.h. Coates.

Middle English Monstre, from Anglo-French,
from Latin Monstrum, from monēre, meaning to warn.

Mon•ster

Usually connotes something wrong or evil; a monster is generally morally objectionable, physically or psychologically hideous, and/or a freak of nature. It can also be applied figuratively to a person with similar characteristics like a greedy person or a person who does horrible things.

First Known Use of the word Monster: 14th Century

Merriam – Webster Dictionary

**But Monsters of all kinds have been
around since the beginning…**

CHAPTER I

1: The Beaten

SHE WAS BEATEN into unconsciousness and he was about to commit murder.

In a panic and as if surprised to be waking up at all, Lily leaned forward while trying to open her eyes. It did not take her long to figure out that she did not have the strength to open them all the way nor to keep leaning forward. So she gave up on both endeavors and let her pillow break her fall. Tilting her head slightly she noticed a white blur behind her lids, just to the right. Since the bathroom and the window were both in that direction, it led her to one of two assumptions, it was morning or the bathroom light was left on. Either way, she blamed its unwanted brightness for feeding the slow but constant pounding in the back of her head.

Lily moaned.

Hearing herself seemed to cause the throbbing in her head to accelerate. Awareness had become momentum and bits of memory presented themselves like flashcards. Which was fine, since she was in no position to have the levies break and flood into her head to drown her in conclusion.

Then I'll know the whole story.

"Yeah," she seconded with a sarcastic and throaty whisper.

Suddenly she fell quiet and trembled slightly.

Is he in bed now?

Her tongue stole whatever moisture she had left as her heart began to follow the beat of the horror playing out in her head. She slowly moved her hand to his side of the bed. He wasn't there, so she listened for clues.

Again nothing and she sighed with relief.

Then rubbing the pain in her temples she almost wished he was there to knock her out again.

And there it is, the epiphany popped in her head.

"Right," Lily said hoarsely. Rick had hit her, more than once if remembered correctly.

Trying not to think too hard, she began piecing together their argument, but she was stumped on how it had started. The only thing she could remember for certain was that he knocked her out to end it.

She rolled over, inadvertently setting off a harrowing chain reaction of pain. "OH MOTHER OF GOD!" she exclaimed with full solemnity, but it was projected no higher than a whisper. Ending with a sarcastic laugh Lily quickly segued into a painful chuckle of awareness. "Okay Lily, you don't have to move right away," she said lying still for a moment.

How long have I been out? An hour? A day? And what did we fight over this time?

"Ha, fight," she blurted with a stutter of built up phlegm. Her feeble attempts to block a punch were not the makings of ESPN's top ten.

Her back started to tingle as little sprouts of hurt decided to blossom, and as she turned her head as if she could look at them, a tight burning clamped down on her neck.

Suddenly memories rushed forward sporadically and clips of Rick throwing her against the wall, grabbing her by the hair and even choking her took center stage. Then all she could remember was everything going dim until her last thought was *I have to put the laundry in the dryer* and then her world fell into that horrifying shade of darkness.

The air around her was becoming thick as her head filled with a dizziness that spawned panic and she knew that she did not want to go unconscious again.

Calm down, she thought to herself.

But the panic was not leaving. Instead it was intensifying and she knew why. So Lily mustered all her strength and called out, "Honey? You here?"

The words tasted like poison in her mouth and the repulsion of it made her nauseous, but there was no reply. And like every other time this happened, he was gone.

Meanwhile, on a happier note, Lily achieved the ability to squint out of her left eye and finally realized that the white blur was actually the bathroom light. She attempted to recreate the miraculous achievement with her right eye to no avail. It felt like tiny weights hung from the eyelid. "Shit, something is wrong with my eye," she said and then remembered. *Of course something is wrong with my right eye, that's where he landed his left fist.*

She gazed into the room but was only able to make out obscure objects that looked foggy and muddy at best.

So she laid back and remembered some more. *I lost my balance when he clocked me in the eye and I fell and hit my head off the coffee table.* Checking the back of her head for confirmation she found a rather large bump. *He picked me up and threw me up against the wall and started choking.*

Her lips vibrated as she exhaled. "He must have put me in bed after I passed out. How sweet," she said with a heavy helping of sarcasm.

One mystery was solved.

But the bigger question of whether it was night or day was still lingering in obscurity. Lily would have to wait. And as she waited she thought, and as she thought she became disappointed, not just with the situation but with herself. "This is getting old," she said trying to overcome the cry building up. Then a single tear escaped her eye and her breath choked. "I just want to be loved," she cried and quickly followed it with a loud sniffle that turned into a laugh of self-pity. "I'm such a cliché."

Then as Lily turned herself carefully to her side she noticed that it was dark past the window. So Lily leaned out from the bed and peeked toward the alarm clock on her dresser. Trying to ignore the sharp pain in her neck she saw the fuzzy red digital lights that did not give her any clue of the time. They just sat there, like a big fat red blur.

"Probably almost time to get up anyways Lily," she coaxed as she pushed herself from the bed and found that her steps automatically stuttered. Bending over slightly for her overshirt was enough for agony to rake across her back and cause Lily to yelp before freezing statue-like. *Wonder if my health plan will cover this?*

That comment in her head reminded her of Todd and Martin, her two best friends who just happened to be her bosses. Who also just happened to bug her on a daily basis to move in with them, since best friends who happen to be bosses tend to query about bruises and scrapes and are usually privy to certain situations. And although she'd practically been living there lately, neither would call it official until all her stuff was there. *And they aren't going to let up now.*

"No. They're not going to settle for a couple of nights to let Rick cool off this time."

And there it was, she thought with a saddened smile.

That was the start of the argument. Lily had been thinking seriously about moving in with Todd and Martin, thus giving her a counterfeit sense of courage. So when Rick began yelling that she should be home with him and not with those two *fags* as he liked to call them, Lily made her thoughts known. That was the end of the yelling part of the argument and the beginning of the physical part.

Lily knew she had to tend to her wounds but also knew that she had to think fast. She had to go or stay, but if she was going, it had to be today. The thought of Todd seeing her in this condition played out in her head like a soap opera, including Todd sending Martin over with gun to rid them of the evil Rick. And since Martin actually served in the Marines and kept a gun in the store, it wasn't out of the realm of possibilities.

"Come on Lily," she half-heartedly cheered herself on. And before she knew it, her painful shuffle to self-assessment was almost done. Lily was also grateful that the bathroom light had been left on. The painful task of not having to raise her arm that would stretch her back, even if only slightly, was a pleasant and grateful surprise.

So Lily looked at herself in the mirror over the sink and could not help but question the authenticity of her eye. The purple crayon puff forming at the top of her cheek looked like something a mother would make for her kid at Halloween. Turning on the hot water Lily drenched the face cloth and started to pat her lips. Gingerly guiding it over the stale blood she cautiously caressed the large sore that bubbled from her lip. Wincing as the hot cloth touched it, Lily opened her eyes and caught it in the corner of the mirror. She stood silent and still for a moment and stared at it.

It was a bloody hand print that seemed to be waving at her from its spot beside the light switch. Lily just didn't know if it was saying goodbye or welcoming her back.

Staring at herself in the mirror and then shifting her gaze to the hand print she decided to give the reflection a smile, taking pity at the swollen face smiling back. She inhaled deeply. Ashamed at what she was about to say, she let it all out in one breath, "I don't want to see you no more."

It was time to leave, and Lily began to sob. Making her way back to the shower she used the mirror on the outside door to see the full scope of the newly painted canvas that was her back. Lily adjusted it so she could bounce the reflection off of the mirror over the sink, allowing her to get a full glimpse while she brainstormed on how she would get all of her stuff out of the apartment. Lily didn't know if her thoughts were normal, because as she looked at her red and tender flesh she was actually wondering how big of a flash drive she needed to get all her pictures off of the laptop? Then she wondered if she should just take the laptop?

"Wait," she yelled out. "They're all on my cloud storage," she explained to herself and laughed, but her laughter quickly dissipated to tears. "I don't, need a flash drive."

The weight of reality started to get heavy.

"I don't think I can do it," she confessed to the mirror with a sniffle, her reflection just looked back at her with dismay.

Either way, you have to call Todd and Martin, she thought.

"Why?" Lily asked herself.

You're supposed to work today. Do you think you can handle a full shift like this?

"No."

And they're going to want to talk.

"The talk."

The moving in with them and leaving this asshole talk?

"I know what talk."

Leave him.

"I can't," she said turning from the sink mirror and meeting herself in the shower stall mirror on the outside of the door. "I just can't."

Leave him.

Suddenly she slapped her reflection and stood in shock. Then she began to slap at the mirror repeatedly and screamed in panic, "I'M SCARED!"

She felt dizzy and swayed before catching her balance.

For years Lily had been so sure that if she left him, Rick would eventually find her and he would kill her. Or worse, take her back.

She could not go home, she had none.

Maybe we could move far away, another state. Hell, another country.

"With what money?" she asked herself. Rick controlled all of the money, she didn't even have a bank account. Every week her paycheck would automatically be deposited into his account and every night she would hand over her tips. Of course she hid some, a couple bucks here, a couple bucks there. At that rate, she'd be ready to start a new life in eight years or so.

But she'd made a lot of friends here and she shouldn't have to start over. She was getting to the point in her life that she didn't want to.

"Pills," she interrupted and made her way back over to the medicine cabinet. Opening the mirror and taking three Advil from their little plastic home, she swallowed them, then chased them with a cupped hand of water.

Ignoring the bloody hand print she took her housecoat hanging on the door and slowly attempted to slide it on, as if one wrong move would set off a bomb. But it was becoming apparent she would have made a horrible addition to the bomb squad. "Ow, ow, ow, ow and ow," she repeated until the coat was on. Slowly turning around like a victim of severe sunburn Lilly stood still for what seemed like an eternity and then smiled. "Somewhere in this big old city a real man is waiting for me. He won't lie to me. He won't hurt me or cheat on me. He's just going to love me."

It's a nice dream sweetheart.

"I'm in the mood for dreams," she said looking back at the girl in the mirror.

Lily took a deep breath and exhaled slowly. "Goodbye," she said turning the bathroom light off and closing the door, leaving her reflection to disappear into the darkness.

2: The Murderer

In the small town of Amalfi, Italy, a thunderstorm raged overhead while two Chakans fought below on rooftops.

Mikhail leapt upward through the rain that caused the already immeasurable amount of raindrops to burst into an infinite explosion in all directions. At the peak of his ascent his trench coat still strived to rise into the air while the rest of his body seemed to pause. He fully extended his right leg and growled as his piercing glowing eyes fixated on his target. "MURDERER!" Mikhail roared as he began to plummet.

A loud thud of foot connecting with a chest was shortly followed by the crackling of terra cotta shingles splitting apart as the recipient of the kick crashed into roof. Nathan quickly scrambled to his feet and wiped away the rain and debris.

Mikhail walked along the rooftop, struggling to see the one he accused of murder past the sheets of rain slamming into the clay tiles in front of him. His feet stopped at the very beginning of Nathan's destruction of the tile. The droplets were starting to weigh heavy on his lashes, so Mikhail blinked and suddenly Nathan was gone. He turned to his right, nothing. Then desperately to his left and still nothing. "Coward!" Mikhail called out and began to run, until he came to the end of the roof and then soared forward. Landing on the next roof he kept running from rooftop to rooftop, searching.

Suddenly he stopped. The wind blew past his hair letting it flicker slightly. Then a bigger gust ran past him causing his trench coat to flutter. Millions of tiny droplets erupted in chorus all around him that seemingly aided Nathan in hiding, but Mikhail knew he was here, somewhere.

Mikhail Yaroslav Sviatoslavich was almost one thousand years old, and with him he brought over one thousand years of experience. His father, Yaroslav the Wise, was a mighty Chakan warrior and his grandfather, Vladimir Sviatoslavich the Great, was even mightier. And although Mikhail wasn't as famous as his father or his father's father, he had lived to be almost a millennium for good reason. Mikhail had trained on all of his abilities all his life, garnering a superior reputation and that is why he was chosen, not his father. He was also patient and very calculating, so his next move had to be precise. Of the Five Rings, Mikhail's one enhanced Ring was speed. He also knew that Nathan was rumoured to have all Five Rings enhanced, but of how much they were enhanced differed and depended on who you asked. Besides, Nathan did not have the experience he had, Nathan had not lived for almost ten centuries and Nathan did not love her like he did.

Then Mikhail heard it. It was ever so faint but there it was and so obviously out of place.

Deciding to take a different approach, he bent his legs and leapt into the air doing an almost *a la seconde turn* ballet spin. His eyes practically beamed like a lighthouse, catching all the nearby light and reflecting it back into the night. As he spun, Mikhail was concentrating on noise rather than sight, but had hoped that his glowing eyes was enough of a distraction. And it worked, because he now had a fix on his opponent, but that meant that Nathan was closing in.

Mikhail dropped to the ground in a defensive pose, ready to face the Monster who had none of his experience nor his speed. Even still, Mikhail was almost as nervous as he was excited. "You killed her," he spoke harshly as his whole body began to twitch with anticipation. "I have come long way and I have ignored a lot of orders to bring us both to this moment," he said with a thick Ukrainian accent. His eyes feverishly sought out an image to go with the scent barrelling down on him. "My name is Mikhail Yaroslav Sviatoslavich, son of—"

"I know who you are Mikhail," Nathan interrupted.

Mikhail heard the landing twenty feet behind him and spun around.

Nathan was now approaching him. "And I really don't care."

Mikhail shifted his eyes slightly and caught a silhouette in the shadows. "Nathanial," he whispered triumphantly. "So it will be—"

But before the Ukrainian-born Monster could finish, the silhouette became a figure that was lunging, and much quicker than Mikhail had anticipated. He quickly leaned forward to help anchor himself, but it was not enough to stop him from flying backwards. He could feel the tile below him crumble as the sound of grinding clay erupted all around him.

Finally coming to a stop, Mikhail looked up projecting deadly anger. "I will kill you tonight."

But the smugness of Nathan's smile only deflected it. "You won't, but I'm sure it won't be from a lack of trying."

"I loved her," Mikhail hissed, but all he received was a twitch of Nathan's eye and a sigh that held very little concern within it. Mikhail was growing increasingly agitated. "I knew her since she was just a baby."

Nathan half attempted to muffle his laughter. "And you don't find that a tad bit creepy?"

Mikhail took a deep breath. "You did not deserve her."

"Maybe not," Nathan said lowering his hands. "But at least I don't go around dating babies. That's gross. Pedophile much?"

"You insult me," Mikhail yelled finally picking himself up. The anger in his eyes looked as if it was going to break free. "I loved her. And you killed her."

Nathan smiled. "She was sick Mikhail. And if you didn't see that, well then, you're dumber than you look."

Mikhail nodded. "You made her sick."

"No. She got the Bug. I just ended her suffering."

"She was too young to get the Bug. I spoke to her, she was not suffering, you murderer."

"She was out of her mind Mikhail. I did her and the world a favor. It was law."

"MURDERER!" Mikhail screamed with every ounce of hatred he had and leapt into the air, meeting Nathan with a roundhouse kick that was blocked. Mikhail turned midair with another kick that again was blocked. He saw Nathan kicking towards him and Mikhail planted his own foot on Nathan's to push backwards into a flip, but not before catching Nathan in the chin as a parting gift.

Nathan landed on his ass.

Mikhail landed on his feet. "I was to track you. Report back. Wait for them to come," he explained as claws slid out from under his nails. "But now I'm glad I did not."

Nathan's eyes started to almost flicker, like the ignition of a car starting. "No one is gladder than I," he stated with a grin.

Mikhail raced toward Nathan with blinding speed and dished out a series of fast forward attacks, all blocked and countered. But Mikhail could feel his speed overtaking Nathan's ability to read them. Finally his offence paid off as he caught Nathan's chin and quickly capitalized on it. Backing up slightly Mikhail blurred forward and kicked with all his might.

Nathan flew back into the darkness before he could emit a sound with his arms fully extended.

Mikhail blurred with blistering speed and passed Nathan, stopping just a few feet away from where Nathan landed. "This is one hundred percent personal."

Nathan coughed and tried to inhale as much air as he could. "Yeah, I got that."

Mikhail looked at Nathan with pity. "You know how this is going to end don't you."

"Badly," Nathan said wiping the water from his eyes.

"So you do know," Mikhail said while growing a smile.

Nathan grew a smile of his own. "I meant for you."

"No my friend. Tonight you will die."

"Jesus Mikhail, you're like a cheesy *James Bond* villain," Nathan said propping himself up onto his elbows.

"Go fuck yourself," Mikhail growled as his eyes started to glow a bright green.

"We could just talk," Nathan suggested rolling over to his side and placing his elbow on the ground so he could prop his head up with his hand. Then almost sounding sincere, "Maybe bake some cookies. Find something girly on Netflix?"

Spitting on the ground Mikhail rolled his head on his shoulders and matched Nathan's sincerity. "We could have a tea party and give each other hand jobs too."

Nathan laughed. "Whoa cowboy, let's see how good those cookies are."

"You seem really cocky for someone who is getting his ass kicked," Mikhail said and then let out a loud growl and before Nathan could even offer a smart-ass response, lunged.

Nathan impeded Mikhail's attempt to tackle him and lifted him straight into the air. "And why do you think that is Mikhail?" he yelled over the pouring rain. Then Nathan hurled Mikhail down into the rooftop as the architecture let out a loud buckling cry for help. Nathan lifted him back into the air and this time let go, sending Mikhail soaring through the storm until landing with a hard thud on a higher rooftop beside them.

Mikhail quickly scrambled to his feet and turned to see Nathan already landing on the roof. But Mikhail had no plans to wait and see what the murderous Nathan would do next, so he let out a lion-like roar before charging forward.

Thunder rolled across the sky and approaching lightening illuminated the hard rain falling on the two Monsters fighting below.

Screaming in a fit of rage, Mikhail threw punch after punch followed by swipe after swipe only to have them deflected and countered. He sped up his assault, becoming an obscured multicolor pinwheel of special effects. Mikhail did not know what was more infuriating, the fact that Nathan was blocking everything he was throwing at him or that he was now doing it so effortlessly.

Then, lightning ripped through the sky striking an old weathervane just off to the side sending an explosion of sparks to flutter in every direction.

Seeing that Nathan was distracted Mikhail seized the opportunity and thrust forward with his claws. He caught his foe's neck and watched with a gluttonous exhilaration as a long line of blood was sent free falling into the air. But his exhilaration was short lived.

Springing from Nathan's neck were tiny red veins that lassoed into the air, catching every drop of blood and retracting it back into his neck.

Watching in amazement at the incredible healing ability Mikhail suddenly felt himself soaring backwards through the air courtesy of a kick. Finally coming to a stop he felt the pole that held up the weathervane bend effortlessly as he and it both crumbled to the tiles below. Tangled up in the old rusted instrument, Mikhail jerked violently until ripping himself free and stumbling forward. Unfortunately it was right into an oncoming fist that stopped the Ukrainian dead in his tracks.

Now it was Nathan taking advantage with a devastating uppercut.

Mikhail instantly felt the slow motion feel of flying up and backwards. Then he watched in horror as Nathan barreled down on him with a speed that might have even surpassed his own.

Nathan grabbed him by the legs in mid-flight and spun Mikhail around in the opposite direction, abruptly changing his course with all the momentum of a locomotive. Nathan blurred again and was able to catch up to him. He put both of his hands firmly on Mikhail's back and slammed him into the tiled roof, causing it to explode and crater while the structure bellowed.

Mikhail cringed as his body wrapped itself in tin and wood until the cocoon finally swallowed him and the roof leaned inward.

As the roof creaked in protest from the sheer force, it suddenly burst and Mikhail dropped through the ceiling to the concrete floor below. Dust billowed around him as blood leapt ahead of his distressing moan.

Nathan dropped through the almost comical man-shaped hole in the roof and landed on his feet without a sound. He stepped back watching the water pour into the abandoned warehouse and onto the old Ukrainian. "Had enough?" Nathan asked stepping forward.

Mikhail arched himself and then sprung to his feet. "I loved her," he growled with a rabid determination and swung his claws wildly.

Nathan leaned, tilted and moved it seemed all at once, easily evading the Ukrainian's offensive attempts. And as Mikhail turned his gaze back in preparation to his next attempt, Nathan plunged his hand into Mikhail's chest. His claws found the heart pumping expeditiously and wrapped themselves around it before Mikhail even knew what was going on. Then in a blink, Nathan severed two pulmonary veins, punctured the left atrium and applied enough pressure to the right ventricle that Mikhail's heart stuttered and then began racing intermittently. Nathan let go of the heart and withdrew his hand in a wet and bloody retreat.

Mikhail kept moving forward, swinging as he fell to one knee. He quickly stood up and stepped forward but then fell back to his knee again. Awkwardly looking up at Nathan, he was not quite sure what had just happened and finally fell onto both knees, clutching his chest. He coughed and watched as more than a mouthful of blood spewed out in front of him. He tried to speak but was stifled by confusion and something that resembled pain.

Nathan dropped his arms and let his claws retract. "If you stop now, you might heal."

Mikhail looked down at the pool of blood growing in size in front of him and then at Nathan. "No, I won't."

"You're right. You probably won't," Nathan reaffirmed. "And when you said that you ignored orders to bring us to this moment. I'm assuming you are referring to Marcus. So how long does that mean I have?"

Mikhail's head bobbed a couple of times before he looked up, the anger fully returned. "I now regret it with every fibre of my being."

Nathan smiled sarcastically. "So what's that, a day? Two?"

"Fuck you!" Mikhail sprayed with an exclamation of blood.

Nathan just shook his head. "If I knew you were going to be a dick about it I would have just ripped it out."

Mikhail's head started to get heavy and he had to let it bow. "At least I know Marcus will hunt you down to the ends of the earth for what you did," he said letting his head rest.

Nathan patted him on the back and stood up. "Going on thirty years now Mikhail."

Mikhail fought to stand and with a cry of determination he succeeded. "I would go to the After as a warrior," he said fighting to keep from returning to the floor. "Not like wounded animal bleeding out on ground. And burn me, please. I do not want to come back once I am gone," he pleaded, referring to the belief that fire sealed their door to the After.

"You just wished me a horrible death and now you're asking for favors?" Nathan said and then offered him a sympathetic frown. "Plus, I don't smoke."

Mikhail gave him a perplexed grunt.

"Matches, I don't have matches," Nathan elaborated.

Patting his pocket Mikhail smiled. "Zippo," he said and took a deep labored breath. "We will continue this in the After."

Nathan drew his right hand back.

"Wait," Mikhail interrupted. "May my eyes look east when I burn, so I may say goodbye to my father. And my grandfather. And my homeland."

Nathan sighed. "Anything *else*?"

Mikhail looked into his eyes. "Say her name."

With one hand on Mikhail's shoulder Nathan drove his other into the defeated warrior's chest. The last of the bones that were intact snapped and splintered as his claws plunged forward. He again wrapped them around the slow beating heart and leaned into Mikhail. "No," he whispered and wrenched the heart out of the body, causing a suction of flesh to back up and then rush forward until exploding into the air. "But when you get to the After, you can tell her I said hello," he said as his teeth sank into Mikhail's heart. Flesh and muscles burst apart with bite after bite as the Ukrainian's eyes slowly turned to a gaze of milky white.

Mikhail thought it was fog falling over his eyes but he was actually seeing another place merge with the warehouse. In this other place it was not raining, but rather the sun was shining and the sky was blue. He was in a field and he could see nothing but untouched nature in all directions. In the warehouse the rain that poured in from the hole in the ceiling was the dominant noise. But in this other place, it was only peaceful with a faint sound of a blowing wind. Then as a cry from an eagle cried out overhead, the sound of rain started to dissipate. Mikhail turned and saw a figure walking towards him and blinked. The warehouse was fading and the After was now trembling violently to replace it. Her hand reached out and he chased to touch hers.

In the warehouse Mikhail dropped to the floor, lifeless. He had crossed the Bridge from the Now and into the After. Leaving one world and entering the next.

3: Hopefully for Good

Lily sat awkwardly on her big overstuffed comfy sofa chair realizing that it wasn't so comfy. At least not when you've just been beaten. In actuality it was downright uncomfortable, like she could have bought it from the Spanish Inquisition Furniture Outlet. The idea made her smile as she imagined people walking into the Torture Outlet, being greeted by sales monks who were all guaranteeing that this year's furniture was the most uncomfortable since the first store was open during the Inquisition. Their commercial would be playing on a wall of TV's with a well-known Cardinal offering a free torture rack with every living room set. Meanwhile hunchbacked henchman were in the back loading the delivery trucks.

The whole thing made Lily giggle and she finally began to feel relaxed.

Todd walked into the living room and looked at her with confusion. He turned toward the hallway. "Come look at this. Bitch has had the fuck beaten out of her, but here she sits, giggling and looking all goofy and shit."

Martin showed up in the living room with a box. "Do not be making the fun," he said in a thick Latino accent.

Lily started to get up. "Please let me help," she said waving someone in to help her up.

Todd stepped toward her with a steely glare. "Get your beaten ass back in that fucking chair." Then he smiled, "We got this."

Martin chuckled. "We?"

Todd's face distorted, apparently finding Martin's comment petty. "Fine. Martin's got this."

Lily was starting to feel bad. "Let me help, the sooner we get this done the sooner we can get to the store."

"The store she says," Todd laughed. "You ain't going to no store."

"Why?" Lily asked, but already knowing the answer.

Todd rolled his eyes. "It's not Halloween Lily. You can't be serving the customers looking like Quasi-fucking-modo."

Lily began to pout. "You're an ass."

"Hey," Todd continued, "if we had a tower, you could drag your lumpy bruised ass up there and bang the shit out of the bell all day long."

The whistle for the kettle went off and Martin headed for the kitchen.

"You're not very sensitive," Lily smirked.

Todd laughed. "Do it, say—**I am not an animal!**"

"That's the Elephant Man," Lily said and threw one of the big comfy chairs pillows at him.

Martin brought back a tea with him. "Here you go Lily. And you are not the Elephant Man."

She accepted it with a big heartfelt smile and then stuck her tongue out at Todd.

Todd looked at Martin and offered a scowl for not bringing him one and then turned back to Lily. "And don't you worry, Jeanette is covering the store."

Martin picked up another box with a look of surprise. "You did nothing but complain about Jeanette being left alone in the store the whole way over here."

Todd frowned and placed more of Lily's stuff on top of the box that Martin was carrying. "I know my dear, but we don't want to make Lily feel even worse. Especially when our coffee shop goes up in flames because we had to leave that halfwit on her own."

Lily laughed. "You are so mean."

"I know," Todd laughed back, "but it's because I really do hate her."

Lily took another sip. "Why? I love Jeanette."

Martin was still holding the same box as Todd kept piling things onto it. "He likes to have someone to bitch about."

"I could bitch about you," Todd suggested as he put an old looking vase on top of the box.

Lily interrupted. "That vase isn't mine, it's an antique. It was owned by Rick's great grandmother or something."

"Oh, okay," Todd said swinging his hand across the vase and sent it crashing to pieces on the floor.

Martin huffed. "Why you do that? You know Lily is going to get the blame."

Todd rolled his eyes. "Then I'll leave him a note. I *owe* you a big old anal rape, with my fist."

Shaking his head Martin flatly returned. "You are not going to leave him the note that says you are going to do the rape to his ass with your fist."

"I can leave anything I want," Todd argued with a tone of a five year old.

Lily watched as Todd and Martin began to bicker and was glad that they were there. They turned the scariest moment in her life into— well, still the scariest moment in her life, but having them there seemed to give her the strength to actually go through with it. Hopefully for good this time.

Todd picked up a picture off of the floor, he recognised it and placed it back in the middle of two other pictures of her family.

Lily did not want to be mean but coughed to get his attention. "I'll be taking those with me."

"Oh fuck, right," Todd berated himself and took all three down.

Bringing the rim of the cup to her lips, she sipped that annoyingly loud sip that was always followed by the just as annoying *Ahhh!*

Todd hated when she did that. "I am going to let that slide."

"Thank you," Lily said not hiding her joy.

Todd was already past it. "Look at this coffee table, littered with empty beer bottles. Cheap beer too. Shit, they smell the worst. And how the fuck does one person fill two ashtrays on opposite ends of the table?" Todd asked no one in particular. "What does he do, wait for one to fill up and then go lie on the other end of the couch and fill that one up?"

Lily held back her laughter, since it hurt to laugh. "I kind of like it when you get all angry."

"I'm telling you Lily, if that mother fucker was here right now, I would fuck his shit up."

Lily's laugh couldn't be held back any more. "Really?" she cried and then winced in pain.

Todd joined her. "Well, Martin would fuck his shit up."

"Okay, that I can buy," she said making herself calm down.

"Wait a minute. You saying I couldn't throw down if need be?" Todd said and started to demonstrate his type of martial arts, a type that the world had never seen.

"Martin was in the Marines and can throw down. You'd have a better chance at surviving a hoedown."

Martin walked in and stared at Todd still demonstrating his unsanctioned Todd-Fu. "Will you please stop? The poor girl has been through enough already."

Todd turned left, then right and then gave Martin a kick that hardly got off the ground. "Are we done yet?"

Martin frowned. "Yes, *I* am almost done."

Todd handed him the three pictures and then bowed. "About fucking time."

Martin's frown turned into a grimace as he walked away complaining to himself in Spanish.

Todd smiled at Lily, "How's your tea, baby?"

"Actually, pretty awful."

Todd laughed. "The man can bake the shit out of anything, can't even make a cup of instant."

Lily smiled, but inside she was getting more and more terrified. Martin was almost done and then it would be time to go.

It was as if Todd saw it on her face. "I know its way easier for me to say, but don't worry. Everything will be okay."

"I know," she said and took another sip.

Then Todd looked at some pictures with Rick and his buddies. "And who knows, maybe he won't even make it home."

"What do you mean?" Lily asked.

Martin was passing by and decided to enlighten her. "He means maybe Richard will end up dead. Naturally or act of God."

"Or diabolical plan from a master mind evil genius," Todd said with his fingertips from both hands pressed together in front of his face.

Lily and Martin looked at each other and started to laugh.

Todd started to rearrange some things on the shelves. "You can't tell me you haven't thought of it. Sitting here some nights, your phone goes off and you briefly, and I'm just saying briefly here," he said turning around with one of Rick's *I'm sorry* gifts in his hands, a little pudgy porcelain pig princess. First Todd held out the Pig Princess. "Keeping?"

Lily shook her head. "I hate all of that stuff."

Todd immediately dropped it from his hand and continued. "As I was saying. You hear the phone ring and you wonder if it's a call to tell you they have found that piece of shit dead and need you to go down to the morgue and identify the body. Maybe it's horrifyingly mangled or horribly charred."

Lily paused and then admitted with a little smile, "Maybe once."

Even Martin looked at her and raised his eyebrows.

Lily frowned. "Or twice."

Todd turned around like a bad actor in a detective movie. "Aha! You homicidal whore."

"Hey," Lily said and then pointed at him. "I thought about it. It sounds like you've planned it out."

Martin continued on with his work. "Planned it—He has sketches of different scenarios at home," he said and then started to trail off as he walked down the hall, "seriously, they could be evidence in a murder trial."

Lily let out a laugh that brought on some hurt from her injuries but she ignored it. She needed the laughs regardless at how painful they were.

Suddenly her phone rang and Lily looked at Todd with a mixture of humor and horror.

Todd looked more horrified than her until he spoke. "Holy fuck it's the morgue, the piece of shit was crushed by a falling fucking piano."

"Stop it," Lily said.

Todd turned and begged, "Can I come and see the body with you?"

Lily glared at him and then grabbed her phone. "It's Jeanette. Have you been ignoring her calls?"

"No," Todd replied immediately, "just had the ringer off."

Lily threw him her phone.

Martin came by once again. "Just one more and we can *vamonos*."

Todd threw the phone to Martin, who caught it on top of the box. "It's for you."

Martin put the box down and picked up the phone with a disappointed look directed specifically at Todd. "Hello Jeanette."

Todd ignored the look and continued with Lily. "So wouldn't that be simply super fantastic?"

Lily took another sip of her tea. "Rick getting crushed by a piano?"

"Sure, there is Rick walking down the street, whistling his *I'm going home to beat Lily* song."

Lily laughed in her tea first and then replied. "Really, it's an actual song."

"Well, mostly instrumental," Todd said as he started to whistle and re-enact. "Then out of nowhere, a fucking piano drops on his head, literally sending his head into his asshole."

"Seems befitting."

Todd was not done. "Then I come out from the building, and bend down and play, Dun-Dun-Dunn, on the keys."

Lily and Todd just laughed and laughed.

"Okay," Martin interrupted, "we can go."

Suddenly the laughing stopped and Lily just looked at them. She could not move, she couldn't even say anything.

Todd mustered a smile and then hit Martin on the arm. "Well just don't stand there, be a gentleman and go help her."

"*Si*, sorry Lily," Martin said rushing to her side where he waited for her patiently.

Lily held her breath and reached for Martin.

He helped her up gently, and then when it looked like she could carry on without him, he ran and grabbed her coat and shoes.

Lily's hands began to tremble and then she felt them being taken and covered. She looked up and saw Todd smiling at her. Not sympathetically, but as if he admired her.

"Look Hooker," Todd said taking the coat from Martin and started to help her put it on. "Now I know this is the third time."

Lily nodded nervously.

"The first time you lasted what—half the day?"

"Give or take," she said putting her second arm into her coat.

Todd zipped her up. "The second time you lasted three days."

"Sounds right," she said as her breathing grew erratic.

Todd found her eyes and started to breathe calmly until she followed the pattern. "I am not letting you come back this time."

Lily nodded again and lifted her foot to let Todd put on her shoe.

Then Todd grabbed the second shoe. "And I know that's scary, but I promise. I mean really promise you Hooker," he said finishing up the shoe and standing up while taking her hand. "You don't ever have to be afraid again."

"Okay, Pimp."

Martin finished looking around the apartment one last time. "Okay, you ready?"

Todd smiled at her. "I think we are."

"*¿Tuviste la charla?*" he asked Todd.

Todd nodded. "We had the talk."

Both men stepped out into the hall and waited just outside the door.

"Do you want a minute?" Todd asked.

"No," Lily replied immediately. She walked out and let Todd close the door behind her.

Hopefully for good.

CHAPTER II

1: A Bloodhound in Italy

IN A BACK ALLEY behind some markets and warehouses in the town of Amalfi, a rather large muscular man walked in a casual but expensive suit. He looked out of place, but he was right where he was supposed to be, just one day too late.

He was an Elemental. A powerful Monster species believed to be what humans referred to as Greek Gods. Now this particular Elemental who was walking casually in an expensive suit behind some markets in the town of Amalfi, was very powerful.

He gazed up the wall and then double checked to make sure there was no one in the vicinity before raising his hands. And as his irises turned from a dark brown to a bright yellow a line of brilliant red raced around the iris until it was a full outline. Out of nowhere an immense gust of wind flooded into the alley and lifted him to the top of the building like he was rigged to a special effect. As he came to the top he stepped off of the wind like it was an invisible elevator, crushing the old clay tiles under his feet due to his colossal size.

Then his nose twitched, beckoning him to pursue a lead that took him to an old bent weathervane. Upon closer investigation, he found blood.

Gently scraping the old rusted pole he collected enough flakes of dried blood to place on his tongue for a diagnostic test. "Chakan blood," he declared with a smile. The blood was still fresh, but it tasted very old. He knew it had to be Mikhail's, but where there was some blood, there could be more, and some of that could be Nathan's.

Merrick looked around, hoping to see or smell a different scent of blood, but all he could smell was the same scent that was on his tongue. "Stupid Ukrainian," he said quietly.

How did you think this was going to play out Mikhail? Nathan was born not with just one Ring enhanced, but with all Five Rings enhanced. You fucking moron, he thought as he stood up. "Complete and utter stupidity my Ukrainian friend."

A voice came from the other side of the building. "Agent Merrick?"

He spit the taste of Mikhail's defeat out of his mouth and dropped down on the opposite side of the building. His eyes returned to a more acceptable dark brown without a red ring around them as he circled around the building to find an older man in a long beige trench coat covering a cheap suit. "Ispettore Bianchi," Merrick assumed and offered his hand.

"Agent Merrick," the detective said accepting it.

Merrick smirked, but just slightly, as the Ispettore tried his hardest not to wince when they shook, since he liked to add just a little extra pressure to his already forceful grip.

Then from the old walkway came a younger gentlemen running in the same style of trench coat that covered an even cheaper suit. "Ispettore Bianchi, Ispettore Bianchi," the younger man called out in distress.

Inspector Bianchi excused himself with a smile from the agent and walked toward the younger man, losing the smile. "*Ciò che è esso?*" he asked a little agitated for being disrupted.

"*L'uomo che ha lasciato la città,*" the younger officer exclaimed holding up papers, claiming to have information on some young men who had recently left the area.

Understanding them completely Merrick's eyes widened, just shy of ecstatic.

Taking the papers Merrick watched Bianchi looking them over, already becoming anxious as to what they said. He moved toward them coyly and asked, "What man left the city?"

The old Inspector looked up from the papers looking a little embarrassed. "Agent Merrick this is Vice Ispettore Rossi, Vice Ispettore Rossi this is Agent Merrick."

Vice Ispettore looked up in awe and wondered how he could have missed the imposing man towering over him.

"This is Agent Merrick from Interpol, he is the one who requested the information on that list of names you were given," Bianchi revealed to the still flabbergasted Vice Ispettore.

Vice Ispettore Rossi replied like a child meeting a real life superhero, "Interpol!"

Merrick extended his hand and Rossi hesitated.

"What are you waiting for?" Bianchi asked.

Rossi turned to his superior. "He might break my hand," he said and laughed.

Bianchi did not look impressed. "Maybe he is insulted now and he break your head?"

"It was joke," Rossi defended to Bianchi and then turned to Merrick. "Really. You just so big."

"Don't worry about it," Merrick assured him. "But the men who left the city?"

Rossi still looked like a kid at Christmas and turned to Bianchi. "*Qual è l'interpol facendo qui?*" Rossi asked with excitement.

Bianchi lifted his head at Rossi and instructed, "In English, don't be rude."

"That's okay," Merrick offered.

Bianchi shook his head and gave Rossi an eyebrow raised that looked like it was spurring him to go on, in English.

"I am sorry, my English not so good. We only found one name on your list Agent Merrick. Nathan Caesar,"

Merrick could not believe it. *Cocky bastard doesn't even hide his name anymore.*

Vice Ispettore Rossi continued. "The funny thing is that we only found that by interviewing people. Apparently he was well known around town, but there is absolutely nothing on a Nathan Caesar living here."

"What do you mean?" Bianchi asked.

Rossi turned to his superior. "Well, supposedly he owned a few businesses in town, but his name was not on any of them. Even the villa he lived in was under a company name."

Bianchi thought for a moment. "And this company name?"

Rossi smiled nervously. "Which one? Each business and the villa was linked to a different company. Even the utilities were all linked to, what is the words?"

Merrick laughed. "Offshore?"

Rossi snapped his fingers. "Yes."

Bianchi shook his head. "There has to be something, what about identification?"

Rossi frowned. "Nothing with that name. Nothing that links ownership to anything to any name. Just corporations and numbered accounts that just lead us to the offshore business accounts."

Merrick thought that there had to be something. "What about flights, train tickets, credit card purchases?"

Rossi just shrugged his shoulders again. "We suspect he is gone. But we believe he had other aliases because a Nathan Caesar has not come up on anything."

"Fuck," Merrick muttered to himself. Nathan could have left by any means and then from any number of countries.

"If you no mind me asking," Rossi started and leaned in. "What does Interpol do here?"

Merrick sighed and continued with his facade, since he was really here on behalf of the Immortalis Corporation. The same corporation that hired Mikhail to track Nathan and report back, not to engage and have his ass handed to him. But for Merrick to be able to walk among the authorities without question, Merrick was an agent of Interpol. Which was easy, since the Immortalis Corporation controlled Interpol. "We believe what happened here was perpetrated by an individual we've been trying to apprehend for a very long time."

"So what did happen here?" Rossi asked while looking around.

Bianchi looked at Merrick. "There is very little evidence out here, but there is blood inside the warehouse."

"May we?" Merrick asked already starting to walk.

Nodding Bianchi followed him to the far end of the building.

Bianchi held the door open and Merrick thanked him silently with a smile and continued inside. Then before Bianchi could follow, Rossi walked right past him, smiled and added a wave to his silent thanks. Bianchi only inhaled deeply and rolled his eyes as he caught up to Merrik and Rossi standing around a large pool of blood.

Bianchi gave Merrick the rundown. "So, all the doors are unlocked, we have a large amount of blood, as you can see. We don't know how it got there," he said and then stepped clear of the blood and pointed upwards. "And we haven't figured out how that was done," Bianchi said referring to the large hole in the ceiling.

Rossi almost laughed. "It is much like the Coyote and Road Runner cartoon, it looks like a man went through it like this," he said raising his arms and legs outward.

Bianchi pulled Rossi away. "You are a cartoon."

Merrick carefully stepped around the edge of the bloody pool, looking from it to the hole in the ceiling repeatedly. "So, we have a large pool of blood down here and a large hole up there," he said looking at Bianchi. "No body, or bodies. No signs pointing to a body being removed."

"None," Bianchi collaborated.

Merrick smiled. "None down here," he said slowly tilting his head back up the hole in the ceiling.

Bianchi followed his gaze and then frowned. "You think the body was taken through the hole in the roof?"

"I don't know," Merrick said vaguely.

Bianchi looked again. "But why tear out the ceiling? Why not just go through a door?"

Because they ended up in the warehouse by coming through the roof. Nathan just used it again to add a layer of confusion for you idiots, Merrick thought as he just shrugged at Bianchi.

Bianchi called another officer over and started giving instructions as he pointed to the hole in the ceiling. He then barked at Rossi. "Get someone in here now. I want this blood analyzed."

Rossi turned around immediately and pulled out his phone.

Merrick didn't have to lean down to sniff for clues, the pool reeked of the Ukrainian. He also felt sorry for the blood worker that was going to spend weeks trying to figure out this puzzle. He doubted they ever saw Chakan blood before and knew all of the samples would eventually be considered contaminated and then scraped.

Rossi looked at the large pool and then back to Merrick. "This is a lot of blood."

Merrick nodded. "It most certainly is."

"Well, when we get the blood work back, maybe we get a lead," Bianchi said with a hopeful tone.

Merrick spotted something in the thick pool below him. Unable to find the words he gestured for the anonymous object until finally finding the word, "Pen, please."

Bianchi nodded to Rossi who reluctantly handed him what appeared to be his only pen.

Bending down Merrick dipped it into the large puddle of blood and began to twirl it as if he hooked a long piece of spaghetti. But it was not pasta. Standing up he brought it to his eyes and confirmed it was a small piece heart. He almost tasted it out of instinct, but caught himself just in time.

"What is that?" Bianchi asked while raising his head to study it with Merrick.

Obliging him, Merrick held out the pen so he could take a closer look.

Squinting, Bianchi tried to come up with an educated guess until finally he looked at Merrick and shrugged his shoulders.

Merrick replied as if letting them in on a dark secret, "A piece of the victim's heart."

Bianchi jerked back from the pen with a look of disbelief, but he saw the seriousness in Merrick's face and returned to observing the pen with a look of repulsed curiosity.

Rossi did not hear what they were saying and asked, "*Che c'e?*"

"*Un pezzo di cuore,*" Bianchi explained frankly.

"*Cuore,*" Rossi whispered becoming saddened and placed his hand across his chest.

"A psychopath," Bianchi offered, and then looked to Merrick who confirmed it with a nod.

Merrick handed the pen back to Rossi who then darted out of the warehouse, most likely in search of an evidence bag he thought and then instructed Bianchi. "I want a phone call from you personally when you get the test results back."

"You are not taking the case?" Bianchi asked staring from Merrick to the blood. "Do you think we will ever find the body that belongs to this?"

"I hope so," Merrick lied and then offered a hopeful, yet all be it fake smile. But Merrick knew exactly what happened to the body. Nathan removed and most likely ate the heart, which is just as much Chakan custom as it is necessity. The heart is not only nourishment, but it also creates what they call a Bridge, their way of leaving their current Now and getting to the After. The door is shut or the *Bridge is crossed* when the heart is pierced, at least for Chakans. Merrick always thought their ways a bit theatrical. *Not like us Elementals. We ride a fiery comet through the Cosmo's and burst's into the After among a choir of thunder and lightning.* "Because that's not pretentious at all."

Confused with Merrick's comment Bianchi turned and asked, "I'm sorry?"

Merrick looked his way and just shook his head. "Nothing, just talking to myself."

"I don't know what else to say Agent Merrick," Bianchi said stepping out of the warehouse and into the warm afternoon sun.

Rossi was running back to their direction. "Agent Merrick-Agent Merrick," he called out waving his phone. He stopped in front of them with his finger raised, seemingly out of breath. "Sorry, un minuto."

Bianchi just shook his head.

"Here is a list," Rossi started and then took another deep breath. "If Nathan Caesar left Italy, these are the flights that left the Aeroporto Internazionale di Napoli in the last 24 hours."

If he left by plane, or from that airport, Merrick wondered but thanked Rossi nonetheless.

Another officer handed Detective Bianchi a clipboard. "It says here they linked some of the businesses with a local bank," he said and then looked at Merrick. "There is money in these accounts, he will try to withdraw this, no? Then we can track the money."

Merrick knew Nathan didn't need money and that he would not be coming back for a while. He was also pretty positive that Nathan knew who Mikhail was working for. "I'll be in touch," Merrick said handing Bianchi his card. He said his goodbyes and even though he would have liked to stick around and play investigator or even take in the beautiful coastal town, he had gotten what he came for. He would report back to Marcus and hopefully be called back home.

Walking down the path, he felt the vibration of a message notification and waited until he was past the crime scene unit. Pulling out his cell phone he quietly instructed his phone to, "Read message."

"Sightings of Target. Unable to confirm. Flight to Tokyo already booked. Meet twins at the Bar High Five and they will chaperone you during your visit. Would you like to reply?"

Merrick was going to Japan.

"Fuck!" he yelled.

"I do not understand, would you like to reply?" the female voice on the phone asked again.

He looked down at his phone and had to fight every urge to throw the device into the sea, but instead he made his way to the parking lot. "Do not reply," he said and then pocketed his phone.

CHAPTER III

1: The Battered and the Beasts

WALKING OUT OF the bathroom, Lily headed down the hall and peered into the bedroom. She saw that he was still sleeping so she opened the door, but just slightly. She wanted her hoodie but didn't dare wake him. Lily just hoped that today wasn't the day a creak had made its way into the hinges. The clock on his nightstand read 5:32 am. "He'll definitely kill me for sure if he wakes up," Lily whispered.

She scoped the room and found her hoodie in the closet that had its doors wide open. "Fucker," she hissed and began to tiptoe silently through the room. Creeping closer to the closet her heart stopped as a low creek made its way up from underneath her left foot. "Shit," she murmured and stood absolutely still.

Not a grunt or a groan, not even a disruptive roll came from the bed.

With a silent sigh of relief Lily proceeded without incident until she was standing in front of her hoodie. Thinking that the quickest way to get the hoodie would to be just pull it down over the hanger, Lily began to pull. Now why she didn't just take the hanger off of the pole and remove the hoodie like an adult instead of like an eight-year-old, would be the focal point of a later debate.

Already committed she began pulling the sweater down over the arms of the hanger, creating a tension that began to build substantially. And then, in an instant the tension was gone, the hoodie just draped lifelessly in her hands. The hanger however did an energetic spin and then leapt to freedom into the air. What happened next was usually reserved for cartoons and hilarious YouTube videos.

The hanger, which now resembled more of a makeshift bow, rocketed across the room and collided into the wall with the springier bottom. It ricocheted back across the room a bit slower, but with enough momentum to reach the other side. The noise of all of this was enough to wake him and he was now sitting up against the headboard. The hanger then hit the picture frame in just the right spot for the mock painting of Hercules battling the Nemean Lion, which instead of a ferocious mythical Greek creature lunging at Hercules was replaced by a picture of a fat tabby cat, to begin wobbling.

The hanger dropped on the bed in front of him and he looked at Lily, totally unaware of the painting losing its grip above him. "Lily?" he asked.

And that is the exact time when the picture let and came down cracking him over the head with a loud wooden thump.

"Holy shit," Lily whispered in disbelief.

"LILY!" the voice came roaring from the bed as he shot up and then right back down again, holding his head with a look of confusion and anger.

Lily didn't even answer, nor did she wait for a follow up, she just walked away as if it was a crime scene. As she headed down the hall toward the kitchen she grimaced as "*Qué pasa Lily*" blasted from behind her. The Spanish from the bedroom got louder and more blasphemous as Martin yelled several times about how this was to be his day to sleep in. Seeing Todd reading his tablet she tried to look as inconspicuous as possible.

He took a sip of his coffee and the look on his face screamed instant coffee. "Good morning Lily."

"Morning," Lily said with an eager panic.

Todd looked at her and then towards the yelling. "Wouldn't know anything about the Spanish curse words coming from my bedroom would you?"

Lily frowned and slowly shook her head but her facial expression was that of a town busy body ready to burst.

"Look at you," Todd said taking another sip. "You look like Lassie wanting to tell Ruth that he caught Timmy masturbating down by the well again."

Lily could not hold it in anymore and let it out in one breath. "I found my hoodie you keep stealing—you dick—and yanked it off the hanger and it flew across the room and it bounced all the way back across the room hitting your picture and then Martin sat up and saw me but the picture fell on Martin's head because remember he was already sitting up," she said with her face beating red and took a long deep breath and exhaled, "And it was f—ing hilarious."

Todd raised his head a little and turned his ear towards the yelling coming from down the hall until it finally stopped. "He's like a little jalapeño, getting all angry and shit," he said and then suddenly adopted a look of terror.

Lily turned around and then backed up from Martin.

Todd signaled Lily to get a move on and then asked his infuriated partner, "What are you doing up sweetheart?"

Martin scoffed while gingerly touching the top of his head where the picture landed. "Because I bleed Todd. Not just from where the picture landed on my head, but I bleed from my soul. I bleed from the heart break from being up at five-thirty in the morning," he recited and then suddenly drove his index finger into the air. "When I was promised! That I could sleep in today—You do remember telling me I could sleep in today don't you Todd?"

Todd was dumping his coffee out in the sink and turning off his tablet. "It does sound familiar."

Martin nodded with a Travis Bickle frown. "Well, being up from the bleeding on the head is not sleeping in. Is it?"

Throwing his tablet into his carryall Todd frantically looked for his keys. "Well no Martin, it is not."

"No it is not," Martin repeated seemingly getting angrier. "Now—"

But Todd cut him off before he could begin. "Oh no honey, we got to go and open the store," Todd said as he gave Martin a quick kiss on the cheek and ran to the door squeezing past Lily, who was still fighting to get her other shoe on. "Hurry up, you slow ass bitch."

"I'm trying."

"Well try harder, unless you want to end up in his breakfast churro," he said heading out the door and giving no cognizance to the soldier's creed: No man left behind.

They made it down the elevator and out onto the street of an empty morning, laughing their asses off.

Todd calmed down somewhat. "That looked like a cartoon the way the hanger hit the wall and flew back to the other side."

Lily agreed and then suddenly stopped laughing. "Wait. How do you know that?"

"Because I was fucking behind you. Only I was smart enough to run when he shot out of bed like a bad batch of guacamole."

"Oh my God, was he mad," she said helping him keep his balance.

"Mad?" Todd blurted, "honey, he was pissed with a capital pee-pee. And you better hope my Hercules versus Kitty portrait is okay," he said coming to a sudden stop and looking like an epiphany hit him. "Let's get a coffee."

"Ah, we're going to open your coffee shop, like—right now," she said.

"But it's like … fifty blocks away."

"It's twelve blocks," she corrected.

Jumping up and down Todd started to whine. "And then we have to make it. Oh please-please-please. I want someone else to serve me."

"First, I make it. Second, you make me serve you."

Todd looked at her with the fakest genuine smile. "And don't you deserve this just as much as I do. Some might say more."

"Yeah, some might say that," Lily said pushing him away. "Fine," she laughed and they started to make their way down the street.

"See, that's why I love opening with you. You're much more fun than that grouchy Latino," he sang, grabbing her arm and starting to skip.

"I hope he wasn't too mad," she said and the instant thought of Martin getting mad made her eye twitch. Suddenly a cold blanket that reminded her of fainting covered her face and her chest felt like it was slowly imploding.

Todd stopped while holding her arm out and started to look her over. "What's wrong girl?"

Lily just shook her head.

It seemed that Todd didn't buy it. "If you think we would ever, ever—and honey I mean *ever*, kick you out," he said, apparently able to read Lily's mind. "Well you would be a bitch for even thinking it."

"I know, it's just that you both had to change your entire lives for me and he was so mad this morning. I guess I'm kinda freaking out a little," she said, trying to be honest.

"What!" he snapped. "Ha! I would kick you out before Martin would," he divulged and took out his phone. "I can prove it, we'll call and ask him."

Lily reached for Todd's phone. "No! He'll kill us both," she yelled and started to giggle.

Todd wrestled with Lily and got the phone close to his mouth. "Call Martin," he yelled at the screen.

The phone made a couple of little beeps and informed him, *Calling Martin.*

Lily yanked Todd's arm toward her. "Cancel call," she yelled.

A couple of more beeps and the phone informed her, *Call Canceled.*

"Dammit Lily," Todd argued as he continued to wrestle and had to turn his head to the very right to just get his lips to the side of the phone. "Phone, tell Lily to stop it."

The phone made a few more beeps and then responded. *Sorry, can you say that again?*

"Nice going Lily," Todd strained as Lily kept pushing his face away from the phone. "You made my phone stupid."

"Okay," Lily said letting up. "I believe you. You won't ever kick me out."

Breathing heavy and trying to straighten himself up, Todd pocketed his phone and cleared his throat. "That's all I was trying to say."

Continuing to walk along the barren streets, finding a coffee shop that was open this early was starting to look doubtful, even to Todd. "I don't think we are going to find a coffee shop that's open yet, Hooker."

"I think you're right, Pimp," she agreed, although not surprised since their shop wasn't even open yet.

Todd was already moving on. "Anyways, like I was saying, you should plan on an extensive stay," he chimed quite prissy. "I mean, until you meet a guy and get married. And even then I still think the two of you should stay with us. At least until you save up enough to buy your own place."

They both suddenly stopped and started to laugh.

"Just saying, if you can stay with Mom and Dad for a while," Todd interjected.

"You're the mom right."

"Hello," he said giving her his prettiest smile.

Lily rested her head on his shoulder. "Thank you Mommy. And it's been amazing lately, no midnight phone call, no two hour marathon of buzzing the intercom, no drunken idiot screaming on the street below at three am."

Tugging on her shoulder with an appalled disposition he asked, "Yeah, what the fuck was that? Like a drunken hillbilly version of Streetcar Named Abusive," he chuckled. "I mean, it's been six months, move on loser."

Lily giggled along with him and didn't want to bring how all of those silly things Todd just listed off were absolutely terrifying. So she changed the subject. "I don't think I'll be ready for Mr. Right anytime soon."

"Bitch please," he said turning to her. "You telling me you haven't eyed up any man coming into the store?"

"Nope."

"Not that David, the fireman. He's hot."

Lily shook her head. "Not interested."

"He looks like he has a huge cock," Todd said holding out his hands like he was describing the size of a fish.

Lily slapped his arm. "Can you be a little crasser?"

He ignored her. "I have. What do you inch-estimate how big he is?" Todd asked with a stereotypical lisp.

"Nice," Lily laughed.

"You like that. I think I should patent that."

A loud thundering crash rang out into the brisk morning causing Lily to jump, followed by an almost as loud yell of "HEY!" that made her jump again.

Turning nervously Todd saw that it was only a construction worker who seemed to be yelling at a co-worker. Watching her shudder he quickly put his arm around her and yelled back at the workers. "Little early to be yelling isn't it fellas?"

"Fuck you," a voice yelled back automatically.

"Fuck you too!" Todd replied heatedly.

"Who's yelling now asshole," the voice called back pursued by the laughter of co-workers.

Gently squeezing her he guided her onwards, "Just a big old dumb construction worker."

"Okay," she said taking a deep breath.

"Do you need to stop?"

Lily offered him a half smile. "I'm okay. Really."

As they journeyed farther away from home and getting that much closer to making their own cup of coffee, Lily thought she recognized someone. "Is that Ms. Johnson?" she wondered aloud and placed her hand just above her eyes to get a better look.

Squinting, Todd saw that it was. "What the hell is that old bitch doing up this early in the morning?"

Ms. Johnson seemed to be going through some papers while she stood at the front doors of the apartment building she owned. Her husband had bought the building over forty years ago with some mid-size lottery money. When he died some years back, Florida Johnson just kept on running it herself. Being in a favorable area and turning a bunch of small apartments into a few extra large ones, attracted a lot of people with money and it turned into a sizeable retirement income. She was also a regular at Sips, frequenting the coffee shop enough throughout the day to stay current on all of the tabloid gossip and local juicy stuff.

Lily yelled out. "Hello Ms. Johnson."

Perking up, Florida looked around and caught Lily and Todd walking up the street. "Lily," she said cheerfully giving them a wave. "Hello Todd," she said matching the cheeriness.

"Wonderful day isn't it?" Todd asked.

Florida chuckled until they got within normal talking distance. "I don't think the day has even started."

"What are you doing up this early?" Lily inquired.

"Have to show the apartment."

Todd's face sprouted envy. "The big one on top?"

"Mm-hmm. And they are looking for something immediately."

"It's a bit early to look at apartments," Lily said.

Trying to put her papers in order Florida agreed. "A bit early for a lot of things."

A police car flew down the street causing Florida and Lily to take notice.

Todd however, was still looking up at the building. "The one for five grand plus utilities?"

"Todd!" Lily said smacking his arm for being rude.

"What? It's listed," he said.

Florida just laughed. "That's the one."

Whistling, he looked up at the building again. "Single, family, what's the scoop?"

"Todd," Lily blurted with surprise at his unbridled tenacity and slapped him again.

Florida was not surprised. "Single, business owner. Of what I do not know, but sounded very gentleman-like," she said, smiling slyly at Lily.

"Yeah, gentleman-like," Todd agreed raising his eyebrows to make fun of her.

Lily started to get embarrassed. "That's nice."

"Please, girl," Florida said with an inquiring tone. "How long has it been?"

Todd answered for her like a tattling child. "Oh it has been a long time."

"Mm-hmm. Although I don't think he means what I meant," Florida said looking Todd over. "Little pervert."

Todd just laughed.

Then the older lady reminded her. "We women have needs Lily."

"Yeah," Todd said holding his finger and thumb together to make a circle. He then took his other hand and using its finger he made it go in and out of the circle.

Florida frowned and shook her head. "I meant companionship."

"I thought that was companionship," he said still running his finger in and out of the circle.

Lily tried to hide her giggle. "You're an idiot."

"What is wrong with you, Todd Jacobson?" Florida asked with a disappointed gaze.

He just shrugged, finally taking notice of another police car flying down the street with its lights silently flashing. "What the fuck is going on?"

"Probably has to do with that murder that took place last night," Florida said shaking her head.

"Murder?" Lily asked, watching the squad car speed down the street.

"Mm-hmm, another young man," Florida said sorrowfully. "And this one happened a little too close to home if you know what I mean."

Todd turned to Lily. "I heard the first one looked like something ate him," he said running his finger down her face and giving her a creepy constipated stare.

"Ew," she said, pushing his hand away.

"Ripped his heart out and ate the whole thing," he said trying to touch her face again with the same finger.

Lily slapped it away. "If it was ripped out and eaten, how would you know?"

Todd thought for a moment. "Internet."

Florida changed the subject. "Anyway, I will do a bit of reconnaissance on the single wealthy man this morning and be down for my tea with a full report," she said taking her keys out of her purse.

"Okay Ms. Johnson," Lily said smiling.

In his snotty tattle-tale voice, Todd said, "Bye, Ms. Johnson."

"You have my tea ready," Florida called out from behind them.

"I will," Lily replied with a wave, then she and Todd continued on their way.

Todd turned to Lily. "Your luck, the single wealthy man Ms. Johnson tries to hook you up with will turn out to be the monster eating Chicago."

2: The New Tenant

Nathan watched as the man and woman who were talking to his morning appointment disappeared down the street and then turned his gaze to Florida. He waited and watched as she looked around, most likely for him.

A moan floated up from the ground.

Nathan looked down. "I'm afraid we'll have to pick this up in a little bit my friend," he said promptly bending down and delivering a quick but sufficient punch to the man's head. The body slumped back to the concrete and Nathan used his foot to sweep the arm back under some garbage. He straightened himself up and then walked out towards Florida. "Mrs. Johnson?" he called out in the form of a question, already knowing who she was.

Spinning around a little startled, Florida looked him over and then smiled. "So you're my morning appointment," she declared with hospitality.

"Yes, ma'am, I am," he said offering her his hand and then stopped when he noticed blood on his knuckles.

"Well then..." she started until she became distracted and seemed to gaze at him. "You got a little smear or something on the side of your mouth," she began and finished by rubbing her own cheek in the hopes that he would mimic her.

Another police car flew by with its sirens on and Florida turned automatically to watch.

Nathan blurred his hand across his face and the smear on both his cheek and knuckles were gone. *A little amateurish don't you think Nathan?* He then offered his newly cleaned hand as Florida turned back around. "Caesar. Nathan Caesar, but please call me Nathan."

"I'm sorry," Florida offered taking his hand. "Damn police have been going up and down this street all morning. Probably found another body."

"What is this city coming to?"

"Amen," Florida agreed. "Well anyways, let's take a look at the apartment."

"Shall we," Nathan said holding out his hand for Florida to lead the way.

They entered the building through two sets of security doors, past the mailboxes and down the hall to the dark wooden stairs.

They only made it up a couple of flights when Florida had to stop and catch her breath. "No elevator," she said breathing a little heavy. "But you're a strapping young man, this should be no problem for you."

"Not at all Mrs. Johnson," he said patiently waiting.

"Ms. Johnson, honey, Max passed away years ago, bless him. And you can call me Florida," she said and started slowly start her ascent again.

Reaching the top Florida was definitely out of breath and once again declared a time out. "My Lord, you had better be taking this place. If I have to walk up these stairs one more time to show it, I might be going down in a gurney," she said almost mournfully. "Those boys will be earning their paycheck, yes sir," she snickered as she made her way to the door and began to unlock it. "Put on a little weight these past few years," Florida said opening the door and letting Nathan go in first.

Walking into the huge open apartment Nathan stood impressed. He could tell the floors were hardwood and not just camouflaged to look that way. The openness was immense, it had a small bar to the left and to the right a tiny one-wall kitchen with a freestanding breakfast nook. The rest of the area was vast and surrounded by windows. "It's wonderful," he admitted. "The online pictures were nice, but they do not do it proper justice," he said walking in a little deeper.

"Mm-hmm, now I know the rent is a little high, but it's a nice clean building in a nice clean neighborhood."

"It's perfect."

Florida pointed to the wraparound staircase. "Over here is the stairs to the bedroom, but I'll wait right here. Done enough climbing already today."

Walking up the circular stairs, Nathan was pleasantly surprised to see it was large and just as open. The entire back window practically took up the entire wall. "I love it," he said picturing his things in different spots.

Then from downstairs Florida called up, "No closets up there. This was the first and last apartment I let my son renovate. And everything you see here now, was redone by professionals. After I saw what he did to this place I thought for sure the testing we had done on him when he was a boy was wrong."

Nathan let a laugh escape and called down, "Nothing an armoire and a few cabinets can't fix."

Florida agreed. "Yes sir, absolutely. My son would look at me like I was from another planet if I said to put it in an armoire— What's an armoire, Ma?"

Coming down the stairs he stepped off the last step and decided,
"I'll take it."

"Oh, my feet thank you. My lungs thank you and I'm pretty sure
this old heart thanks you."

Nathan took one more look around and smiled. "It's perfect," he
said reaching into his coat pocket and producing a check. "And it's
only a few blocks from my store."

"Store?' Florida asked looking intrigued.

"Yes ma'am, I'm actually opening a bookstore."

"Bookstore, huh?"

"I have deliveries of books coming all this month. Even have my
brothers coming down with some more delicate first editions."

"First editions, that's the original print of a book?"

"That's right, they can be quite sought after."

"How sought after?" she asked playfully.

Nathan thought for a moment. "I sold a first edition of Harry
Potter and the Philosopher's Stone to a very nice woman in Italy for
ninety thousand lira."

Florida jerked in disbelief. "Dear Lord."

Nathan laughed. "It's only about fifty-thousand American."

"For a book?"

Nathan smiled. "Like I said, they can be quite sought after."

"Nice young attractive man like you. Successful business, now a
very nice apartment. Some of that Harry Potter money," she said
patting her pocket holding the check. "What about a wife?"

"Nope, just me."

"Not even a girlfriend?"

"No girlfriend."

"Might have to try and set you up Mr. just Nathan," Florida laughed.

"Well, please be gentle," Nathan jokingly pleaded as he wondered
just how grateful would that person really be once they learnt that
they were set up with a real life Monster.

"Come on downstairs and we'll start the paperwork, get you a
mailbox key and security code for the doors."

"All right, sounds great," he said holding the door open.

After finishing up with Ms. Johnson, Nathan left his new building
and headed back to the alley where he saw that the garbage he had
left the body under was interrupted.

"Shit," he said lifting some bags and cardboard to only see that the body was gone. He blurred in every direction, ripping cardboard and garbage bags out of the way until he finally conceded. Nathan looked down both ends of the alley, breathing heavy while his eyes started to beam an emerald blue. "Fuck," he murmured as his fangs punctured the air. "This is not good."

CHAPTER IV

1: ~~Bumps~~ Screams in the Night

LILY AND JEANETTE walked down the street that was once lit by the sun, but now they were fenced in by the darkness that crept into the city while they were in the movie theater. Their only light came from some dimly lit lamp posts overhead.

Lily hadn't liked Jeanette when she'd first started working at Sips, but Jeanette's ability to get under Todd's skin, even when she deliberately tried not to, made it fun. Plus she was a hard worker and with five kids, she never missed a shift. Within weeks Lily went from disliking her to making a loyal and sweet friend. "That was a horrible movie," Lily said, blaming Jeanette since she picked it. "We should have just gone straight to the party."

Jeanette laughed. "Yeah it really was. But the guy was hot."

Suddenly as if that was his cue, a very attractive man in a suit without a tie bumped into Lily.

"I'm so sorry," the man said and offered her a smile.

Lily returned it shyly.

Just as he was about to say something, a bang rang out from the same direction he came from and they all jumped and turned towards it.

Lily noticed his expression had become almost panicked as his eyes frantically scoured the street and buildings on both sides.

Finally he turned back to Lily and Jeanette. "I'd love to stay and try to be charming and witty, but maybe some other time," he offered, seemingly in a hurry. Then he turned around. "If a good looking chap comes by here looking for my description. Tell him I went that way would you?" the hot stranger said pointing in an opposite direction. "He's a friend of mine and I'm having a little fun."

Lily and Jeanette both agreed.

"Goodnight ladies," he said and took off heading towards the main street.

As they both stood a little confused Jeanette sighed. "That guy was way hotter than the one in the movie,"

Lily gave it a little thought and then elaborated. "Kind of looked like a buff James Franco."

The man was now almost a block away but turned around and smiled at Lily, as if he had heard her compliment. Lily knew it had to be a coincidence.

Jeanette seemed to be having her own thoughts as she watched him. "Fuck Lily, you're such a cockblock."

Lily turned to her aghast and amused. "How am I a cockblock?"

"Because you're here. If you weren't he'd be dragging me down that alley there and bending me over a garbage can."

Lily now looked at her with humorous astonishment. "Oh my God Jeanette. A little worked up are we?"

"I'm sorry," she apologized, "I haven't had any in a really long time. Five kids will do that."

Lily laughed. "Are you looking for kid number six?"

"Hey," she started with a sly smile, "I'm just looking for a little something-something, you know?"

Lily slapped her arm. "Isn't that how kid number five happened?"

Jeanette stopped as Lily kept walking. "That's how all my kids happened," she laughed and began to catch up. "And I gave them names. I don't just walk around yelling at numbers you asshole."

Suddenly from behind them, a loud scream rang out into the night causing both of them to turn around and stare silently.

Jeanette backed up into Lily. "What the fuck was that? Do you think it was that guy?"

"I don't know, but I think we should get going."

"I fucking agree," Jeanette said grabbing Lily's arm and pulling her toward their previous course.

"Wait," Lily said coming to a stop and causing Jeanette to jerk backwards. "Maybe we should call someone."

"Okay," Jeanette agreed and began tugging on her again. "When we get to the party."

"But what if they need help?"

Then as an argument that would resemble a cheesy 80s slasher film was about to break out, three men appeared from the alley.

One screamed again as the other two tried to touch his hair.

The scream wasn't the same, Lily thought, *or was it?*

The man with the hands-off hair then yelled at his two friends who just laughed as they continued down the street.

Lily and Jeanette watched them walk away for a bit and then turned to each other.

Jeanette started to laugh nervously. "Are you shitting me?"

Lily looked back. "I'm not sure the scream from before was them."

"I have an idea," Jeanette said getting overly sarcastic. "Let's walk down these dark alleys and see if we can find where the scream came from."

As they turned around they walked right into a second attractive man.

"Careful," the new man said grabbing Lily by the arm and helping her keep her balance.

As she straightened herself up she took one look at him and immediately introduced herself. "Hi, I'm Lily."

"Smooth," Jeanette sarcastically mumbled.

He laughed. "Hi, my name is Nathan and I'm so sorry."

"That's okay," Lily said almost spellbound. "Seems to be happening a lot this evening."

Nathan looked puzzled. "I'm sorry?"

"No," Lily said trying to piece the puzzle together for him. "I just literally bumped into another gentlemen, like two minutes ago."

"Yeah," Jeanette agreed. "Men just bumping into damsels in distress all over the place."

Nathan smiled. "Well, on behalf of men everywhere, sorry."

Wait," Lily stated. "Are you looking for a friend of yours?"

Nathan nodded. "In fact I am."

Lily wanted to take a time out and just look at the new stranger. Something was different about him and she couldn't put her finger on it. He was gorgeous, but it went much deeper than just that.

"Was there more," he asked as if he was expecting a bit more from her.

Lily shook her head. "Yes right. He wanted us to tell you he went that way," she said pointing right. "But he went that way," she tattled pointing behind them. *Wow, we totally narced for this guy.*

"I thank you ladies," Nathan said and looked like he leaned in swiftly and took a quick sniff of Lily's neck. "I'm sorry, you smell really nice."

Lily felt at least fifteen years fall off of her intellect and she was suddenly a giggling teen mess. "Thank you."

The scream filled the night again, but this time it was more distant.

Lily watched as the new stranger turned around towards the scream and then back up seemingly to shield her. At least that's what it looked like and that was what it would look like when she replayed it in her head. "We heard it earlier, we were going to call someone," Lily explained and then saw a bright blueish light coming from in front of the stranger. *Wow he must have a bright screen on his phone.*

Nathan turned around with no blueish light to be seen. "I'll check it out when I go get my friend," he said to the both of them and then looked directly at Lily. "And thank *you* for snitching."

"I know," Lily grimaced. "I would not do well as a spy at all."

Jeanette bit her bottom lip. "I would have made him interrogate me," she said as both Lily and Nathan turned and looked at her. "Did I say that out loud?"

Nathan just snickered a little and continued with Lily. "No-No. My friend will get a big kick out of it when I finally catch him."

"Up to," Lily said thinking he missed a couple of words in his comment.

"I'm sorry?" Nathan asked.

"You said catch him. You mean catch up to him. The other way sounds like you're chasing him to beat him up or something," Lily said and wished that she didn't.

Nathan just grinned. "Or something."

Jeanette coughed, obviously trying to get Lily's attention. "The party, Lily."

Lily turned to her, apparently still a teenager. "What?"

"We have to go to that party," Jeanette reminded her. "But maybe our new friend would like to come?"

Lily's eyes widened in terror as she stared at Jeanette with a look of sarcastic wonderment. "Really."

"I would love to," Nathan said. "Unfortunately I really do have to catch up to my friend."

Lily felt an entire mountain of relief slide off of her back. She wasn't sure if she was ready to flirt with a man all night and she really did not want to put it to the test, not just yet.

Nathan smiled and then looked at Jeanette. "Plus, you really shouldn't just go around inviting strangers to your home," Nathan started as his own smile grew. "I could be the serial killer everyone is talking about."

Lily turned to Nathan. "Yes! Thank you," she said and then stopped short of looking back at Jeanette and asked. "But you're not, right?"

"But I'm not," he assured her.

Lily turned teen instantly. "I believe you."

"But maybe I'm a monster with glowing eyes and fangs," he said letting his grin linger.

Jeanette laughed. "You mean a vampire."

"Don't be silly," he said to Jeanette. "There is no such thing as vampires."

Lily just couldn't help herself. "If you're ever in the neighborhood, we work at Sips—"

"I've passed it a few times," Nathan interrupted. "I've been meaning to go in."

Jeanette added, "Lily is actually the residential tea master."

"Is she," Nathan said smiling. "That's perfect, because my kind have actually been known to kill for a good cup of tea."

"Your kind?" Lily asked coming out of her dream like state.

"Yes, tea lovers. We love tea," he said almost automated.

"That's really a weird thing to say," she said as if it was a thought to herself.

Nathan agreed. "It really was wasn't it?"

But he was too charming to hold any level of grudge. "Tea lovers would kill for tea?"

"Well," he started while thinking at the same time. "It'd have to be really good tea, but yes."

"That is some hardcore tea aficionados," Lily laughed.

Then with a straight face Nathan confirmed. "Oh we really are."

They both laughed until the scream rang out again.

Nathan just casually looked over his shoulder. "You ladies should get going. May I walk you to your party?"

"We're just over there," Lily pointed disappointedly.

"Well then," Nathan said with a nod. "Until high tea," he finished, but as he started on his way he quickly turned back catching Lily by the eyes and offered her a large honest bashful smile. "Ladies," he signed off with and started to lightly jog away.

Lily wasn't trying to be mean when she tuned Jeanette out as they began making their way to the party again. She even nodded and offered an agreeing Mm-hmm to not be rude, but the stranger had awakened something in her. *Shit, I didn't even get his name.*

"So do you think he will?" Jeanette asked.

Lily shook the distraction out of her head. "Sorry?"

"Do you think he'll come to the store?" Jeanette asked like it wasn't the first time.

"I don't know," Lily answered, but she hoped and inside she was making that *hope so* a priority over all others. Lily had not thought about being with another man never mind dating one. Sure, she noticed an attractive man when he walked into the store or passed her on the street, but that's as far as her imagination had let her get. Suddenly her imagination was erupting with thoughts and scenarios about things she probably shouldn't be thinking of right now as her and Jeanette made it to the building doors.

2: Run Boy Run

Nathan kept looking behind him and waited until they weren't looking before slipping into the shadows. He saw them look back and was pleased that Lily looked disappointed. He would have liked to continue the conversation if that scent of blood that he was following didn't start to fade. Then as he saw that they entered the building he was off, blurring through the shadows.

He had been chasing this Monster all night and was sure that when he caught him he would get the answers he needed. But this one was quick, a lot quicker than this type of Monster should be.

Nathan knew something was going on in the city and that he was wasting time talking with baristas and flirting with tea masters. But if this Monster was the type that Nathan thought it was, there were more around, a lot more and nesting like cockroaches.

Racing down an alley he stopped halfway and sniffed the air, letting the slight glow in his eyes follow his nose. Then he blurred another thirty feet to a dumpster that was sheltering a half dead body.

The almost dead man looked up. "Monster—Fangs with the eyes—It hurts so much, please," the homeless man cried, seemingly trying to brace his entire torso so his insides would not fall out.

Nathan didn't need heightened senses to hear the blood squirting between the man's fingers or to see the man's innards barely being held back by dirty hands. "Guess I should have knocked you out a bit harder the other day."

The man on the ground looked up and recognized who he was talking to and started to hyperventilate. "You!"

Nathan bent down. "Sorry old timer," he said and with a celery-like crunch Nathan had twisted the man's head on an angle and severed the spinal cord.

The homeless man slumped over letting his hands drop to his side, which in turn let his insides slide out and spill over his lap.

Nathan heard the hurried sound of footsteps fleeing from behind him. He spun around with his eyes glowing and saw the Monster he had been chasing all night running away. *Must have thought he lost me,* Nathan thought and blurred after him.

Nathan was quicker and catching up, as he watched the Monster turn down another alley he knew he would be on him in just a ...

Nathan stood in the alley where the man had turned down, but he was gone. "Dammit," he cursed to himself and then heard the clang of metal fire escapes being climbed. He looked up and the Monster was making his way up the building. "Son of a bitch," Nathan said and leapt to a ledge and then again across the alley to another building. He criss-crossed from building to building gaining height each time and catching up to the Monster who was only using the fire escape.

As Nathan leapt from the opposite building to put himself on the same platform, he saw his intended target stop and slam his foot onto the metal. Hearing a loud clang he then heard the sound of steel letting go of brick and the whole platform that he was supposed to land on was falling to the ground underneath him. "Fuck!" Nathan cried as his hands extended to grab onto something. Anything.

Nathan howled through his clenched teeth as his side caught the jagged railing and tore his flesh open. Reaching for another railing he was able to grab it just long enough for him to dislocate his arm. Letting go his face pressed and dragged down the brick until a smack from a concrete ledge pushed his head away, putting him into a somersault. Nathan stopped the spinning by kicking away from the building, but right over a hand railing that he hit directly with his chest and snapped his sternum. It held him for only a partial second and buckled inward, dumping him towards the ground where his left knee caught the dumpster in the alley and shattered. Automatically clenching the knee he shifted his weight and it caused him to fall from the dumpster to the dirty alley floor.

As he landed with a loud thud he felt all the air in his lungs being sucked out as everything went foggy. He could only endure, painfully waiting for his Healing Ring to do its work as he suddenly heard something big falling onto another dumpster, just down the alley from him. Nathan blinked rapidly to focus as the bones in his body started snapping back into place.

He fucking fell too, Nathan said to himself, seeing a body fall from the other dumpster to the ground and lurching its way towards a main street.

Nathan got to his hands and knees, reeling from the pain he pushed himself up, yelping in pain. *Must have been a really bad fall.* He looked ahead and saw that the Monster had made it across the street and into the next alley. Worrying that he was about to lose him again Nathan took a deep breath and then heard a loud snap internally putting his sternum back to one piece. Staggering to his feet Nathan's eyes ignited and he was blurring down the alley towards the busy street.

Milliseconds from the busy lit up sidewalks, Nathan leapt into the air. He straightened himself until he was spiraling in an arch over an unsuspecting woman crossing the street on her phone.

"I don't care, I just told him I had to work early in the morning," the woman said looking like she felt something above her and looked up to an empty night sky.

Nathan soared into the alley with a tuck and roll back on to his feet. He was far enough in that no one saw him and he let his fangs violently puncture through his gums. His blue glowing eyes searched for the Monster that he had been chasing all night. The city made it very hard to pick out smells but he believed he found the one he was looking for and ran towards it, then stopped. Catching it out of the corner of his eye he looked down the alley to his right and saw the Monster running in a different direction from the scent. Then he heard clanging and looked up, only to see what looked like the same Monster. "What the fuck?" Nathan asked, but he quickly figured it out. Like he feared, there were a bunch of them and they had been using each other to throw him off. This is why I've been having so much trouble finding this prick tonight, he thought letting a low vibrating growl escape. "Because he happens to be them," he whispered and went with his first instinct, blurring straight ahead.

His target had ducked and weaved through a seemingly endless maze of alleyways to the empty streets in an industrial area. The Monster ran out onto a main street looking like he tripped, but recovered and ducked into another alley.

"Got you," Nathan said as he crossed the main street and into the alley, going head on towards an oncoming manhole cover. The round disc of iron and concrete whirled towards him as he grabbed it like a frisbee and spun around ready to release it, but there was no one to throw it at. He tried and listened for any clue but again, there was nothing. *What the hell?*

He sniffed the air, but it was too confusing. Nathan looked up and blurred to the first few connecting alleys but found nothing. "Shit," he said and finally dropped the manhole cover.

CHAPTER V

1: Oh Brothers Where Art Thou

A COUPLE OF DAYS LATER and in the early morning, halfway across the city an old cube van was creeping down the street. Inside Louis sat in the passenger seat rocking back and forth while fidgeting with the seatbelt and Bo, who was a monster of a man, kept both hands on ten and two driving very meticulously.

The behemoth behind the wheel read the street signs at the intersection and then turned to his brother. "I think we're getting close."

"Thank da Christ," Louis said in his deep Cajun accent.

"Sure are a lot of books," Bo said referring to the cargo.

It was true, the van was stuffed with Nathan's books that were handpicked and put into special climate controlled storage on top of the extra individual care. Less valuable books were being delivered by regular delivery services, but these rare treasures were being hand delivered by his two brothers. Two brothers that were adopted into Nathan's family well before Nathan was even born, so they didn't feel adopted to him at all.

Already amused with his reply Louis started to chuckle. "Too bad not a pop-up book in da lot."

The giant in the driver's seat took a deep breath and exhaled trying to manage his anger. "You sure are funny, Louis. Yes sir, funny-funny-funny."

The Cajun began to laugh. "You know I joke Bo-Bo"

Bo quickly changed the subject. "So you think Nate is here for good?"

"Here is a hoping," Louis said and then remembered, "and you don't be bringing up da Italy thing neither."

Bo rolled his eyes. "I know Louis. I *was* in the room when Mom and Dad said it."

"Yeah but you really dumb, so I just be reminding you."

Bo took a moment to silently calm himself.

"I just saying, it still probably da sensitive subject."

Bo seemed to not want to get into a debate and changed that subject. "So why do you think that Mikhail character tried to kill Nathan?"

Louis thought quickly. "Same reason any Monster try and kill baby bro."

"I don't get it," Bo said and then responded to a car honking at him by waving it to pass.

"Okay," Louis said getting comfortable. "All da Chakan—"

Bo cut him off. "If you go into a twenty minute lesson on the Chakan scale of power and irregular powers and how Nathan has five irregular powers, I'm gonna punch you in your damn face."

Louis paused for a moment and then cautiously continued. "So I think dis Mikhail guy had a thing for da same girl."

"Oh," Bo dragged out. "Didn't anyone tell him about Nathan's Five Rings?"

Louis turned to his brother. "Obviously he did not get da memo."

"Well that is a crappy way to find out the truth," Bo said shaking his head.

Louis got an inquisitive look on his face. "So Bo, you think you can take little bro?"

"No," Bo said immediately. "I mean, if it was just a feat of strength sure, I am stronger."

"Yeah, but all of your other Rings suck."

Bo shook his head. "Grant it, they're not enhanced, but they aren't shabby either."

"Please Bo-Bo, even when you do da blurring you is slow as shit."

Bo leaned over and quickly slapped his Cajun brother in the face and laughed. "Yeah, quick enough to bitch slap you."

Louis just rubbed his face and giggled. "I wasn't ready you big monkey."

"So you think you could take Nathan?" Bo asked.

"Let me tell you something Bo," Louis started in melodramatic tone. "I am very fast."

"I know Louis. Speedy Gonzales fast," Bo indulged.

"Fuck dat," Louis said. "I am da Goddamn Road Runner."

"Testify," Bo said getting in on the fun.

Louis was now into a rhythm. "I got da endurance to go all night long if you know what I be meaning."

"I do," Bo said still smiling from ear to ear and then suddenly he was frowning. "And that is just gross man."

Louis sat up straight and seemed to be completely offended. "Why that be gross?"

"Cause I live with you and I don't never see no women come home with you. Which means you're going all night long at yourself."

"Fuck you Bo, I get da plenty."

"Un-huh," Bo agreed sarcastically.

"Don't you be worrying about dat."

Bo smirked. "Only if we shared a room."

"Thousands brother, all of dem completely satisfied, yes sir," he confided.

Bo was trying to keep his eyes on the road. "See you got that delusional Ring."

Louis continued. "And you know my Omen Ring be pretty good."

"Is that so," Bo contested. "I think my Omen Ring is way better than yours.

Louis smiled with a hint of deviousness. "Da mentally handicapped guy working at da Walmart can read da situation better than you."

Bo was not impressed. "So I guess you know that I'm about to smash your head into that dashboard."

Louis looked aghast. "You be referring to me being da mentally handicapped guy working at da Walmart?"

"I'm saying if you don't shut up, the mentally handicapped guy at the Walmart is going to be your supervisor."

Louis smiled. "Dat don't sound very politically correct Bo-Bo. I think da right way is da special needs."

"Oh now Louis, when I punch you in the head with this big old mitt," Bo said holding up his more than sizable fist. "Things like that won't concern you no more. *No*, you'll be more concerned about what kind of pudding you'll be having for desert."

Louis started to laugh. "But I already get concerned about da kind of pudding I get for desert."

Bo howled while slapping at his steering wheel. "Oh I know you do," he laughed and continued slowly along the street while upsetting the morning traffic. Ignoring the honking and yelling while he looked for any sign that he was getting close to Nathan's bookstore, he made a casual observation, "Some people are so rude?"

"You drive like da Ms. Daisy—I honk and yell too."

"Ms. Daisy was not driving. She was driven, by a Mr. Morgan Freeman."

Louis just rolled his eyes. "What were we talking about?"

The van made another turn and slowed right down.

"I never really know with you Louis," Bo said bringing the van to a stop and putting it in park.

Suddenly a joyous but demanding voice rang out beside them. "You're late. Park around back," Nathan said heading back into the store to meet them around back.

Louis stuck his head out the window in protest. "Hey! What about da hello, or hey bros, nice ta see you?"

Nathan gave him the finger as the door shut behind him.

Louis turned to Bo for some support.

But Bo just smiled. "He's looking pretty good."

"Maybe you work up da courage and ask him out on da date."

Bo's smile faded to a grin. "Maybe I work up the courage and snap your neck."

The van took a long slow U-turn going back up the street and turned left. The back street was empty and Bo just had to drive until he saw Nathan hold out his hand to stop.

Hopping out of the passenger side Louis took a big stretch and then opened his arms as he walked towards Nathan. "Come give me da hug you fucker."

Nathan gladly did.

"I miss you bro," Louis said grabbing his cheeks and pinching them together until his mouth resembled a fish.

Nathan replied as well as he possibly could with his cheeks mushed together. "I-missed-you-too."

Two massive arms engulfed Nathan and lifted into the air away from his Cajun brother. Now his cheeks were mashed together with Bo's thanks to the massive bear hug. Nathan could barely hear the muffled giggles of his Herculean brother. "I missed you Nathan, did you miss me?" Bo asked still squeezing his brother in his arms.

Louis thought he resembled more of an animal being slowly killed by constriction on one of those Animal Planet shows. Seeing his brother's face start to change to a dark shade of purple obviously prompted Louis to save his little brother. "Okay, you gonna break him for Christ sake."

Nathan dropped to his feet and instantly began seeking the sweet vitality of air. Taking a deep breath he paused to let the blood start flowing to all the proper places. "So," he began prematurely and waited a moment and then finished, "how was the trip up?"

"With this cooyon," Louis said rolling his eyes.

Not registering his Cajun brother's comment, Bo continued to answer with full pleasantries. "It was a delightful trip, beautiful weather and—" he stopped short and turned to Louis with a hateful look only a brother could project. "I'm gonna break your face Cajun. Don't call me a cooyon!" Bo growled abruptly and then went calm and continued. "It was a lovely trip, thank you for asking."

"Where is da refreshments bro?" Louis asked looking around.

"We're in an alley you moron," Nathan shot back.

Louis froze sarcastically. "Oh, they inside then?"

"No," Nathan said a little defeated.

Bo popped his head from behind the van. "I am famished Nathan."

"Yeah," Louis said raising his eyebrows. "We only stop to eat five times dis morning."

"Okay-Okay," Nathan surrendered both verbally and physically with his hands raised. "There's a coffee shop just up the street, it has a full menu. I'll go and get us tea and something to eat," he said with a dash of condescendence.

"Good, I'm hungry," Bo yelled coming around the van with boxes.

Then at the same time Nathan and Louis responded. "You're always hungry."

They turned to each other smiling and both said, "Jinx!"

Nathan then slapped his brother in the face. "Infinity."

Louis held his cheek while waving his finger back at his brother. "Dat was da good one. I can tell it is going to sting for da while."

Nathan laughed and started walking. "Just start unloading the boxes. I won't be long."

2: Welcome to Sips

The store wasn't exactly busy, except for the group at one table that was filled by the staff, Lily, Todd and Jeanette, plus one patron, Florida. The staff was enjoying the down time while they all were trying to decide who would be a better suitor for Lily. There was the dashing young businessman now renting out Florida's very posh and expensive apartment, or the very rugged and handsome stranger Lily and Jeanette had met the other night.

Jeanette got up from the table. "I'm just saying he was hot, like take me home and do me on the kitchen table hot."

"Ew, your children eat at that table," Lily cried.

Jeanette rolled her eyes and before she disappeared into the kitchen she added, "I'd obviously clean it after."

Sipping at her tea Florida continued her argument. "I'm just saying, my guy has a lot of money and he is gorgeous. He owns that new book store opening up,"

"Imaginations?" Todd asked.

Florida snapped her fingers and pointed at him. "That's the one."

Todd educated the table. "I saw the sign going up a while ago. I have been waiting ever since for it to open," he said looking at Lily. "Sorry Lily, bookstore owner? I'm siding with Florida."

"And he's single," Florida added.

Jeanette was still rooting for the stranger. "So he's a stuffy suit wearing nerd."

Florida interrupted with a caustic laugh. "Nothing nerdy about this boy honey."

Then Todd took the accountant role. "Fly apartment. Lots of money. Owns his own business. All good qualities in a potential mate," Todd directed to Lily.

"Potential mate?" Lily asked becoming very conscientious. "What are we, *Wild Kingdom*?"

Todd excused his attention from Florida and turned to Lily. "Um, yes Lily. Even the hippo wants a mate with the best water plants in the area. The lioness wants the lion with the shadiest tree. The girl bears want the boy bear with the largest honey pot."

Jeanette reappeared from the kitchen grabbing some dishes from a table and informed him, "That's Winnie the Pooh."

Todd just ignored her as she disappeared back into the kitchen and continued. "Whatever, you don't think cashing in those Disney royalty checks gets Pooh Bear all the bitches? Hooker please. Up to his neck in bear pussy."

"Todd!" Florida snapped.

"Oh I'm sorry Ms. Johnson," he said apologetically patting her shoulder. "I meant bear va-jay-jay," he corrected while pointing downwards at Lily's privates.

Watching Lily swat Todd's hand away, Florida couldn't help it and smiled. "What is wrong with you boy?"

"Come on people, bear va-jay-jay. That's funny," he said giving Florida a kiss on her cheek.

Jeanette reappeared again. "It's probably a sexual harassment case."

Todd tuned obviously stunned. "Bitch please, I'm gay."

Lily shook her head. "I don't think that matters."

Todd looked to Ms. Johnson, who agreed with Lily.

Todd turned back to Jeanette's direction. "Don't fill the other subordinates' heads with ideas."

Lily became perplexed. "Subordinates? It's just me and Jeanette."

Todd looked at her with a huff. "What about Mary-Anne?"

"She's not here, and she's a teenager who comes in every other weekend and holidays."

Todd rolled his eyes. "Don't be a bitch Lily, and Jeanette, don't be a whore."

Lily returned to the previous conversation. "So let's go back. My options are the stranger, who for all we know could be the Chicago Serial Killer."

Todd leaned into Florida. "You know, I really hope they come up with something better than the Chicago Serial Killer."

Florida smirked. "Maybe when someone other than homeless people get killed."

Todd nodded. "That's right, homeless people deserve a proper named killer too."

"That is not what I meant," Florida said looking up to the ceiling.

"Maybe if they give him a snappy killer name," Todd said grabbing his tablet. "People might start caring."

"Here we go," Lily said preparing herself.

Todd thought aloud while he scrolled through headlines. "The Vagabond Exterminator. The Transient Cut-throat."

Lily just shook her head trying not to giggle. "What happened to you as a child?"

Jeanette yelled out from the kitchen, "Gross, I don't want to hear that story."

"The Bum Assassin," Todd said ignoring them and then looked up from the tablet. "That sounded like a porno movie I would order."

Florida laughed, but still smacked his arm.

"I got it," Todd declared. "The Hobo Hacker."

"You—" Lily started and then cut herself off. "That's actually not bad."

Florida glared at her. "Do not encourage this boy."

"*Okay*," Lily said trying to get the conversation back on track. "So my choices are, the Serial Killer."

Todd coughed deliberately.

Lily rolled her eyes. "The Hobo Hacker."

Todd showed them the tablet. "I tweeted it and I already got three favorites and a retweet."

Jeanette appeared back at the table and held out her phone. "This guy called you an idiot."

Todd pushed her phone away. "Shut up Jeanette."

Lily continued. "Or the rich business man," she said and then paused. "Who Florida says is hot."

Florida looked at Lily who was already giggling. "What the hell does that mean? Because I'm old I don't know what hot is?"

Jeanette started to rub Florida's arm. "Yeah, you kinda got those grandma eyes. You know, the ones that think the fat ginger kid with freckles is handsome."

"Girl, I have been defending you all morning." Florida asserted.

Suddenly the door chime rang out and Nathan walked through.

The table was silent and then as if they practiced it, Florida and Lily both stood up. They both noticed that they both stood up at the same time and gave each other a comparable look of inquisitiveness.

Slowly taking her eyes off of Florida, Lily raised her hand and gave Nathan a little wave. "Hey."

Florida was not as shy. "Hello there Nathan," she cheered and walked around the table to meet him.

At the table Jeanette and Todd watched eagerly.

Nathan approached Florida. "Hello Ms. Johnson. How are you?"

"I'm fine, just fine."

Lily was confused. "How do you know one another?"

Florida looked equally confused. "This is Nathan. He's the nice young man that rented the apartment.

Todd turned to Jeanette and tried to keep it to a murmur. "We've been talking about the same guy. I told you."

"Oh," Jeanette realized and then murmured back, "you didn't tell us nothing."

"Shut up you whore," Todd hissed and nudged her with his elbow.

"I am not a whore."

Todd raised his speech to a robust whisper. "You have five children with six different men."

"That doesn't even make sense," she said in a normal pitch and slapped his arm.

Suddenly the two of them were at the table and exchanging frantic elbow nudges. Only a cough from Florida snapped them out of their cat fight and they both turned to see Lily, Florida and the man that they were all talking about staring at them.

Todd was the first to react. "No I will not sleep with you Jeanette. I keep telling you I'm a HO-MO-SEXUAL!" Todd reprimanded her and got up and left.

Jeanette just stood dumbfounded for a moment and then just decided to get up and head to the kitchen without saying anything.

Florida turned to Nathan. "I know it seems like an insane asylum now, but they have the best desserts I have ever tasted."

Nathan smiled. "Well they made such a big deal about this place the other night that I just had to come and check it out," Nathan exaggerated.

"The other night?" Florida asked.

Lily nodded at her. "This was the stranger that Jeanette and I bumped into."

"Get out," Florida said and then roared with laughter. "All morning arguing and this is him," she said to herself as she headed to the door. "I'll be damned."

Nathan looked a little bewildered himself. "Am I missing something?"

"Absolutely," Florida said and then never elaborated. "Do me a favor Nathan, have the tea. It's to die for."

"I will," he said and then raced to open the door for her.

Suddenly Todd appeared beside Lily startling her. "Mmm, and he's a gentlemen."

Lily pushed him. "Will you go away?"

"Well aren't we a little sour patch bitch," Todd said heading back to the counter.

As the door shut behind Nathan Lily walked backwards while looking at him and smiling. "So—Tea?"

"That would be good," Nathan said not letting his eyes veer from hers.

"Well then, just let me get set up and we'll—" she stopped short after she backed up into her own table. Lily quickly turned around to see if she knocked anything over and flung her arm with the turn, which caught a jug of water that went aerial until it hit the wall. *SHIT!* She slowly turned around and saw that Nathan was at least attempting not to laugh. "I just need a minute."

"No problem," Nathan said and started to back up. "I have to order some food anyways."

Lily picked up the jug and wiped up the water. "Okay Lily, he's just a guy who wants a tea," she said softly trying to calm herself, except her mind wasn't helping. *No, he's a totally hot guy who flirted with you the other night and now he's here.*

Jeanette appeared. "So do you think he's here to ask you out?"

"What? No," Lily cried quietly.

"He's even hotter in than I remember," Jeanette said eyeing Nathan up like she was picking out her dinner.

"You're not helping."

"If you don't want him can I have him?" Jeanette said in a joyous hush.

Lily's eyes widened in disbelief. "No."

"So you do want him?"

Lily started to push her away. "Go away Jeanette or I swear."

Nathan made his way back to the counter. "Nothing seriously damaged I hope."

Lily smiled without looking up. "Just my dignity," she said trying her best to avoid any type of eye contact.

"It's a very impressive tea station. I can't even smell the spices or dried fruits," Nathan said.

Lily knew she had to look at him sooner or later. *One ... Two ...*, she counted to herself and raised her head. "I sometimes like to put a little spices out just for the customers to smell, but places who have all their ingredients out in the open—"

"Are just putting stale ingredients in the tea," Nathan finished.

Lily smiled. "Exactly."

"So is it true that you have a masters in tea?" Nathan asked in fun.

Lily laughed while putting on her apron. "I make a pretty good tea."

"Then I can hardly wait."

Suddenly Lily remembered. "Did anything ever come of those screams?"

Nathan looked like he was caught off guard, but his expression settled. "A completely inebriated gentlemen who lost his phone."

"Oh," Lily said a little surprised. "I guess I'd be really upset too if I lost my phone."

Nathan's pocket started to vibrate and he pulled it out and read the screen. "I am so sorry, I really do have to take this."

"No problem," Lily assured him and watched as the hot stranger that Florida called Nathan stepped outside to take a call. She just stood at her counter watching every twitch of his nose, every blink of his eyes, every word she couldn't hear coming from his mouth. Oh my God look at that mouth, she thought becoming aware at how intoxicating he was. Then from behind her came Todd's voice.

"Wow, the dirty thoughts that must be going on in there," Todd said staring at her head.

She closed her eyes, dismayed at the shattered delusion. "What?"

"Here's the teas he wants," he said handing her the order.

"Thank you," she said taking it.

Todd just stood beside her. "Some heated thoughts going on up there."

Lily just smiled slyly.

"That's what I thought Hooker," Todd said returning to an abnormally amount of boxes of deserts.

"That's a lot of deserts," Lily said.

"I know, I guess he has a lot of people working at getting his store ready," Todd said and went back to packing the boxes up.

Lily just returned to look at Nathan through the window and then looked at the order. "Nice," she said reading the teas Nathan wanted.

3: The Spoils from Plunder

Taking another box of books Louis jumped out of the van and took them inside of Nathan's new store while also adhering to Nathan's strict rule of no blurring in public.

Bo on the other hand was hoping to see Nathan's imminent return any time now and waited at the end of the alley. "There he is," he yelled waving his brother over to prove he wasn't lying.

Nathan was easy to spot since he was the one with boxes piled past his eyes weaving left and right through the busy sidewalk. Bo watched in terror as his oncoming food took quick and sharp turns to avoid collisions with human traffic, making it look like it could all tumble at any second.

As Nathan finally approached the alley, Louis relieved him of some of the burden and asked sarcastically, "Get enough?"

Bo eagerly followed like a lap dog as Louis became increasingly frustrated. "Shoo-shoo Marmaduke," he yelled kicking at him.

Bo waited for him to set the boxes down and then picked him up as if he was just a box full of packing peanuts and put him off to the side. "About damn time Nathan, I was really starting to get worried."

Louis rolled his eyes. "Yeah your safety be all he talking about."

Bo started to look through each box, most likely to make the prudent decision on what to eat first. "Oh these just look delectable," he said tilting the box to Louis. "Look at those cupcakes."

Louis gave Bo a patronizing smile. "And look at all those sprinkles."

"Yeah," Bo agreed, "I do like cupcakes."

And here is the tea," Nathan said handing his colossal brother the first cup.

"That's what I'm talking about," Bo said putting down the deserts and popping the lid off of the cup. "I could smell these before I even saw you."

It was a fact that Chakan had very heightened senses of smell and taste, making them appreciate all kinds of properly spiced foods. But they absolutely reveled in the copious tastes and aromas of properly prepared tea.

Bo took a cautious sip to register the taste and then let it linger. Finally he swallowed. "Yes sir, watermelon mint chiller white tea," he said enthusiastically taking another sip.

Louis was almost pouting. "Can I please—" he stopped short, watching Nathan already drinking his. "Really? You be fucking with me right?"

Nathan smiled and handed one to his brother.

Louis took the tea and peeled the lid back. As he inhaled the aroma he was surprised at how bold and individual it smelled. Taking a sip he followed his large brother's ritual before swallowing and then following it with a mouthful. "Oh hot damn that is da good tea there."

Nathan was actually thinking about keeping the others all to himself, but decided they probably already smelt it. "I got more," he declared holding up the second tray.

"I know," Bo said taking a cup. "Wonder-berry chocolate truffle oolong tea," he said, now conflicted.

Louis looked at Nathan. "These teas are da shit bro."

"The lady who made them is like a local celebrity when it comes to her teas. I actually bumped into her the other night, she's really nice too. A little shy but really sweet. Her friends are really nice too. I only got to talk to her for a bit when you called, and …" Nathan trailed off when he realized his brothers were just staring at him. Nathan tried to change the subject. "So how are Mom and Dad?"

Louis turned to Bo. "I think he be liking dis lady who make da tea?"

Bo agreed and then suggested, "Nathan got a girlfriend?"

Louis pointed back at his bigger brother that led to both looking at Nathan and singing, "Nathan got a girlfriend, Nathan got a girlfriend."

"Real mature," Nathan said taking another sip of his tea.

Louis repositioned himself by hopping beside his brother and threw his arm around Nathan's shoulder. "You want I should give you da tips on asking this lady out?"

Nathan smirked. "Even if I did need tips, what makes you think I would ask you?"

"Who you gonna ask? Giganto over there?" Louis asked.

Bo gave him the finger and triumphantly stuffed a whole cupcake into his mouth. "Hot damn, they taste better than they look."

Watching as Bo popped a second one in like they were peanuts, Nathan started to worry he might choke. "Careful there Bo."

Smiling ear to ear with his mouth full, he began to pronounce dramatically on purpose. "Please, well-Prepared, Pleasantly scrumPtious and absolutely Palatable," he said as crumbs exploded from his mouth. Unable to get out of the way of the outpouring of tiny cake pebbles Nathan held up his arms to umbrella himself against what he could.

Louis decided they did look delicious and reached for the box. Out of nowhere a thunderous smacking sound echoed throughout the store and he retracted his hand that was now throbbing.

Bo stood in front of the boxes and declared, "These are mine!" Then slowly stuffed another one into his mouth.

Louis was still rubbing his hand. "I think Nathan buy them for everyone," he said attempting once again to take a cupcake, but was stopped short as the big man raised his hand, intending immediate consequences.

"I said Piss off Pecker head," Bo yelled, letting crumbs fly until the baked goodness in his mouth turned on him and he started to choke.

Louis pointed with a look of vindication. "Serves you right fat-boy," he scorned as his brother's shade turned a color bordering on grim.

Nathan walked over to his brother and put his hand on his shoulder to get his attention. "Okay Bo, ready?" he asked as Bo nodded with panic. Going behind him, he raised his hand. "One, two—"

Nathan didn't even wait for three and brought his hand down with a blinding speed that even made the air crack before it smacked Bo's back.

Bo tripped violently forward they watched as an almost fully intact cupcake flew out of Bo's mouth and landed on the floor. Taking a moment for the proper color to return to his face, he took a deep breath and exhaled. "That..." he tried. "That's ..." he tried again but still could not finish.

"You're okay buddy," Nathan said rubbing his shoulders.

Shaking his head, Bo pointed to the ground. "That's still mine."

"All yours," Nathan said holding his hands up and surrendering all claims.

Louis just shook his head in disbelief. "You like da animal Bo."

Ignoring them, he walked over and grabbed the cupcake off of the floor and tempted fate once again.

Nathan laughed as he suddenly for the first time felt home. "You know, I really missed you guys."

Louis grinned as if Nathan's declaration was an invitation to let him in on something devious. "So once we get da books up, maybe me and da big guy stay da night."

"That'd be great," Nathan said, but now thinking that something was up.

Louis waved Nathan to follow him. As they made their way out to the back Louis leaped inside the van and began digging behind the passenger seat. Coming back out holding a large jug that looked like something out of an old prohibition cartoon, he smiled devilishly.

Nathan however smiled in disbelief. "Maggie gave that to you?"

"Gave?" Bo answered with a cynical question and holding a second box of cupcakes.

Nathan's eyes widened in horror. "She didn't give it to you? You stole her whisky?"

The two brothers weren't denying it.

"Wow. It's official," Nathan said conclusively. "You are both certified idiots," he said holding up the jug and becoming a little frantic. "You know you're dead right? And I'm dead for just knowing about it."

"Then you probably don't want to know that we have five more of them," Bo said a little saddened, as if he agreed with Nathan's declaration.

Nathan was both terrified and impressed. "You're both out of your goddamn minds. Six?"

Wrapping his arm around his frightened brother, Louis recited some of his wisdom. "Why worry today about da consequences of da tomorrow?"

Bo sighed. "Which is great for today. Not so much for the tomorrow, when we go home and get our asses handed to us."

"Why you so scared?" Louis asked Bo. "You just as strong as dat Bruti."

Their adoptive sister Maggie was Bruti, another species of Monster. Bruti for the most part are known to be a pretty passive and mostly joyous Monstrum bunch, but they are also known for their love of alcohol, stubbornness, quick temper and unnatural strength.

Bo smiled half-heartedly. "It's not just the strength. It's her meanness. Its borderline horror film."

Nathan nodded bitingly. "That is true. Remember what she did to us that time I came home for a visit and we lost her Dawson Creek tapes?"

"Oh yeah, da Dawson incident," Louis said putting his hand gingerly over his nipples. "She gave me da titty twister so bad, my left nipple still can't get da fully erect."

Bo just looked confused for a moment and then roared. "I will say this, Louis usually does get it the worse."

"That's because he antagonizes her," Nathan said setting down the jug of whiskey. "When her tapes were destroyed, he blurred away and then spent the rest of the afternoon singing the, *I don't want to wait* theme song from the trees."

Bo laughed. "That was funny."

Nathan agreed, partially. "Yeah, but he had to go home eventually."

Louis frowned. "Dats when she got da nipples."

Nathan started to pass boxes to Louis. "Let's finish up here and we'll head over to my place."

Even with Nathan's detailed specifications it would take them less than an hour to set up, meaning that soon they would be drinking and laughing long into the night. His homesickness was subsiding.

But what Nathan really felt like doing was going back to Sips and ordering another tea.

CHAPTER VI

1: Welcome Back Neighbor

"WHY THANK YOU," the first older lady said cheerfully walking into Sips.

"My pleasure," Nathan said still holding the door open for the second elderly lady, who wasn't so merry.

The first lady turned to her less pleasant friend and said, "Such a polite young man, isn't he Pearl?"

Pearl seemed to be skeptical and frowned. "Pfft! His clothes has douche bag written all over it."

Nathan kept his smile. "Actually that's fashion's big spring line this year. Douche Bag by Calvin Kline."

Pearl's frown turned into a scowl. "Oh great, a smart ass."

Nathan waited until they were both turned around towards the counter and then let his eyes widen in disbelief. Then it hit him, first he turned his head in an attempt to avoid it but it had already made its way to his eyes. They began to water and he twitched from side to side as the heavy presence of cologne surrounded him. He tried to look casual as he waited in line and tried to avoid the onslaught of aroma. And then, after what seemed to be a hundred questions about the different coffees and desserts, the two ladies made their way to the register.

Todd lit up like a Christmas tree when he saw Nathan. "Well, hello there neighbor."

"Todd," Nathan remembered from yesterday and offered his hand.

"Nathan," Todd replied, proving his memory was just as good.

Nathan smiled. "That smell?"

"Finally someone noticed. You like it? Chanel Antaeus, a little pricey for work, but better to be an exclamation mark then a question mark," he said laughing lightly at himself. "Can I ask you a question Nathan?"

"As long as I can get a tea," Nathan answered.

"You look a little young to own a bookstore," Todd said seriously.

Nathan looked like he was waiting. "That's not a question Todd, more of an observation."

Todd thought for a moment. "Right. Okay, why is such a young man running a used book store?"

"I love books," Nathan replied immediately.

"So do I," Todd said and fell to his elbows with his palms in his cheeks. "There is nothing better than a good book," he said looking off into some past memory. "I would have to say, *Treasure Island* is my all-time favorite."

"It would be hard to argue with that," Nathan said, finally adjusting to the air pollution that was Todd's cologne.

"I mean, I loved *The Time Machine, To Kill a Mockingbird*."

"Good ones," Nathan agreed.

"*Catcher in the Rye, Frankenstein, Moby Dick*."

Nathan decided to interrupt since Todd seemed to have an entire library he could ramble off, "I will actually have a pristine first edition of *Treasure Island* on display."

"Shut your ass, *Treasure Island* is one of my favorites. If I had a really bad day at school, that would be my go to book," Todd said with a look that said he was ready to be transported back to his past again. "And I can actually see the first editions?"

"Absolutely, they'll be encased in glass, but yes," he assured him.

Tilting his head a little, Todd's eyes widened as he waved Nathan closer, as to keep it on the down low. "Can I touch it?"

Nathan looked at the weird obsessive look in Todd's eyes and got a little worried. "We're still talking about the books right?"

Todd stared at him silently and was making Nathan even more uncomfortable, until all of a sudden he burst into laughter. "Yes, the books," he roared. "*Treasure Island* was probably the first book that I read. Well that wasn't authored by Dr. Seuss, or a *Choose Your Own Adventure*. The first time I actually read it, I literally flipped right back to the beginning and read it again." Todd leaned back in for more, *on the down low.* "They must be worth a fortune. I read somewhere, a first edition of *Moby Dick* in mint condition is worth—" he stopped short and waved Nathan in closer, so as not to be rude when he let him in on the dollar value. "North of a hundred thousand," he said and then nodded as if to confirm it to be true. Then, just in case he wasn't sure as to what hundred thousand he was referring to, he clarified. "Dollars."

Staying in close proximity Nathan replied back. "Actually, it's a little south."

"Still," he said with an *Oh My God* eyebrow raise and a whistle that started low and then pitched high to low again.

"Well, I'll be open soon, so you'll have to come by."

"That would certainly be a delight Nathan," Todd said.

Martin called out from behind the cash register. "Novio, how much for the lovely ladies?" He also looked as if his patience was being tested.

Nathan knew that Pearl knew that he had tried beating them to the door, hence the *douche bag* comment. So he was hoping that this was going to make up for it. "Please, I got that," Nathan told Todd. One would think he was trying to make up for something, maybe almost running them over trying to get to the door first? "Just add it to my bill."

Todd yelled over to Martin. "Martin honey, don't charge the lovely lady. And you don't have to charge Pearl either."

Nathan gave the surprised women a wave.

The lovely lady turned to Pearl. "Now would a serial killer do that? I told you he was a nice young man."

Nathan turned back to Todd. "Serial killer?"

Todd smiled awkwardly. "I'm assuming she's pegging you as the cities murderer."

"Of course he would Phyllis," Pearl pursued. "That's how they lure you into their basement."

Nathan turned to Todd again. "I don't even have a basement."

Pearl continued. "Or their van. Then they drive you out into the woods to have their way with you."

Still looking at Todd, Nathan felt compelled to reassure him about that as well. "Don't have a van either."

Martin stepped in. "I'm pretty sure the nice man is not our serial killer," he said receiving an agreeing nod from Phyllis and a "Humph" from Pearl.

"Serial killer?" Nathan asked.

"Haven't you heard?" Todd asked.

But Nathan only shook his head, almost overselling his bewilderment.

"It's been all over the news for weeks sweetie, we have a serial killer on the loose," Todd said and with a few swipes showed him the headlines on the tablet.

"Alleged," Martin corrected.

Todd smirked. "Please, the Hobo Hacker is a serial killer."

Martin shook his head. "Not this again."

Todd swiped and tapped at the tablet. "I totally coined the phrase. Look at that," he said holding up his tweet. "Look at all those favorites and retweets."

"Impressive," Nathan said.

Todd started to read the tablet. "The last murder victim was found not too far from here. Scary."

Nathan seemed to fall into a deep thought, until Todd snapped him out of it.

"Well Nathan, what can I get you?"

2: A Tea, Maybe My Heart?

Lily stood at the sink doing dishes and with a bit of concentration, could make out the conversation by the cash register. Then she heard the two ladies pondering if the new customer that paid for their coffee and dessert was a serial killer as they walked away to sit down. *Shit, I missed something*, she thought and concentrated a bit harder. But before she could even begin to peace it all together Lily heard Todd calling out to Martin, "Honey, call her grace."

"I'll grace him," she muttered withdrawing her hands from the sudsy sink when Martin yelled out, "Hey perezosa, tea time!"

Lily walked out of the kitchen looking like a mess and a little pissed off as she threw a dish towel over her shoulder. She was about to yell at

Martin for calling her *lazy* when she saw Nathan standing by Todd and gave a silent shout out to the universe. *Thank you.*

Then like a vinyl record being violently scratched, the reality of her situation came screaming back into her head. *I look like Cinderella. And not the good Cinderella riding the pumpkin to the ball, the white trash Cinderella covered in trailer park grime.*

Leading Nathan to the tea station Todd cut off Martin before he could say anything. "And don't you be going and calling me lazy, I ain't Lily, I'll kick your Latin ass all the way back to El De-wherever the hell it is you came from," he said and added a stern finger. He then turned to Lily with an enormous smile. "Lily, you remember Nathan."

"Hello," Lily said meeting his eyes and feeling her whole body melt. Including her tongue. *My God you are beautiful,* she thought loudly in her head as he was looking at her, waiting for her to speak. Time was ticking on, she had to say something, anything. "Umm, well hey," she practically squeaked. Lily decided to bring it down a few decibels. "How's it going?" she asked in an almost Darth Vader impression. *Concentrate Lily,* she attempted to calm internally. Then with a quick breath she let out a normal, "Hello."

"My dear Lord," Todd said under his breath and started to drag Martin away.

Martin noticed but wasn't as subtle. "What is wrong with Lily?" Martin asked being pulled away. "Is she sick?"

Lily found herself staring, so she desperately searched for something to say, but it wasn't working. Instead she was trying to block a flurry of dirty thoughts and the longer she stared the dirtier they became. *What is going on, I don't want a relationship. Not even a sexual one.*

"Tea!" Todd swooped in, "you make tea and Nathan would like some."

Lily looked at Todd and started to pull out of her downward spin. "Yes," she started and turned back to Nathan, "yes I do."

Todd held his hand out. "This is Nathan. You made tea for him yesterday. You know, the day before today. We had tacos for dinner and we watched reruns of Golden Girls and then we—"

"*Okay*, I got it," she said while knocking the carnal vignettes out of her head, or at the very least paused them.

Todd waited for Nathan to sit down so his back was to him. *So hot*, he mouthed to Lily and quickly began jabbing his finger through a circle he made with his other fingers.

With a stiff face and bulging eyes, Lily gave the hint for Todd to go away. "So Mr. ..."

Nathan smiled. "Caesar, but I thought we were on first name basis?"

They were, but it seemed like the best thing to say since the alternative would have the three words *Do Me Hard* in it. Actually it would probably be just those three words. *Seriously, what is wrong with me? It's like I've been possessed by the horny spirit of a gay coffee shop owner*, she thought getting off the topic again, which was Mr. Caesar's tea. "Wait, did you say your name is Caesar?"

Nathan agreed. "Yes I did."

"You don't hear that name a lot. At least not off screen," Lily said feeling both amused and clever. "What could I get you Mr. Caesar?"

"Please, just Nathan. I was actually wondering if you knew how to make a golden monkey black tea," he said.

"I thought you were going to ask for something difficult," she declared and turned on the burner. She began grabbing tins and containers to prepare his request when she glanced up and saw that she'd made him smile. Which of course caused the dirty thoughts to start their engines, but she quickly cooled them finding that Nathan seemed genuine with a kindness in his eyes. *Okay, that's not cooling them at all.* Neither did her observation on his rugged demeanor that made him seem older than he looked. In a, *I already conquered life* type way. Lily thought for the word. *Dapper.* She could feel his eyes on her and it was making her lightheaded. *What about Rick?* But as Nathan smiled at her, Lily could feel her fear melt into obscurity and then answered herself, "Fuck him!" Unfortunately that time she answered out loud.

"I'm sorry?" Nathan asked.

Lily stood there hovering over the boiling water with a look of astonishment. *Shit, what do I say?*

What would Todd do?

He would lie.

Really?

Oh yeah, a whopper.
Should I?
Well, we gotta say something.

Then she smiled. "Sorry, Todd and Martin want me to work this weekend and it's like the tenth," she paused thinking that ten was over exaggerating. "I mean third weekend in a row, and I was arguing in my head. Sorry that it spilled out verbally like that." *Not bad, I wish I could clap.*

Nathan grinned. "Well then you're right, fuck them."

And just like that the past was banished to a dirty little corner of her mind. "Yeah," she smiled back and dumped the scolding water. She placed the sack in the empty pot and noticed that Nathan was about to ask her a question, so she quickly answered. "Moisture."

"Moisture," he repeated.

"That's where you're probably making your mistake."

Nathan smirked. "What makes you so sure I'm making mistakes?"

"Please," Lily returned. "The sack is dry—"

"Ha!" Todd blurted out a couple of tables over as the rest of the women with him giggled.

"Real mature," she called out and then turned back to Nathan. "I'm guessing it is dry when you're putting it into the pot right?" Lily asked and waited for Nathan to nod. "Let it moisten in the first pot, like letting the pores open. This way you're not trying to coax the flavor out once in, by pressing on it. It'll just flow out all on its own," she said lifting her head and seeing him deep in thought. Realizing that she'd been rambling on for a bit now on the subject of tea, Lily decided to change the subject. "So Mr. Caesar, are you of Roman decent or any relation to the original?"

"Guiles Julius Caesar?" he guessed.

Lily started to chuckle. "Yeah, that guy," she said while dumping some unmarked spice to a pile of leaves and twigs.

"Well first of all, the name Caesar was already ancient and highly respected before Guiles came along. The suffix—AR, was highly unusual in the Latin language, which means it's also likely the Caesars's origin is that of non-Latin. So it wouldn't be truly Roman..." he said trailing off. "I'm sorry. I just took us to a whole new level of boredom."

"No...Maybe," she giggled.

"Water's boiling again," he said and pointed, seemingly trying to change the subject.

Lily took the sack that was now moist and dumped it into the kettle that was boiling and continued the lesson. "Let it boil for a couple more minutes and trust me, the flavor will explode." Grabbing a large cup from the shelf and a lid she put them beside the kettle. "Now you know it tastes better in porcelain?"

"Of course."

"Milk or sugar?" she asked reaching for them in slow motion.

"No, thank you."

"A purist," she said and then began to pour. "Good ... I thought I was going to have to hit you." Grabbing two tea cups from the lower shelf she poured the rest of the tea through the strainer and filled them.

Lily watched as Nathan gently took the saucer and placed it in front of him. Then he put his index finger through the handle up to his knuckle. Placing his thumb on the top of the handle to direct the cup he then put his third finger underneath to secure it. Letting the weight rest on his third finger, he let his fourth and fifth finger curl back towards his wrist, correctly holding his tea cup. Stirring the tea gently and dispersing the flavor throughout, she noticed he never let the spoon touch any part of the cup. Removing it, he gently placed the spoon on the saucer behind the tea cup and to the right of the handle.

Lily would have been impressed if he had just remembered to take the spoon out before taking a gulp. But watching this gorgeous man use proper tea etiquette was a huge turn on, and she already heard Todd in her head, laughing. Thinking he was going to lift the saucer with the cup still on it she held her breath. Lifting the cup off the saucer his eyes did not leave the task at hand. Lowering the cup he glanced directly into her eyes and smiled, making her want to swipe everything off of the counter, rip off all of her clothes and invite him to take her right then and there. "Hmm," she pleasantly sighed, letting the warmth flush over her.

Nathan apparently noticed her expression and leaned forward. "Do I have something in my nose?"

"No."

"My teeth then?" he asked "Did I spill some on my shirt?"

Lily attempted to cover up the fact that she was staring at Nathan like he was a slab of beautiful prime rib sitting pretty in the butchers showcase. "No—no, I'm just surprized you drank your tea correctly."

He chuckled. "My mother would be *ecstatic* to hear that."

"You should see how Todd drinks his tea," she said nodding to direct his attention behind him.

Turning around Nathan watched Todd over-embellishing a popular song on the radio and trying to twerk in reference to some joke he was telling. Martin was already walking away in embarrassment, but everyone else was laughing. "I could only imagine," he chuckled.

"You actually looked pretty suave."

"Well, thank you."

"Well, as suave as one can look while drinking tea," she clarified.

"Right," he agreed. "Believe me, years of practice and a *lot* of correction."

Out of the corner of her eye she saw that he was actually checking her out. It was quick, but Nathan was definitely looking her over. And when he noticed that she was watching, he gave her a quick semi-embarrassed smile that confirmed it.

Nathan stood up. "Thank you Miss Lily, for the perfect tea and company."

"Well you're welcome Mr. Caesar."

"Please, just Nathan."

"Right, just Nathan," she said with full giddiness.

Lily watched Nathan go to the counter as Martin rang up his tea. She watched as he reminded Martin about the two ladies he said he would pay for and Martin corrected his total. Then Nathan refused the change and turned around, where he caught her eyes instantly, perfecting the action with a smile. She smiled back. *I want you so bad*, she thought and decided it more prudent to just offer him a wave.

Todd also noticed Nathan was leaving and leaned back in his chair. "Now remember Nathan, when I come over to your place, you said I can touch *it*," he said and then returned to the table and explained his joke through his own laughter.

Suddenly Lily remembered and called out, "Hey just Nathan."

Nathan turned around.

Lily wanted to ask him if he was busy this Friday, but could not muster the courage. "You never answered me about your name."

Nathan smiled. "Am I related to the original Julius Caesar?"

Lily quickly nodded and waited for him to reply.

"As a matter of fact, I am," he said taking his sunglasses from his pocket and putting them on.

"Really?" she asked, thinking that maybe they should have been talking about that instead of tea.

Walking out the door and before it shut he replied, "Really."

CHAPTER VII

1: Cried Their Victims ... Nevermore

THAT NIGHT in another city, Jenny sat with her phone on her ear talking the night away. Jenny lived in a very upscale apartment building and had, since the age of fourteen, started to babysit for a lot of the young parents in the building. And why not? She was responsible and even though she was now sixteen, she did not have a nightlife, at least not a real one. Her clients paid the average going rate, but like it was stated, this was an upscale apartment building and no one liked to be out done by one another, so for the most part, they tipped very well.

She heard the key go into the lock, which was a clear indication that Mr. Gable was home so she started to get up. "About time," she said rocking enough to propel herself off of the couch. "Not like I don't have shit to do," she bitched into the phone as the voice on the other end pitched high and feverishly while Jenny agreed, "I know!" The voice asked her something new and Jenny rolled her eyes. "No, you whore. I don't unbutton my shirt to get tips. I babysit, I don't work the pole," she explained as the voice on the other end laughed. "I'll call you when I get home," she said and then waited a moment. "Shut up, I live in the same building, it takes me like two minutes." Turning off the phone and throwing it into her backpack she started towards the hall "Shit, where—"

But before she finished her sentence she found her tablet and tucked it under her arm. She had planned on reading a new book she had recently downloaded until Becky called and ate every possible minute of the night.

Then a voice apologized as the door closed. "Sorry again Jenny," he said taking off his long coat and hanging it in the closet. Jonathon Gable threw his phone on top of the cubbyhole unit in the hallway and continued. "I should have known better," he admitted walking into the living room. "I really hope I didn't keep you from anything?"

"Don't worry about it Mr. Gable," she said giving a quick look around for anything else she may have forgotten.

"And Chrissie was okay?" Jonathon asked.

"Chrissie was great," Jenny assured him. "We had a blast."

"Good," he said reaching for his wallet and following Jenny back down the hall toward the front door.

"So you still need me for next Saturday?" she asked.

Jonathon thought for a moment. "I'm not sure if I'm going to have her next weekend. Can I let you know by Wednesday?"

"No problem, I just have the Baker's kids on Friday, so just let me know."

"Perfect," Jonathon said handing her an already counted amount of cash, tip included.

Jenny took the small stack. "Thank you Mr. Gable."

"Thank *you* Jenny," Jonathon said making it back to the door. He opened the door while waiting for Jenny, who was back at the bar counter putting her tablet into her backpack. "So I'll call you and —"

As he turned into the doorway, two people were standing in front of Jonathon Gable's now open door. One was a man in a black Coburn Great Coat who wore a white dress shirt with a silk black Kentucky tie underneath. His hair was frizzled and shooting out in all directions, while his black goatee was trimmed and properly manicured.

Beside him was a woman who would have been stunning if she didn't have a look in her eyes that screamed that she had just escaped from the set of a movies insane asylum. She wore all black, leather in the front and in the back while the sides from neck to toe was spandex, presumably to make the outfit more flexible. Her hair was an extreme horse mane ponytail that started at the beginning of her hair above the forehead and made its way back, making an intricate line of small ponytails all strewn together.

The male in the coat asked. "Mr. Gable?"

Jonathon looked at the man peculiarly. "Yes—how did you get into the building?"

The man in the black Coburn looked up and his eyes went from a dull brown to a snake-like yellow, complete with black diamond pupils. "It *really* doesn't matter Mr. Gable," he said without hesitation and grabbed Mr. Gable by the neck. Lifting him off of the ground he casually walked him back into the apartment. The woman in mostly leather with a bit of spandex followed with her bag and closed the door behind her.

After the sound of the door being locked to apartment 14A, the hallway was completely silent and empty.

Inside 14A Jonathon's legs kicked as they tried to find the ground while his hands frantically grasped and pried at the stranger holding him by the neck. He even tried to speak, but nothing translatable came out.

"What's going on," Jenny asked with an equal amount of shock and confusion, fear was still a moment or two behind.

The almost attractive woman, if not for the insanity in her black-rimmed eyes, passed the two men, placed her bag on the bar counter and headed right for Jenny. "My poor little puppet," she crooned and then shot forward grabbing Jenny.

Jenny did what anyone would do, she struggled. "Get the fuck off of me."

Suddenly the woman in leather and spandex, but mostly leather, slapped Jenny across the face and sent her sprawling onto the living room floor. She laid on the ground holding her knapsack as she began to cry.

Jonathon followed, looking like cargo being delivered by a forklift. The stranger in the Coburn dropped him to the ground where Jonathon gasped for air and rubbed at the pain. "Who—are—you?" Jonathon cried gruffly.

The woman looked at Jonathon lying on the floor. "Think of me as *You're* and him as *Fucked*," she said grabbing her bag and pulling out what looked like a mini tripod.

"My name is the Raven. And the ravishing specimen working over there is my one true everything, the Crow," he said and gave the Crow a smile before returning his attention back to Jonathon. "Now before you ask, it is a common misconception, but there is a difference between Ravens and Crows. We are also Monsters. Not as in bad guys who do bad things," he began and pointed towards the Crow. "Real—life—Monsters."

"What?" Jonathon asked as he turned to the Crow who had the same shade of yellow eyes and watched as a forked tongue flickered out from between her lips as she smiled. "Oh my God," Jonathon gasped. "What do you want," was the only thing Jonathon could think of asking as he watched poor Jenny struggle just to get to her hands and knees.

The Raven took a step back and bowed slightly while twirling his hands. "But to kill you of course."

Jenny was able to lift her head. "What are they talking about Mr. Gable?"

"Well my dear. Mr. Gable makes his living by finding ways to cheat people out of their insurance claims. Which lead to quite a few people dying."

Jenny looked at the Raven and then to Jonathon. "What?"

"Oh yes, quite the rapscallion," the Raven illuminated.

Wishing he had his phone on him, Jonathon decided to bluff. "You have ten seconds to get out, or I'm calling the police." Suddenly he found himself clutching the better part of his nose and right eye as he fell to the ground from a hard jab, courtesy of the Raven. "Jesus Christ," he cried and checked his hand for blood.

The Crow finished setting up the phone on the tripod and tapped the record button. "Every single one of those people you let die by manipulating their insurance claims had families Mr. Gable."

"Yes Mr. Gable," the Raven said and then added, "families that had to watch their loved ones die. Some of them might say, slowly murdered by you directly."

Jonathon looked up at the Raven, still holding his face. "I didn't kill anyone."

The Crow started to walk toward him. "Found each other online and started a little group."

The Raven smiled. "A group who had insurance policies for their loved ones. Paid their monthly premiums, for their loved ones. And when you screwed them over Mr. Gable, do you know what they didn't have? Enough money to save daughters and sons. Nor could they save wives or husbands," he listed off as Jonathon grimaced.

The Crow smiled. "But they had more than enough money, once pooled together. Enough to hire two Monsters."

Jonathon looked faint. "You're going to kill me."

The Crow laughed.

"No Mr. Gable, not for the money they paid," the Raven said and smirked as his eyes lit with insanity. "We are going to kill your daughter so those poor people can see you suffer as they did."

Jonathon got to his feet and began to back away slowly shaking his head. "Don't hurt her."

"*Don't hurt her*," the Crow mimicked as she looked to the Raven. "It already begs. How unpleasantly pathetic, even for a human."

The Raven's smirk turned into a full blown maniacal smile of pure lunacy. "Then we're going to eat you alive so those people can see *you* punished."

Maybe just desperate, Jonathon ran to the cabinet across the living room. He went directly for the top drawer where he kept his already loaded .38, which was more than high enough to keep out of reach of children. But when Jonathon turned around with a newfound confidence it was quickly erased.

The Raven seized him by the wrist and squeezed until a sound like bone being tightened by a vice grip popped into the air and Jonathon fell to his knees. "Braver than I thought," he admitted to the Crow and squeezed a little harder.

Jonathon cried out as he struggled to hold on to the gun until the painful pressure finally made him drop it. But in one last effort he kicked out his leg and sent the gun spinning towards the babysitter and yelled out, "Jenny!"

Jenny dropped to her knees and planted her palms on the floor letting let her fingers act as a net. Snatching the .38 up she fumbled while turning it around so she was holding it correctly and then rose to her feet, turning towards Jonathon and the man who called himself the Raven.

During this time, the Crow resembled something like a strobe light as she finally took notice of Jenny and moved towards her. It was as if she bobbed to the right and then she would disappear for less than a second, a blink maybe, reappearing a few feet away. Then she bobbed to her left and as a blink in time passed, she reappeared another few feet away, or in this case, closer to Jenny. The Crow bobbed one more time and disappeared as Jenny was turning around with the gun toward the men, but this time the Crow reappeared right behind the babysitter. She leaned in and blew Jenny's hair away to expose her neck and produced two fangs that fell from the top of her mouth like they were on hinges. Then like lightning the Crow struck fast and furious.

"Ow—what the fuck," Jenny cried out clasping her hand over two little puncture wounds now on her neck.

The Crow began to circle her. "My poor puppet. Why don't you use the gun?"

Jenny looked at her and then down at the gun.

"You barely have the strength to lift it," the Crow said and moved in closer.

Jenny finally got the gun up as her eyes became watery and bloodshot.

The Crow was able to get face to face as Jenny tried to point the gun.

"You've been bitten," the Crow said putting her hand over top of the babysitter's hand and then gently pushing them both down. "You don't even have the strength to pull the trigger. And in about five seconds you won't even have the motor skills to hold onto it."

Jenny tried to raise the gun again but suddenly it fell out of her hand.

Jonathon just looked on as all the hope that was in his eyes faded into horror.

The Crow watched as Jenny's eyes started to blink frantically. "Right now your vision is starting to get blurry. Look," she said wiping a string of drool from Jenny's lip. "You're already salivating."

Jenny dropped to her knees as her whole body started to lightly convulse.

The Crow bent down beside her. "The usual purpose of the bite is to paralyze the victim. But where some poisonous bites release an anesthetic that numbs the feeling of pain, ours do not. And although it is not lethal, it is for the purpose of keeping our meals silent and still."

Jenny began to convulse more violently and fell over onto the floor until she gave one final kick. Then she just laid there, breathing and watching, unable to speak and unable to move.

"What?" Jonathon asked.

The Raven adjusted his attention. "I am sorry," he said genuinely as Jonathon sat on the floor, "but we really are Monsters. We're Anguis, which is Latin for snake. A name given for our similarities."

The Crow interrupted him. "I think he is more confused about the eating part."

The Raven looked at her and then to Jonathon. "Of course, my apologies. You see Mr. Gable, like your larger snakes, we are one hundred percent carnivorous."

Jonathon stood confounded in a state of terrifying wonderment. "If it's money you want, I have money," he offered.

Shaking his head the Raven frowned. "That is not how this works," he said turning to the Crow. "They always try to negotiate."

The Crow bobbed left and then right and strobed until she ended up in front of Jonathon. "The child Mr. Gable."

"I won't," Jonathon stated with a father's bravery.

"He doesn't have to," the Raven said and grinned with delight as he nodded in front of them.

They turned around.

Wiping the tears from his eyes Jonathon held out his arms and managed the best smile he could muster. "Come on honey, come to Daddy."

Still tired and holding on to her teddy, the little girl started walking toward him raising her arms so she could be picked up.

The Raven smiled at the Crow. "Yes my dear. Come to daddy," he said and reached into his coat and produced a sickle.

Jonathon saw the creature with the snake-like eyes holding the razor sharp question mark walking towards his little girl and stood up with all the bravery he needed. His little girl had her arms open with the expectation that daddy was going to pick her up and Jonathon was not going—

Suddenly Jonathon side stepped to his left while holding the side of his neck. "What the fuck?" He fell to one knee and quickly looked toward his little girl. His eyes began to blink furiously as he tried to say something, but he couldn't put the words together.

The Raven approached the little girl and raised his left arm.

Jonathon went to stand but could not and fell again, this time to both knees.

The Raven didn't even look back, he only stepped in front of the child and brought down the curled blade, swiping across the child's neck with a deep slicing sound. Without breaking his stride he turned around and walked back to Jonathon as the thump of her little girl head hit the floor.

Jonathon began to convulse as tears streamed down his face.

Rolling along the floor the head stopped just a few feet in front of Jonathon, the expression of sleepy confusion never changed. It was so quick and clean that the blood still contained itself as the headless body kept walking towards its father, still holding on to its bedtime teddy.

One step as if still whole.

The second step and the teddy is let go.

A third step and the blood seeps over the neck like the cup is full.

A fourth does not finish. And the little body in pink pajamas crumbled to the floor, lifeless.

Jonathon dropped to the floor and lay on his side, crying silently.

The Crow had made her way over and was now bending down beside him. "Make no mistake Mr. Gable. This is going to be painful beyond any comprehension."

The Raven holstered his unstained sickle and stood above him. "Whether you pass to your After favorably is a judgment reserved for after Death. But you have ruined your last life for money Mr. Gable," he said removing his coat and laying it on the couch. "For we are not just messengers—no. My word is final. Because we are also your executioners, your composers of the True Silence. Your sentence is death Jonathon Gable."

The Crow nestled her mouth at the nape of his neck and raised her lips to his ear as saliva dripped from her fangs. "Quoth the Raven," her hot breath hissed while her forked tongue flickered at his ear, and then she said the last word he would ever hear. "Nevermore."

Suddenly they were grabbing Chrissie's body and ripping chunks off with their teeth as Jonathon could only lay there and watch. Their mouths snapped and jerked until they were widened enough to fit child limbs in whole. Blood splattered and pooled, and still Jonathon could only lay there watching. They hissed and snapped at each other, playfully fighting for chunks of flesh and then they were done.

With the child that is.

They slowly turned to Jonathon with their cold yellow eyes and flickering tongues. He lay there as they sniffed and licked until the Crow struck at his leg and drew blood that ran down paralyzed flesh in two lines. Then she struck him, taking a piece of flesh with her retreat. The Raven bit into Jonathon's side and wrestled to free a much larger chunk. And the phone recorded it all.

And there off to the side, laying on the ground paralyzed was poor Jenny. But worse than that, she could not close her eyes, she could not pass out and she could not turn away. Jenny could only lay there as Jonathon was savagely eaten alive, in incredible pain and without the ability to express himself. She could only wait there and wonder how long she had left until it was her turn. Wishing with all her might, that Mr. Gable had not been running late this evening.

CHAPTER VIII

1: The Enemy's Camp

ACROSS THE ATLANTIC, a large castle nestled itself in the middle of rolling green hills on one side of it and a lake on the other. It was bustling with crowds and modernism that made it almost look carnival-like. Yet in a small window, the smallest of them all, Marcus held a saucer in his left hand while blissfully taking in the aroma from the cup in his right. The almost out of place window seemed to offer him the best of both views, the rolling green hills to the left and the crystal blue water of the lake to the right.

"Marcus?" she asked from behind him.

Ignoring her he finally took a sip of his tea and then looked outside again, this time with a look of envy.

"Marcus?" her voice called out again. "What do you want us to do?"

He turned around holding out his cup. "This tastes like piss."

The woman frowned. "You made it."

Marcus smirked. "Doesn't change the fucking facts my dear. And you just asked me what it is that I want you to do."

"Not what I meant," the woman in the white blouse named Carmon said. Her top was complimented by a well-made and hand-pressed grey skirt that matched her high heels, from a store that normal people had never heard of, least of all could afford. She finally huffed while taking her phone out from her pocket and tapped the screen feverishly. Then she pocketed the phone. "Merrick is getting nowhere."

"Too obvious fucking conclusion. And might I add, as I predicted," Marcus pointed out and walked to the middle of the room. There he placed his cup of less than mediocre tea upon a grand oak table and waited.

Carmon walked over to an abnormally large screen that took up almost the entire northern wall and punched a few keys on a terminal. The screen lit up with a world map and she waved her hand in front of it and a bright green dot appeared over Italy, the Amalfi Coast to be exact. Moving her hands around she brought up a virtual keypad that she could use her finger to punch in a code of numbers. "His progress so far," she said and suddenly red lines raced to tiny red dots all over the map, all in Asia. Turning to Marcus she smiled sarcastically. "As you can see, thirty two sightings and Asia is still coming up empty."

"You just fucking told me that," he said, seeming to be more concerned with other matters.

"Yes, but what I am trying to get to is," she said and paused while she swiped and pushed in front of the giant screen. Suddenly news headlines from Chicago papers and Internet sites popped up in front of the world map. They were all of murder stories, mostly of homeless men. "We've been monitoring the news and social media and there have been an unusual amount of them in Chicago."

Marcus smirked. "Well, Chicago has never had any shortage of violence."

"No," she agreed, "but our sources are describing them as vicious, like animal attacks."

"Is it being reported as such?"

Carmon shook her head. "All factions have been censoring the media for the most part, until a joint investigation is complete. Should hold for a while. Some early conspiracy adopters have popped up on the net, but nothing grabbing any real public attention."

Through the door walked an elderly gentlemen who looked exactly like a proper butler should. His face never diverted from his task as he set down a tray holding a new pot of tea, milk, sugar and the appropriate sized spoons. He gathered the other pot and cup and left the room without a word.

Marcus started to pour and then looked at Carmon. "Tea?"

"No thank you," she said and continued her swiping and pushing into the air in front of all the virtual imagery. Then a bunch of oversized pictures popped up and Carmon cleared them all away except for one. "Then we got this," she said pointing to a large photo of one body on a street in Chicago, surrounded by police and onlookers behind the police tape.

"Okay," Marcus said taking a sip and looking more content with the taste.

Carmon closed her hands on one person in the picture in particularly and then opened them to zoom in on that person. "This one matches a picture of Nathanial from two decades ago almost perfectly."

"Almost?"

Carmon nodded. "Sixty four percent."

Marcus took a deep breath while scepticism creeped over his face.

"Remember," Carmon led her pre-emptive strike with, "The picture was taken by a cheap phone and found online," she said adjusting the picture to not be so blurry and then turned around to face him. "And when was the last time we had a lead that was sixty four percent positive?"

"True," Marcus murmured as he squinted to focus in on the person who was supposed to be Nathanial.

Carmon swiped the picture to the side to reveal the map. "The Amalfi Coast was fifty-fifty," she said and then reached forward, grabbed the air and pulled back as the screen zoomed in just 600 miles from Chicago. "Home sweet home."

"Family," Marcus whispered, almost becoming intrigued.

"I don't think it is a coincidence that we received thirty two sightings, all within territory controlled by the Order and not one of them remotely confirmed. Yet, this picture shows up in Chicago, just six hundred miles from his family's home, and his father, Julius calls to request a meeting at his home. After unofficially fighting with us for almost a century. Why now?"

"And that little prick tried to kill me. On two occasions." Marcus added.

Carmon nodded. "Corporate espionage, attacks on our properties, our investments and two assassination attempts. And now he wants to meet to *bury the hatchet*?"

"Taking me for a fucking optimist," Marcus said taking a sip. "Bury the hatchet? Right into my ass as soon as my back is turned. That dirty double-crossing cocksucker."

Carmon seized the momentum. "We need to get Merrick out of Asia."

"Well that I agree with," he said walking towards the giant screen. "I've been waiting almost three decades to catch the little cocksucker. My perverse desire to have Nathanial Caesar served to me on a plate, straight from the oven consumes me."

"They say revenge is dish best served cold," she said as an almost consolation.

Placing an antique chair down facing away from the screen he sat on it backwards. "So they say," he said and then slowly turned his head towards her. "But how the fuck would I know? Do you see me eating *anything*? Hot or fucking cold?" Marcus raged as spit flew from his mouth. "Because right now I'd settle for Luke—Fucking—Warm!"

Carmon just shook her head as a beep rang out from her phone. "It's Merrick."

Marcus wiped his mouth and took a sip of his tea. "Mmm—put him on the screen."

Carmon tapped her phone and then swiped at the large screen in front of them. Suddenly Merrick was in his own window within the large screen in front of them. Carmon placed her hand in front of it, closed her fingers to grab it and moved it off to the left side of the screen. Merrick was sitting at a table in what looked to be a dirty hovel that resembled a restaurant.

Marcus looked on in disgust. "Where the *fuck*, are you?"

Merrick gave him a look of sarcastic joy. "Not sure. Some shithole in the southern part of Laos, on the border of Cambodia."

Marcus nodded and then smiled. "And your chaperones?"

"The creepy twins had business two shit holes over. Left me here to grab a *bite*," he said using the last word in his sentence to look down and direct them to the plate of questionable food in front of him.

Carmon's face recoiled in disgust and then she turned her attention back to Merrick. "We're trying to decide if your current assignment is still worth pursuing."

"I feel pretty confident that Nathanial is not in Asia," Merrick said pushing his plate off to the side. "And as lovely as it's been, I believe that I would be better utilized following a lead on a different continent."

Marcus took another sip of his tea. "Carmon believes he might be stateside."

Merrick thought about it. "Home is where the heart is."

Carmon grabbed at pictures and documents on the screen while dropping them in an email. "I'm sending you the file now."

"Sorry Marcus," Merrick apologized. "I should have gone to Amalfi first, instead of Mikhail."

Marcus shrugged the notion off. "I needed you in Moscow. No, I should've listened to my gut. I fucking knew it was too personal for that Slav, but I allowed sympathy to cloud my judgement."

"We'll get him soon," Merrick assured him as he began playing with his phone, judging by the email notification he was opening Carmon's file.

"Soon—it's always fucking soon," Marcus complained. Then out of nowhere he stood straight up while simultaneously kicking the antique chair up into the air. Holding his tea in one hand Marcus grabbed the chair with his free hand and whipped it across the room. The chair screamed through the air as it flew past Carmon, who did not move or blink even though it came close enough to cause her hair to flutter. She only cringed slightly as the chair exploded into kindling behind her, against the back wall.

Marcus didn't miss a beat. "I need to take something other than *soon* from this goddamn, cock sucking, cunt licking, and disastrous anal raping of a fucking kerfuffle."

Carmon and Merrick both just waited patiently and quietly.

Anger surged through Marcus' beating red face. "Fucking Ukrainian," he said taking his long stare away from the screen and directing it at Cameron. "I mean you were there. I did tell him to report, right?"

Carmon barely nodded.

Marcus took in deep labored breaths to try and calm himself. "Do you know they use to call his father, Yaroslav the Wise? And he was a fucking pig farmer."

Merrick covered his mouth to hide his silent laughter.

Marcus' face was getting red again. "But at least the pig farmer can follow instructions, obviously a trait not passed on to his dim fucking son," he said looking to Carmon again. "Could I not have made it any more fucking clear? Find Nathanial—report back." He started to pace and debate in his head as he nodded and pointed his finger into the air. "I know the dumb cunt loved her. But so did I, she was my daughter. Even I wouldn't attempt to fight him on my own. He was born with all Five Rings enhanced. What was he thinking? I mean, did his Kievan mother fuck a monkey? How did this mentally defective dimwitted cunt, live for a thousand years?" he asked taking a large breath and holding it. He exhaled while staring into an abyss of inconclusiveness, until his face twitched and an agonizing expression poured over his face. "I mean, before I give myself a fucking brain aneurism."

"You had—we had no way of knowing that Mikhail—"

Marcus took three forceful steps towards her and pointed his finger. "Do not mention that fucking cunt's name in my presence anymore. Ever!"

"Maybe putting Yaroslav on this now would be wise," Merrick said trying to elevate the situation. "He'll definitely have extra incentive since Nathanial killed his son."

"No," Marcus said almost completely calmed. "No, you'll be handling this directly from here on out."

"Of course," Merrick said and nodded.

Marcus took another sip and his face soured. He spit the cold tea back into the cup and then threw it to the floor. Walking back to the teapot he started to pour. "How long will it take you to get stateside?"

Merrick stood up and threw down a handful of overinflated currency. "Leaving now," he said and started to walk away.

Carmon and Marcus watched as men from an adjacent table got up and invaded his barely touched plate.

Merrick's movement was televised on screen, and as soon as he walked out of the hovel and started to look around, Carmon and Marcus could see the street littered with thousands of locals in a sea of chaos. "I have to settle up with the Order, but I'll be on a plane by the end of the week," he explained and then looked at someone not in frame. "Taxi?"

"Good," Marcus said a little more upbeat and turned to Carmon. "Contact the Raven or that fiancé of his. They should be in that general area. And set up a meeting place, I believe the slithery cocksuckers are partial to St. Louis," he said and then turned back to the screen while taking a sip. "At this point they will just be surveillance. Only surveillance. Please make that absolutely fucking clear Merrick."

"Yes sir."

Carmon began typing frantically on her phone. "I hate Anguis, even talking to Snake People gives me the creeps."

"So text them," Marcus said looking around. "Where is my fucking chair?"

"You broke it," she informed him without looking up from her phone.

Marcus thought for a moment. "When did I fucking do that?"

She stopped suddenly and with her eyes directed him to look behind them.

Marcus gazed upon the shattered antique chair. "Right," he concluded with annoyance. "Fucking Ukrainian. From here on out, Mikhail fucking Yaroslav Sviatoslavich, will forever be known as a fucking cocksucker who failed to follow the simplest of instructions and is now explaining himself to his betters, in the After."

"Yes sir," Carmon said and tried to defuse any other outbreaks of anger. "And again, it was pretty elementary."

Marcus lifted his tea and smiled. "Right, elementary. I like that." He put his tea back on the table in fear his next outburst would cause him to spill it. "Where is Mr. Tuttle?"

"The Middle East, we have him sorting out a small energy problem."

"And the German?"

"In Germany."

Marcus went to say something and then stopped. "Really?"

"Yes Marcus, the German is in Germany."

"Send Mr. Tuttle to Ireland, I want eyes on the Wolfhounds."

"Do you think they are helping Nathanial?" Carmon asked.

"Little shit helped them on more than one occasion, usually by fucking me in the ass. But if the Caesars catch wind of us, the early warning will be movement from those mongrels."

"Got it," she said and began typing again.

"And remind that fucking Bruti to be on his best behaviour. That ape loses his temper and he ends up on top of a building, swatting at fighter planes. Like a meaner and less intelligent King Kong. Costing me a fortune in media silence and insurance restitutions."

Carmon laughed. "Will do. And the German?"

"Send him to Scotland."

"Scotland? What's in Scotland?"

"Tyre is in Scotland. I want to negotiate an alliance with him."

Carmon stood still for a moment, almost looking frightened. "I think if we planned it carefully—"

Marcus had made his way to her and shook his head as he put his hand on her shoulder. "No my dear. Death has a certain knack for collecting even the most careful of men. Odds must be stacked," he explained. "If Nathanial is indeed home. We aren't just going to battle with him, but his entire fucking family. The Caesars. That would cost an unheard of amount of money and manpower. And when I say manpower I mean lives. So why waste so much when you can use just one?"

"I understand, it's just that Tyre is very unpredictable," she whispered.

"I know he is. But on this planet," Marcus said taking her phone. He found the screen connected with the bigger screen in front of them and pushed a few buttons. Suddenly a bunch of blue dots appeared in different locations on the world map. "There are some just as, if not more powerful than even Nathanial Caesar. Now some of them hate us and some of them actually belong to the Order. Some haven't been seen or heard from for quite some time," he said turning to Cameron. "Then there is that one being hunted by every Virus Squad on the planet."

She laughed. "Yeah, but we wouldn't want her helping us anyways."

"No we would not," Marcus agreed punching in a code. "But there is one," he said as a blue dot lit up over Scotland. "He hates the Order and as far as I remember, he doesn't much care for the Caesars either."

"Tyre?" Merrick asked while catching up to the conversation.

Marcus nodded. "We'll send the fucking German."

Carmon looked sceptical as well. "But what can we offer Tyre? He doesn't need anything."

Marcus laughed. "Neither does a cat. But you scratch long enough and even the most stubborn cocksucker will jump up onto the couch to see what all the fucking scratching is about," Marcus said pretty pleased with himself. "And I don't believe Tyre needs that much scratching to pique his interest."

"Of course," she said. "But he hates Germans."

"I just need him to give him the message," Marcus said leaving the room.

Cameron turned and looked at the screen. "I'm not sure what that means. What is the message?"

And then on the giant screen a sorry excuse for a taxi pulled up beside Merrick as he laughed. "That I do not know my dear. But I do know that this shit is about to get very interesting."

CHAPTER IX

1: The Bump In

SINCE NATHAN'S VISIT the other day, when he had revealed that he was in fact related to Guiles Julius Caesar, he had found himself revisiting Sips for a grand total of seven times. *Not a lot* some would say, but in fact, only four days had passed and one of those days he wasn't able to go at all. And in that time Nathan had really got to like Lily and he found that he was making excuses just to go and see her. Now today was her day off, but Nathan had a plan and it involved him following her while she was on one of her walks and pretending to bump into her.

They would talk for a while, maybe get a drink and this would segue into him asking her out. It was a simple plan, but a good plan and he had been following her since she left her apartment, like a stalker. A stalker that can leap from building top to building top and stalk her from twenty stories up.

But at this very moment his plan was being ruined by the fact that Lily was about to die—literally. His plan was going up in flames. No—his plan was about to be hit by a twenty-ton bus.

As the bus's horn howled out into the busy morning and the deafening screams of its brakes seemed to grab almost every passerby's attention to some degree. Yet it failed in doing so for one. Sure, a lot of people looked over there while some looked here and some even looked up, but the one person who needed to be aware of the almost twenty tons that was barrelling down on her was Lily. And she was not aware of it at all.

Nathan's mind was ripping through scenarios and questions at lightning speed. He was using the distraction of the oncoming bus and its screeching brakes to give him some much needed punch in his step but kept himself from outright blurring.

He saw no eyes on him at this particular second so he flung himself forward and blurred between a bicycle courier and a cabby, who until 2.3 seconds ago had been arguing. Coming out of the blur Nathan watched as Lily placed her left foot firmly on the street. He could hear the sole of her sneakers crumple the few loose pebbles beneath them as Lily began to back up. Nathan could also see the bus driver bracing himself for the oncoming horror of Lily becoming evening news. He could already smell the chemical burn of rubber materializing into the air as he quickly tried to calculate if he would reach her in time without going into a full blown blur?

2: Earlier

Lily could never bring herself to jog. She wanted to, she really did, but she just couldn't do it. She tried a treadmill, but the thought of running in one spot going nowhere made her inexplicably angry. She had paid for many a gym membership, with no emerging sign of discipline or consistency in her determination.

So, she walked.

She walked everywhere and she loved it. If Lily was with someone, usually Jeanette, she could keep a pace and carry a conversation. If she was alone, Lily had no problem enjoying the colorful city she loved to the tune of her current soundtrack on her phone.

So there she was, walking briskly down the street on a beautiful early morning noticing the sky was already sprouting big fluffy clouds. There was enough of a breeze to make it brisk while overhead the sun shined its warmth, evening things out.

Unfortunately she felt that she had forgotten something and started to slow down. Finally stopping, Lily couldn't shake that nagging feeling, whether it was important or not was still to be determined. Without knowing what she was looking for Lily began searching and patting herself down.

Change, she thought. Just in case she walked too far, like a couple of weeks ago when she walked all the way to West Blackhawk Street and realized she'd walked right past the Chicago Fire Department and didn't even take in any of the manly scenery.

Then her fingers touched change. *Shit, that's not it.*

Lily could not put her finger on it. She also did not realize that she was turning in little half circles, almost as if dancing, waltzing herself closer to the busy street.

My phone? Yes, you forgot your phone dumbass, we left it on the—

The thought was cut off as her triumphant look turned to shocked distress at the sight of a city bus barreling down upon her.

It was the 10:15 and it was bringing the screeching sound of straining brakes being pushed to their limits along with the deafening blast of its horn. And as Lily's *80s* pop played in her ears, the realization of imminent collision rushed to her head and was looking for acceptance. But before she could argue her whole body instantaneously tightened as she seemed to automatically brace herself for the next life.

3: To Save What You Might Eat?

Thirty-six pedestrians were in the direct area, not including Nathan or Lily or the seventeen people in vehicles, which included the eight on the bus. Nathan counted twelve vehicles that could possibly be affected, one hydrant and three storefronts. There were six people he could see directly in the windows so his current plan relied on the bus staying on its current trajectory. Then, considering the speed in which the bus was traveling, the weight, sound of the brakes and having to guess at the added weight of the passengers, not to mention the last time the brakes were changed, Nathan educated that it would stop in twenty meters, give or take.

But Nathan needed to decide right here and now, blur quickly and risk being seen or fall short by two seconds and watch her die. He began to think but her face interrupted. He tried thinking again but only Lily's face appeared in his head and then as if he had no control over his actions he pushed himself and blurred. Within a blink he grabbed Lily by both of her arms and plucked her from Death's surging embrace just as the bus went rushing by them both.

The bus stopped straight ahead and only a hair over twenty meters. The dramatic squealing of the bus brought thirty-six pedestrians looking their way, as well as twelve cars to a halt and one hydrant left unscathed. It also plastered six people against the deli window and a bird who ignored it all while making off with a piece of hot dog bun.

"I would've splattered on the window of that bus," she said as Nathan directed her away from the road. The imminent explosion of her body did not happen and she looked confused as blue tinted clouds of smoke mixed with the smell of burning rubber made her cough. "I mean, the morning commuters would have been screaming at the sight of me sprawled out on the windshield. My arms and legs spread wide and my tongue just hanging out," she babbled on. "Oh shit, I'm going to miss the previews."

That was the last thing Lily said before she passed out.

Nathan waited and listened. He was filtering all the commotion for anything that resembled, *did you see that guy warp speed and save her? Is he a superhero? Is he an alien?* Or even a, *what the fuck was that?*

But no one saw him blur to save Lily's life.

4: Much Later

Like a child waiting for their punishment to be handed down, Lily sat at her table patiently.

Martin however, was the opposite of patient and was pacing back and forth. "How could she almost get herself killed?" he asked Todd, ignoring Lily completely.

"Well I don't think she purposely set out this morning to get herself killed," Todd replied then quickly looked at Jeanette who looked at Lily who shook her head to concur.

Martin nodded vigorously. "That is my point Papi, she doesn't think."

"I'm pretty sure Lily thinks. I think," Todd said giving him a frowny pouty face. "You're just upset."

Martin tried to hide his emotions with another excuse. "I am upset because we got a call from the policeman to go and pick her up and we had to close the store until Jeanette could come here on her day off."

Jeanette spoke up. "It was okay, I didn't mind."

Martin yelled back. "Yes you did, you minded very much."

"Now Bear, I know you're really upset because we almost lost our Lily today," Todd stated while trying to calm him.

Martin was already nodding. "Exactly. I think we should ground her."

Todd looked confused. "Well that is nothing in line with what I said but *FUN*," he said clapping his hands and turning to Lily who gave him a look as if he had jumped on board the wacky train and ordered the Kool-Aid. He then looked at Jeanette who gave him more or less the same look. Pausing for thought, he turned back to Martin. "Now sweetie," he started, obviously realizing that he had just been caught up in the moment. "Lily, while in our care, is actually an adult."

"Is she?" Martin inserted immediately. "Do adults run out onto busy streets in front of buses?"

Todd turned to Lily. "Just give me a second," he said and then turned to Jeanette with his eyes wide open. "Will you go fucking clean something," he yelled and hissed and shooed at her like she was a cat.

Jeanette scurried off to the kitchen while Todd went and talked to Martin.

Lily sat at her table, again waiting when Jeanette peered out of the kitchen doorway. Lily laughed. "It's safe."

Jeanette sat beside her. "God he's a dick."

"I really am sorry you had to come in on your day off."

"It's your day off too," Jeanette informed her. "So are you really okay?"

"Yeah," Lily said going back to work, "So what were you doing when they called?"

"Waiting at the movie theatre for you, dumbass," Jeanette said smacking her arm. "Remember, we were making up for that horrible movie the other night. When you met your knight in shining armor."

Lily stood up straight with a light bulb going off in her expression. "That's what I meant."

"That's what you meant what?" Jeanette asked in less than perfect English.

Lily laughed. "After I almost got hit, I said—I'm going to miss the previews, but I had no idea why I was saying that."

"Yeah well, we both missed the previews."

Then Lily pondered. "I can't believe I almost died over my phone."

"Yeah, but who are we without our phones?" Jeanette said and then smirked. "But who forgets their phone nowadays? Idiots I guess."

Lily appreciated Jeanette trying to make fun of the situation and gave her a quick hug.

Then out of nowhere came a loud hissing sound. "I thought I told you to go fucking clean something. Where the fuck is my spray bottle?" Todd asked making Jeanette jump.

"Okay-okay, I'm going," she said and scooted back to the kitchen.

"I swear that bitch is always where I don't want her to be," Todd said grabbing Martin and pushing him in front of Lily. "Lily, Martin would like to say a few things," he said and then was left hanging in the silence. So he gave Martin a look.

Martin took one more step forward with a look of shame all over his face. "Si. I am sorry Lily."

Lily jumped up. "Oh Honey, you don't have to be sorry. You were totally right, I am an idiot for putting you guys through this. I am so sorry."

Martin turned to Todd who just pointed at him to turn right back around.

Lily continued to apologize. "I'm also sorry you had to close the store."

Martin took a deep breath. "I don't care about closing the store Lily. I got so upset because you are the family. You and Todd are the only family I have."

Jeanette's voice came flying out of the kitchen, "*HEY!*"

Martin smiled. "And Jeanette of course."

Nodding her head like a toddler Lily laughed.

Martin raised her chin to look into her eyes. "You are not like my sister. You are my sister. Not only that, but my best friend. And I don't think I could handle losing you."

Todd was still standing off to the side. "Oh shit, I think I'm going to cry."

Throwing herself into Martin's arms Lily squeezed with all her might. "And you're my brother," she cried with laughter. "And Todd is like the sister I never had."

Martin hugged her lovingly and suddenly they were both being hugged by Todd. Then Jeanette ran out of the kitchen and tried to get in on the action but was thwarted as Todd held out his hand and pushed her back by her face.

As Jeanette finally gave up and Todd let go, Lily leaned back in Martin's arms. "I love you."

"And I you," he said and gave her a kiss before heading back to the kitchen.

Todd made his way back to Lily's table. "So," he said nudging her.

"So," she dragged out shyly and gave him a nudge back, suggesting maybe she had a clue as to his inquisitiveness nature.

Suddenly Jeanette called back out from the kitchen, "You know I'm not scheduled for today."

"God Jeanette," Todd complained loudly without turning around, "will you please shut up!"

Lily laughed as she heard Jeanette complaining to Martin.

"I swear that bitch just tickles my angry nerve," Todd said putting his hand on Lily's lap, "now, where were we? Right, almost hit by a bus—Go."

"Pretty scary," she said diplomatically.

"Thank God a ridiculously good looking man was there to pull you back from an all but certain death."

"What about, pulled me back with his muscular arms," she said turning away.

Grabbing her playfully he spun her back towards him. "How do you know he's muscular?"

She fell into Todd's arms. "Because when he grabbed me and pulled me back he held me in his arms and I could feel his whole body," she confessed as Todd pushed her back up and started a playful cat fight.

Martin sighed at their immaturity as he passed them. "I'm sure you are giggling over Mr. Nathan. But might I remind you, he is the customer. Not the subject of the perverted amusement."

"This from the man who talks dirty to every male lead on the CW," Todd said trying to bring him down to their level. "Talks dirty when I'm there, God knows what he does when I'm not."

"You're horrible," Lily laughed. "God knows what you do when we're not there."

The door chime went off and now a slew of people poured in.

"Meh," Todd said giving an indifferent shrug. "Give me Netflix and I'll watch Magnum P.I. any day of the week."

"You know that show ended in the eighties right?"

"Not up here honey," he said pointing to his head. "That moustache ride will live on forever up here."

Turning to clear some things off her table Lily started to feel a little disturbed. "I don't even want to know what that means." Suddenly she became repulsed. "Oh wait, eww."

CHAPTER X

1: Plan B

SO WHEN NATHAN'S *bump in* plan did not work thanks to Lily almost getting killed, he decided to take the direct approach. It was the next day and he had decided he would just march into Sips and ask her out on a date.

Except Nathan had hit a little snag.

Screams filled the area and they were originating from a young woman on the outer fringe of the park, just a few blocks from Sips.

Quite understandable, Nathan thought. *I am holding her boyfriend's severed right arm.*

The young lady's screams hit such a high pitch that Nathan was surprised more people weren't running, whether it was towards her to offer assistance or away from the whole ordeal. But they did not and continued on with their day.

The howling female now turned to Nathan and pointed an accusing finger at him. She did not stop screaming of course, she had just made Nathan the focus.

I can't think with this fucking screaming, he yelled internally and blurred forward, clotheslining the woman with her severed boyfriend's arm. The young lady did an on-the-spot somersault until landing flat on her stomach and unconscious.

Not five minutes earlier, Nathan had been on his way to Sips completely committed to going through with Plan B. He was nervous and it had taken the bounce out of his step as walked down the street getting closer to the coffee shop. As he played the scenario in his head, no matter what changes he made to it, slight or complex, she was always saying *no*. Even the advantage of imagination would not tip the scales in his favor and he was getting more and more frustrated.

It was during one of these scenarios that Nathan was not watching where he was going and almost plowed into the *now* armless man and his *now* unconscious girlfriend.

"It's got to be perfect," Nathan had demanded of himself as the couple passed him.

"Okay buddy," the male replied and stepped in front of his girlfriend.

Nathan had presumed it was a chivalrous act to protect her. He understood and even thought it was refreshing, offering an apologetic smile as they went by.

The chuckles that came from the young couple were bad enough, since he could hear every putdown and insult they were saying, but the snide remarks about his shirt suddenly had Nathan second guessing his whole wardrobe choice. And when he turned their way he was met with a—*What are you looking at freak?* Followed by a finger.

Even then Nathan had kept his cool, albeit barely, but offered an apology. "Sorry," he said and turned around and began his agonizing walk back towards Sips.

That would have been that. Except, not ten seconds later the boyfriend yelled from what he supposed was a safe distance to avoid an altercation.

"What were you going to do loser?" the boyfriend yelled as his girlfriend laughed and pushed him away. As if she was a mighty lion tamer keeping Nathan safe from any more embarrassing wounds.

Nathan had stopped dead in his tracks. The stress from all of the imaginary rejection and the stress from all of the anticipation of asking her had collided right on Nathan's last nerve. The one in the corner of his right eye and this asshole was the straw that was bouncing on it like a six year old on a trampoline. His eyes twitched with an almost inhuman speed that seemed to ignite the ache in his head that would soon take over any clear sensible thought.

Today is not the day to test this Monster's patience, he remembered thinking.

"That's what I thought, fucking pussy," the boyfriend yelled, which most likely would have been the last insult since they had almost made it to the park.

But it did not matter.

That last comment was sharp enough to cut Nathan's last nerve and Nathan could feel it break as all of his self-control and discipline broke with it. And as control fell, rage bubbled upward and invaded every thought he had. He blurred towards them and within seconds he had grabbed the boyfriend by the shoulder and sunk his claws in. Blood sprayed across Nathan's questionable shirt and when he dove deeper, the pressure caused the blood to spit all over Nathan's face as he roared in satisfaction. Pain didn't even make an appearance on the man's face before Nathan's eyes started to glow and confusion cut to the front of the line.

Meanwhile the girlfriend had backed up in shock and was trying to get an idea of the situation that was thrust upon her. The sight of a Monster who was violating her boyfriend like a scene from a horror movie did not help to clarify things, but she knew it warranted the tried and true high-pitched scream, one that she nailed perfectly.

Before the man could say *What the Fuck*, Nathan pulled out his claws, creating an Old Faithful effect as blood gushed up into the air like a fountain. He then grabbed him by the throat and lifted him as far up as he could, letting his feet dangle before they started kicking to help in his fight for air. That is when Nathan slammed him into the sidewalk and watched as blood leapt from the man's mouth which made way for an agonizing groan.

Nathan could smell nothing but fear and smiled in delight as he gripped the man's hand so tight he could hear all of the little bones inside crunch in unison. He placed his foot on the man's chest and gave the arm two quick jerks. Nathan then roared and pulled until the arm separated from the torso.

Giving no concern for her own safety the girlfriend stood fast, bearing witness to the atrocities taking place in front of her, a hysterical witness but a witness nonetheless.

Bringing us to where they stood presently. She was now unconscious on the ground and Nathan was watching a one-armed man running down the street, blood spraying like a sprinkler toy onto bystanders. Except the bystanders didn't seem to care.

What is going on? Nathan wondered.

Then he heard the sound of a police car and decided this was the perfect time for him to make his escape. As he turned around he just about walked into a parking meter and veered to avoid it, ending up directly in front of a couple of startled ladies who came to a halt. They mumbled to each other franticly as Nathan offered his apologies. "I am so sorry ladies, I—" he abruptly ended, recognizing the two women.

"It's not a lunatic Pearl, it's that nice young man from the coffee shop," Phyllis said. Her friend shrugged, so Phyllis elaborated. "You know, the one who bought our coffee and cheese croissants."

"Oh yes, the serial rapist with the van," Pearl said remembering. "So what's wrong with him?"

"Hmm, I don't know. Maybe he's on meds and forgot to take them," she answered turning to Nathan. "Did you forget your meds honey?" she asked loudly, in case he was actually off of his meds.

"Um," Nathan began as he wiped blood from his face. But as he looked at his hand he noticed that it was disturbingly clean. *What the hell.*

Pearl had her own theory. "Out here staring off into space and not looking where you're going. You look special boy, like you're waiting for the short bus," she explained in all her political incorrectness. "I thought they were out here filming a *Forrest Gump* sequel."

Nathan looked around and saw that there was no blood on the sidewalk, or on the grass. He frantically looked around and found them, some ways away now, but the boyfriend and girlfriend were there, alive and well. He started to chuckle. *I imagined the whole thing. Or I'm in the early stages of the Virus and going insane.* Given that Nathan was almost two millennia away from having to even start to worry about developing the Virus through old age and his Knowledge Ring was nowhere near the enhanced level to contract the Virus that way, he chalked it up to nervous stress.

Phyllis gave him a comprehensive look. "You sure you're not on any meds?"

Lowering his head he began to breathe a huge sigh of relief. "I'm not on any meds."

"Maybe you should be," Pearl diagnosed.

Nathan could not argue. "You may be right," he said. He'd better hunt down something to eat soon. Ignoring his hunger was starting to cause his emotions to become sporadic that manifested into blood lusting hallucinations, and it happened to every Chakan.

Phyllis seemed determined to find him an excuse. "Are you having a bad day honey?"

Then a familiar voice answered for him. "The boy just has a lot on his mind."

Yes thank you, Nathan thought and then looked to see who the familiar voice was.

Phyllis turned. "Florida Johnson, how are you honey?"

Florida stopped, a little out of breath. "Phew—I'm good ladies, I'm good. And how are you Superhero?"

Nathan ducked his head slightly as if he could evade the comment, knowing she was referring to yesterday's bus incident and hoping that it wouldn't become a big deal. "Oh, you heard about that."

Florida laughed. "Everybody has heard about that."

"That was you?" Pearl asked, looking like she was teetering with her opinions.

Florida gave Nathan the once over. "Going to get a tea?"

"I am," Nathan replied.

"Looking mighty spiffed up to be getting a tea," Florida said and then smirked at the other ladies. "Almost as if he was trying to impress someone."

What are you trying to say old lady? Is what he thought. "Just something lying around that I threw on." Is what he said.

Phyllis lowered her glasses. "Seems pretty crisp to have just been laying down."

Pearl snorted. "Ah—yup, trying to impress someone. Most likely Lily, since he's always over there sitting at her station, chatting her up," she explained to anyone and everyone.

With a sarcastic smile Nathan shrugged. "Well, guess I should get going."

"I think I hit a nerve," Pearl said and it brought on a round of laughter from all of the ladies.

Nathan felt he had to stop and defend himself. "Now, I don't know what it is you ladies think you know?"

Phyllis started to rub his arm. "Don't you mind her honey? You seem like a lovely young man," she said turning to Florida. "He seems like such a lovely young man."

"Mmm-hm, he's a sweetheart all right. Always helping me with my grocery bags and daily deliveries," Florida said and then gave Nathan a nudge. "And don't think I haven't noticed the work you did on the roof." She turned to the other ladies. "I'm not going to take my appreciation out of his rent or anything, but I sure do appreciate it," she said and then started to chuckle.

"Maybe he wore the spiffy shirt for you Florida," Pearl said and then she started to cackle. Pearl definitely cackled.

"*Oh*," Florida stated jokingly and started to sashay back and forth with an almost flirtatious smile.

Nathan couldn't help but laugh. "Okay—that's it, I am out of here."

"Don't you mind them," Phyllis said with a smile. "You and Lily will make a wonderful couple."

"*Couple*?" Nathan repeated. "I'm just asking her out on a date."

Florida pointed at him. "So you *are* going to ask her out on a date."

Nathan stood dumbfounded. "What—no—pfft—what?"

All three ladies started to laugh, or cluck depending on which ears you were listening with. And Nathan tried to act normal while casually walking away as if he wasn't the source of their boisterous amusement.

Not realizing how much ground he had actually covered, Nathan looked up and found that he had made it to his destination. Thoughts quickly transformed into agonizing stress as he caught Lily in the window. Suddenly his fear made sense. She was the most beautiful woman he had ever laid eyes upon. Watching her laugh made his heart swell and he felt a little jealous that he was not a part of it.

Suddenly Nathan became very self-conscious about the fact that he would be interrupting whatever fun they were having. He wasn't just interrupting by way of ordering a tea, he was going to do it with a very public display of affection. The heat radiating from his cheeks signaled that his confidence was dwindling, which made way for the return of uncertainty. If he thought about it for too much longer he would talk himself out of it, he needed to act now. So Nathan ignored everything going on in his head and took a deep breath.

2: If You Only Knew

The debate between Lily, Todd and Martin on the subject of whether Nathan Caesar should ask Lily out on a date was still at a lock. Two for, one against. It wasn't so much an against as more of Lily trying to be realistic.

"Yeah well, he's a little out of my league," she said wiping down the table for the third time.

Martin was a little upset with her lack of self-worth. "Why would you say such a thing *chica?*"

"Yes honey, you must have confidence," Todd said sitting up straight and putting himself on display. "I am fucking gorgeous and I snagged me this piece of tight Latin ass."

Martin turned to him holding out his arms aghast. *"Por favor, cuida tu lengua,"* he said telling him to watch his language.

"Querido, there is no one in here, it's just the three of us," he said turning and looking into the empty store. "Excuse my language everyone."

"Okay, don't get so smart, and don't say *querido,"* Martin said.

"It's Spanish, for dear or beloved," Todd explained arrogantly.

"I know what it means. I am the one who speaks the Spanish," he said. "But you pronounce it, queer, queer-do, and it sounds gay."

"We're gay sweetie," Todd reminded him and turned to Lily and started to dance. "Even self-haters gonna hate-hate-hate."

Lily stopped her little dance with Todd and looked at herself. "Look at me, I'm chubby."

Martin rolled his eyes. "You are *curvy.* Much better."

"Yes," Todd agreed. "And no matter what they say, curvy is sexy."

"Well it's nice to know the gay community thinks I'm sexy," she replied and stopped herself from wiping the table for a fourth time. "But the one I want to think that I am sexy, just happens to be drop-dead gorgeous, successful, and do you see where he lives? *Yeah,"* she said and then dropped her shoulders and sat looking frumpy. "I make tea and rent a room from my bosses."

Martin rolled his eyes. "Again with the rent. Renting would imply you give money."

"Hey I give money to help out," she said a little insulted.

"When? When do you give the money?" Martin asked.

Lily turned to Todd with a scowl painted across her face and her whisper matched. "You don't tell Martin that I give you money?"

Todd leaned in as close as he could and whispered frantically. "Shut up and I'll make it worth your while."

"You better," Lily hissed.

"I will," Todd hissed back and slapped her arm. "Just shut up about it."

Lily smacked his arm. "You shut up."

Todd smacked hers again. "You shut up."

Suddenly they started hitting each other back and forth.

"Okay children!" Martin shouted.

Todd began straightening himself up. "Yes Lily, stop being a child," he said and when Martin wasn't looking, he smacked her one more time.

Lily sat up and inhaled deeply. "Every pay I give Todd money help with bills Martin," she tattled in one breath.

"I knew it," Martin said pointing his finger at Todd. "Telling me you get all of those clothes on sale. You lie, you have the extra money from Lily."

"You bitch!" Todd exclaimed while trying not to laugh as he turned to Martin. "And can we stay focused here, Lily doesn't think she's good enough for Nathan. Our Lily, *Martin*, what are we going to do about that?"

All of a sudden Martin was distracted and thinking out loud. "That is not right. Our Lily is beautiful and funny and talented," he listed off.

Lily turned to Todd while Martin was still rambling on. "Wow, nice."

"*Right*," Todd said getting another idea and got Martin's attention. "And the whole Rick thing, she doesn't even know if she's ready to start dating because of that prick."

Martin started nodding angrily. "Don't even get me started on the *Rick*," he seethed and started going on about that.

Todd nudged Lily. "I just thought of that one."

Lily nodded. "That's actually a major concern of mine, but I'm glad my pain and suffering can help you get out of a jam."

"Me too," Todd said putting his arm around her and squeezing. "You telling me that if Nathan, *holy shit* is he hot, Caesar asked you on a date, you don't know if you'd say yes?"

"I'm not *saying* that," Lily admitted sluggishly.

Todd smiled. "I thought so."

"But guys like that don't go for girls like me," Lily said with a shrug. "We're from two different worlds I guess."

Martin had now made his way over and heard Lily's last comment. "What, he is too good for you? He is the—the Tony from the Jets? I am supposing we are the lowly Sharks?"

Todd started to clap his hands. "Oh shit, we are so watching *West Side Story* tonight."

Suddenly the chime rang out, silencing them all.

The man they had been talking about, in between customers, for the last two hours had just walked in. Everyone noticed right away that he looked nervous or apprehensive.

Lily felt her heart sink at the sight of the man she always hoped was behind every chime of the door. But every time it was him coming through the door, like now, she was lost.

"Hello Nathan," Todd said walking out to greet him. "Um, *tea*?"

"In a minute, please," Nathan said politely as he passed Todd while ignoring Martin altogether, but he stopped right in front of Lily. "Hello Lily," he said sounding stilted or overly formal, like he was in an old western and should have said *Well Hello Miss Lily* while tipping his hat.

"Hello," Lily answered and instantly regretted giving him a little wave. "The usual?"

Shaking his head he smiled awkwardly. "I have a confession to make. Yesterday, when you almost got hit by that bus, and I was there to pull you back?"

Lily shifted from side to side with nowhere to go. Not only was she juggling her ample shyness with her lewd thoughts, but now he threw in embarrassment as well. "Yeah," she said, sounding muffled and distant in her own head. That is when she noticed her hands getting that first sheen of clamminess which matched the faintish cold of her forehead. Suddenly her vision became burry as her thoughts kicked in to high gear wondering what was going to come out of his mouth next.

"I was following you."

Because you lost a bet? You're a detective? I'm part of a hidden camera show? All of these and at least two dozen more went through Lily's head. Then the heat started to surge as visions of Rick invaded, amplifying her current symptoms and she began to panic. "Can you excuse me?" Lily asked, but didn't move—couldn't move.

"Please," Nathan said and offered a slight smile.

That smile was enough for her to gain a modest amount of courage and not run. "Okay."

"I had this silly plan," Nathan started. "I was going to bump into you and make it look like a coincidence. Which would have given me the perfect opportunity to ask you something. But then you walked out in front of a bus."

Locking onto his eyes and hearing the rhythm of his speech, seemed to make her feel safe. She could almost see the words jumping past his lips and it fueled her wanting to let go of her past. Suddenly she wanted to dive head first into a future that would be embraced by his arms and what she hoped, no—yearned would be a love that sustained itself by the beating of their two hearts. *Really, am I becoming that girl? Wait, he asked us a question—shit! Wait I remember,* she thought, finding it harder to keep from drifting away into complete fantasy. "Yes, I did do that."

"And I didn't get a chance to ask you," he said, but looking like he was about to succumb to cowardice. But instead, he took her hand.

Lily quickly looked to Todd and Martin who only offered her a well-timed simultaneously shrug. What was once a very awkward daydream filled with silly hopes and maybes, was all of a sudden looking like it could turn into a reality. *Don't get ahead of yourself.* But she couldn't help it, Nathan Caesar's hand was touching hers. *If he asks us out—please, whatever we do don't scream,* Lily silently demanded of herself.

Gently squeezing her hand, Nathan continued. "I think you are the most beautiful woman I have ever met. I think you are smart, funny, strong and not afraid to laugh at your own jokes. Even when they don't make sense, or you're the only one that finds them funny."

Lily laughed in an almost hiccup.

"But I thought you were amazing ever since the first time I sat down and you made me three watermelon mint chiller white teas and three wonder-berry chocolate truffle oolong teas. So…"

"Yes," she whispered hoarsely.

"Would you like to go to dinner with me next Friday? I mean this Friday would be great, but that is tomorrow and I'm opening the store and—"

"YES!" Todd exclaimed loudly and brought everything to a halt.

Lily smiled. "Yes. I would love to," she said with perfect tone and dignity.

"Good," Nathan said releasing her hand. "You'll understand that I will probably be too embarrassed to come in for a while. So I'll see you next Friday, shall we say seven?"

"Next Friday at seven," she repeated.

"I will pick you up at seven. Next Friday."

She watched as Nathan turned around to leave and she wanted so badly for him to confirm the whole thing, but he just tried to avoid eye contact.

Martin turned to Todd. "I forget, weren't we going to invite Mr. Nathan to our little get together Saturday?"

"We were," Todd answered.

So Martin called out. "Oh, Mr. Caesar."

"Nope," Nathan shot back as he opened the door and let a small crowd pass through.

Trying again, Martin spoke up. "Mr. Nathan, I just wanted—"

"Unh-un," Nathan said slipping out and letting the door close behind him.

Lily glanced over at Todd who looked like he was fighting back the tears of giddy schoolgirl as he pointed to the people at the counter and then gave her the *one minute* sign. She sat in her chair in what she could only diagnose as shock. I don't believe he asked me out. She couldn't remember feeling this happy, she didn't know what to say or what to think. But Lily was sure Todd would know, at least she hoped and glanced back at him. Unfortunately he had made a circle with his fingers while repeatedly putting his other finger in and out of it. Nodding, and smiling creepily at her.

3: Just a Reminder

As soon as Lily walked through the door she kicked off her shoes and couldn't care less where they landed. She was tired but extremely happy since the man she had fallen for the moment she'd first laid eyes on him, just asked her out on a date. Half expecting to wake up and realize it was all a dream, she chuckled. "Wouldn't that suck?" Throwing her keys on the breakfast bar she grabbed what had become the community tablet and slid a few screens around. Seeing that they had a bunch of messages she played them and started skipping the ones that started with *Oh my God* or *You won't believe*. Which, so far, was all of them.

"Next message," the program with the British accent said.

"Lily," the man's voice said sounding timid.

Recognizing the voice she immediately dropped the tablet.

But it didn't stop Rick's voice from continuing. *I—I know I shouldn't have called, but.*

Lily backed away, as if he had materialized and was standing in front of her.

I need to see you Lily—I need to talk to you, his voice started to become insistent.

Falling into the chair she brought her knees up to her chin while her eyes refused to blink.

I gave you space. I haven't been calling...it's time to come home baby.

Her eyes welled with tears as she began to shake her head.

Lily!

She jerked in horror to the beat of her name.

Rick's voice became more demanding. *It's time to come home Lily!*

Racing to the counter she tapped the message icon to pause the message and then dragged it to the trash bin. Taking long labored breaths her eyes searched the apartment while listening for any hint of someone being inside. Her moment of happiness was now buried under all of the self-loathing and fear that had just been hiding, waiting for her to let her guard down. Taking a deep breath she walked to the sliding door and began to cry while looking out from the balcony.

Suddenly Lily felt eyes on her and she stepped back startled. As she stared out into the darkness the feeling wasn't dissipating and a large shiver raced down her back that caused her whole body to shiver. She could not see it but she was positive something was there in the night, hidden among the darkness observing, biding time almost. Was Rick out there watching her?

Lily backed away from the windows as if a wild animal was right in front of her and she did not want to make a sudden movement that would lead to an attack. Bringing the tablet up to her mouth she heard something and fumbled. "Fuck!" she yelled reaching and grabbing at the tablet until she finally had a hold on it. Clicking the icon she called out, "Call Sips." The numbers slid across the screen and she waited to hear it ring.

The call connected and started to ring. With a sigh of relief she went to turn around when her eyes found themselves looking out into the dark buildings again and she felt her skin crawl. *Don't be silly*, she thought to herself half-heartedly and heard the line being picked up on the other end. She closed the drapes, just to be sure.

4: It Tickles

He stood on the roof, hidden in the shadows across the street from Todd and Martin's apartment, watching and eating.

"Something about her," he told the woman in his arms as he watched Lily close the drapes. "Shit," he responded and then turned his attention to the sobbing woman he held against himself and covered her mouth with his hand. "Now if I take my hand away from your mouth, do you promise not to scream?"

The woman responded by trying to scream, but it was nothing more than a muzzled whimper.

"That's why I always ask," he said a little disappointed. "I met that lady across the street not too long ago. I bumped into her in an alley. She was with her friend and let's just say I was in a hurry," he said seemingly taking a moment to think. "I think it was her smile. Yes definitely her smile. Ever since then, I just can't get her out of my head."

The girl obviously being held against her will started to cry.

The man hidden in the shadows leaned down and whispered into her ear. "And something big happened today. Now I don't want to say anymore, you know…in case I jinx it," he said with excitement. "I just don't know what my family is going to think?"

The girl began to cough and convulse so he tried to calm her down. "Shh, it's okay," he said and started to gently rock her back and forth. "I know, I know, my family isn't going to be happy, but they say love conquers all. And who knows, I'm still not sure if I want to fuck her or just eat her right up," he said and then nuzzled into her neck, "num-num-num-num-num." He laughed and continued. "I was so excited about today, I was just going to sit up here and watch her while I masturbated." Then he leaned down to her ear again. "But then I saw you," he whispered and then licked her cheek. "I saw you in that restaurant and I just had to have you. Who was that with you, husband or boyfriend?"

The woman started to cry again.

"Doesn't matter," he said pressing his own cheek against hers.

The woman he was holding struggled but he was too strong, so she cried in pain.

He leaned forward and he let his tongue touch the large open wound on her shoulder. The bite marks were all large and open as blood seeped and spurted. His attractiveness had gotten her attention and his charm lured her away from safety. Now she was all his and in the most literal sense as he let his teeth rip into her shoulder as he burrowed greedily into her flesh.

She screamed as loudly as she could but his hand held it in. The muffled cries that did make it out, were alone with no one around to hear them. He chewed and watched to see if Lily would reappear. He then bent down with her flesh still in his mouth and spoke into her ear. "Your flesh tickles when I swallow," he said with a huge smile that peeked out from the shadow. "Maybe that's why you're so much fun to eat."

The woman could only stand in terror and excruciating pain as he laughed quietly. Tortured by his confusing remarks and the fact that she was slowly being eaten to death.

CHAPTER XI

1: Dinner is Severed

THE RAVEN AND THE CROW had checked into a dumpy motel just a few blocks from poor Mr. Gable's apartment building. As the Crow opened her duffle bag she started to put plastic containers into the medium sized fridge beside the table. "Hope Mr. Gable doesn't mind us borrowing his containers?"

The Raven looked up from his tablet. "It's not like he'll be using it any time soon my love, he's dead."

"Yes I know he's dead, but they're still his containers," she said removing a large black garbage bag that looked like a small watermelon was wrapped inside. She placed it on the table and removed the twist tie, then slid the bag over the severed head of Jonathon Gable. "*Hello,*" the Crow said merrily as she pinched his cheeks.

"I understand you bringing his head my dear," the Raven said trying to be diplomatic and then winced as she unwrapped two more heads. "But why the two children's?"

She stood above them and examined them while she thought about it. "I guess I didn't want them to be lonely."

"Are you going to FedEx all three heads?"

"Actually, I'm using DHL this time."

The Raven grinned bitingly. "That is right, our last delivery leaked."

"The client was not happy," she said raising her eyebrows at him.

"No—they were not," he recalled while pouring himself a drink of scotch.

"Soon we'll be able to point our phones at them and teleport them directly to our clients," she said positioning the heads from biggest to smallest and taking a picture.

The Raven took a sip. "Still, we can text a picture, record video and send it to whoever we want all from our phone. Pay a large corporation to deliver our criminal evidence. I mean, whatever did we do before technology?"

The crow fell to her knees and folded her arms as she studied the heads. "I gathered the heads in a burlap sack, and we hand delivered them," she said, taking another picture with the heads turned. Then she quickly tapped a few buttons and it was off with a text, *package on the way, do you want video?* Referring to the head that would soon be couriered and the video of her and the Raven killing poor little Chrissie and eating Jonathon Gable alive was available to be downloaded if they did not want to wait for the thumb drive. Jenny the babysitter was obviously bonus material. She pocketed her phone and continued. "Which meant anywhere from ten miles to a couple of week's travel," she said grabbing the tablet. "The blood always seemed to leak through at the most inopportune times."

The Raven, who had been sitting and enjoying his scotch opened his eyes. "Philadelphia."

The tablet chimed and the Crow started to tap and drag. "Yes my love, Philadelphia. We had to execute Mr. Deering and his entire family and take all of the heads to the client. That was a big burlap sack."

"Oh my," he said as the memory entered his head. "Now that's going down memory lane." He took a longer sip and got up.

The tablet and her phone both chimed simultaneously and she looked perplexed as to what one she should check with. Since the tablet was already in her hand she quickly tapped the message and began reading, then smiled. "We have a new job my love. Looks like it's in Chicago."

The Raven had pulled a plastic container from the fridge and was gnawing at what looked to be Jenny's arm. "Fabulous. Finally some proper nightlife."

The Crow laughed as her forked tongue flickered. "I am so excited."

"I know you're excited my love, but this is going to be a job remember."

With great enthusiasm she began typing their response.

The Raven just chuckled. "And what might the job be?"

Raising her finger to pause the conversation she proceeded to finish. With a couple of clicks she read the original text while waiting for a response. "The Immortalis Corporation," she said with dramatized respect.

The Raven was already impressed. "The House of Crassus, a high paying assignment indeed. Is it an open assignment?"

She shook her head slyly. "To us directly my love. We must be moving up in the world."

The Raven took another bite of the arm and then set it down. Walking back to the open scotch he poured two glasses and handed her one. "The Immortalis Corporation," he said and raised his glass. "If the great Marcus Licinius Crassus is requesting us specifically, well then we most certainly are moving up."

She took a drink with giddy satisfaction. "There are so few proper night spots left in this country my love. And we're getting paid to be in one. If that's just not the cat's meow."

Before drowning his palates in another mouthful the Raven paused, unsure if he had heard her correctly. "Did you say *cat's meow*?"

The Crow just giggled as she buried her head in the tablet, becoming more captivated as she read. Tapping away she was not paying attention to the rustling behind her. "Oh my," she said scooping up the pale fleshy arm and taking a bite. "This just gets better," she teased, her mouth full of Jenny's arm. "We are to meet our handler in St. Louis."

The Raven called out, sounding as if struggling. "This just gets better."

"That's what I said my—"

As she turned around to finish her sentence she was met with a naked Raven. Fully erect his cock seemed to throb, signifying the erection was newly developed and timid to the touch of air.

She spit the flesh in her mouth to the floor. "My-my-my," she said taking her fork and playfully, but forcefully placing it underneath his prick.

He cried out in surprised ecstasy.

Anchoring the fork just under his helmet, she pulled it towards her and he followed as the Crow's fangs flung from the roof of her mouth. Then she weaved to her right in a blink and then to her left even quicker, getting close enough to the head of his cock to let her forked tongue tease it.

"Careful love, it is a one of a kind," he beseeched as the tines guided him.

Inhaling him partially the Crow grabbed him by his ass cheeks and thrust him forward to complete the task.

His eyes rolled in his head. "Oh my love, to this day your ravenous hunger still astounds me."

Sucking harder until he looked as if he would not be able to endure it any longer the Crow withdrew him from her mouth and looked up to meet his half empty gaze and demanded, "Ravage me!"

Wrapping his hands around her neck he lifted her into the air as she gasped for air. Placing his clawed fingers behind the waistband of her pants his eyes went turned reptilian yellow as she struggled to smile. She swung her hand downward and caught his face, and as he turned to meet her eyes with blood running down his cheek, she spit as hard as she could on him.

He jerked her forward to get a feel for the strength of her pants and then in one fell swoop, he violently ripped them from her body completely. The burning sensation of the fabric ripping along her skin caused her to scream through the choke.

He peered quickly behind him and then swiped his arm across the table to clear it of all the clutter. Still holding the Crow by the throat he placed his other hand on the small of her back and flipped her backwards, forcing her to do a somersault. She landed on her feet, but bent over the table, and with the speed of a snake striking out at its prey, he was now behind her.

"Wait," she called out, "the heads?"

Bending over top of her he whispered while his forked tongue followed his words, "Look my darling." Suddenly he took a handful of her hair and forcibly yanked it back.

Elated with arousal and pain she cried out while trying to steady her eyes and fix her gaze at the heads of Jonathan and Jenny that were placed directly in front of her.

"I was going to put the child on display, but I thought that this is not for children to see," he said, referring to the fact that he did not put the young head of Chrissie on display.

"No, it is not," she cried as her body rocked vigorously back and forth on the table. She cried out again as saliva dropped off her lip and ran down her chin. Now grunting and fighting to keep her yellow snake eyes forward, her forked tongue flickered again and again as he pounded her relentlessly.

2: In A(sia) Minor

The black Toyota Crown pulled into the park-and-fly of the Haneda Airport, in the Kanto region of Japan. It sat running as the two Gemini Monsters, Kimiko sat in the passenger seat while Hitoshi, her brother, sat in the driver's seat.

Gemini are a rare species of Monstrum, born always as twins. They have telepathic abilities in the form that they can communicate with each other's thoughts. Impregnation is only possible by mating with themselves and there is always one male and one female at birth. The mother always dies giving birth and if the father does not kill himself, the female baby dies shortly after being born. This supports the part of their myth that they are reborn as each other, but taking turns with gender. This is how they live forever, being born from each other as one another, over and over again. They are sometimes referred to as the acrobats of the Monster world and at other times they are just referred to as the creepy siblings.

Merrick sat in the back, still infuriated after months of run around, but tickled pink to be finally leaving just days of talking with Marcus.

Kimiko quickly glanced into the rear-view mirror. "I am sorry this trip was uneventful Mr. Merrick," she said and looked forward just as quickly.

"I wouldn't call it uneventful," Merrick said calmly, making Hitoshi smile. "As much as I would call it just plain old bullshit. You know you could have saved me a whole lot of time and just told me he wasn't here."

Kimiko still just stared ahead. "We did not know," she said with a hint of sympathy.

Hitoshi smiled. "And even if we did. We are part of the Order, you are part of the Immortalis Corporation," he said and then smirked.

"Besides, look at all the great things we saw together. Mongolia, China, Kazakhstan, India, Sri Lanka, Bangladesh, Cambodia, Vietnam, Malaysia," he said listing off all of their destinations with the expression of a school teacher.

Merrick nodded. "All crossed off my bucket list now, thank you."

"East Timor, Philippines, Taiwan, South Korea, North Korea and of course," he said and paused before waving his hands towards the window, "Japan."

Kimiko looked at her brother and him back at her. Their eyes twitched and their heads turned periodically as if they were having a conversation with each other in their minds, which was exactly what they were doing. Kimiko then turned her head to the side as not to be rude when she addressed Merrick. "Your visit was uneventful, you have our deepest apologies."

Merrick added a dose of caustic to his tone. "Yeah well, what can you do right?"

She turned to her brother with a look of confusion.

Her brother looked at her and then thought for a moment. "It's like, shit happens," Hitoshi said looking back at Merrick for affirmation.

"Yeah," Merrick affirmed opening the door. "I'd tell you to both go fuck each other, but since you're Gemini, you already do. *Creepy motherfuckers,*" he finished while slamming the door shut and heading straight into the airport. It didn't make up for the time wasted searching every corner of Asia, but it felt good.

The window of the Toyota Crown came down and Hitoshi was leaning over his sister and out the window and sang out. "*Sayōnara* Merrick-san."

Merrick just held up his middle finger without even looking back.

Inside the airport, Merrick headed to the counter while inputting a number on his phone. He was greeted with a pretty smile from a pretty agent.

"Yōkoso," she said and held out her hand.

"Konnichiwa, eigo wa dekimasu ka?"

"Yes, I speak English," she said still waiting for his ticket.

Merrick handed it to her and then explained, "I need to change flights."

"Of course Mr. Merrick, where would you like to change it to?" she inquired while typing.

"St. Louis, Missouri, the United States of America," he instructed.

The agent typed away until she looked up and smiled. "I have a flight that leaves in four hours. I assume First Class?"

"You assume correctly."

"One stop at San Francisco International for...one hour and forty minutes," she said and waited to see if that was acceptable.

"That'll be fine," Merrick said handing her his credit card.

She typed again and then waited for the printer to spit out his new ticket. "And how was your stay Mr. Merrick?" she asked still waiting for the printer to finish.

"Hmm," Merrick thought aloud and gave it some serious thought.

As the printer finally stopped and the transaction was approved, the agent tore the ticket from the machine and handed them both back.

Taking the ticket and having given the question enough thought Merrick smiled. "I'm not sure how you say it in Jap," Merrick said growing a very intimidating stare. "But I hope when the next Tsunami comes, it swallows this entire fucking country and everyone in it," he finished as the agent seemed to lose her ability to smile.

She stood behind the counter discombobulated, knowing that this was never covered in her training.

Tapping his finger on the counter he offered, "Jā mata ne." Then he smiled and gave her a wink.

"Itte irasshai," She said, which meant *Go and come back.* But her bewildered and distressed face did not convey the meaning at all.

CHAPTER XII

1: The Quiet Grand Opening

IT WAS FRIDAY MORNING and Nathan sat and listened to the radio.

Another grisly discovery this morning, ladies and gentlemen

That's right Kevin, a third body has been found

Three now?

Yup, police aren't saying a whole lot, but what we do know is that the body is male. And, sadly this one looks like it might be preteen.

Not that anyone getting killed is any less sad

No of course not, my apologies if that's how I made it sound

No-no, but when kids are involved, well, it really strikes another chord

It sure does. And like the others, it too is missing a fair amount of flesh and body parts including…

The heart

Including the heart, that's right

Well for not saying a whole lot, that is a lot of info Jerry

Well it's not like they gave out a name and address

Are you sure

Well, by now maybe, it is the Chicago PD after all

Nathan turned off the radio and rubbed his face into his hands. Not only could this be a big red flag to Marcus, but Nathan's other problem was—Chicago fell under his family's jurisdiction. And he had yet to go and visit his Mother.

He inhaled deeply and exhaled with exasperation, he had just eaten two hearts not that long ago but it felt as if he was already feeling the strain of Chakan fatigue setting in. The same fatigue that caused him to have those blood-lust hallucinations just before he asked Lily out on a date.

Looking around, Nathan sighed and shifted his focus, becoming even more despondent. Not because he didn't think that his store looked good. The hardwood floors looked original even though he'd had them installed. The brown two-tone walls were fine, with the top being winter sky and the bottom desert camel that matched the strategically placed mats. The posts throughout the store had the same two tones, but the top and bottom reversed. Shelving that was hand-carved from mahogany, almost fifty years ago by his brother Bo, then put into storage for this exact purpose, looked beyond perfect.

He had new books and old books. Some read while some were maiden. He had first editions scattered throughout the store with some under glass and others framed. He had no intention for beverage service, but end tables beside big chairs told people to bring your own and stay. He was actually quite pleased with the look of his new store.

What he was disappointed with, was the fact that without knowing it, he almost replicated his coastal store in Italy impeccably. It made him miss the atmosphere of the ageless town. Not to mention all the books that he'd abandoned.

But his mood changed when he thought of the one thing the southern Italian town did not have, it did not have Lily. Just thinking of her modified his mood and he switched on the open sign, smiling at the familiar hum of neon. Unlocking the door he walked behind the counter and dropped to his elbows. He loved being surrounded by books and hoped, as he did most days, that no one would come in. Nathan did not need money. Like his books, he had plenty. He needed a front to appear normal. So if pretending to be normal meant spending day after day reading books, drinking tea and talking to people about books, well then he could not think of a better way.

The only thing that would make this day perfect would be a cup of tea from Sips.

He was faster and stronger than any Chakan he had ever met, any Monster he had ever met for that matter. But even with all his powers he couldn't muster the courage to go back. Even though Lily said yes, he didn't think his fragile ego could take even the slightest hint of second guessing.

Taking a sip of his own tea he scoffed silently. Then, a horrible thought went through his head. *What if our impending date does not go well? Lose the woman, lose the tea.*

Then he began to think about how far he and Lily had come and he started to worry. At first when he had met her in the alley with Jeanette he was very forward because he did not think he would ever see her again. Then he went to Sips for a tea and not only did he start liking her, he liked everyone around her. Then he started thinking about her all of the time, and this was a problem. Nathan wanted to like her, he wanted to see her more and more, but with everything that was going on he was starting to doubt it all. The last person Nathan loved, he ripped her heart from her chest and then ate it in front of her.

Which is always a damper on any relationship, he thought with a frown.

"I'm pretty sure I can resist the urge to eat her heart," he added out loud.

You can, maybe. What about all the other Monsters running around out there? What about all of those Monsters we call family?

"They wouldn't," he started and got lost in thought.

Giving his head a shake he turned his thoughts to another problem. *What about all those Monsters that want to kill us?*

"Yeah, nothing breaks up a date night like a bunch of Monsters foaming at the mouth while trying to rip you limb from limb."

And getting back to family, will they even accept her, being human and all?

"Of course. Well ... Mother is always a question mark isn't she? But what would be the worst thing that could happen if Mother didn't like her?"

Eat her. The absolute worst thing that could happen is your Mother actually eats your Girlfriend.

Suddenly the little shopkeeper's chime went off and mercifully shattered the thought from his head.

Walking through the door was Todd, smiling ear to ear and humming a very recognizable *Disney* movie theme song. He resembled an early twentieth century golfer, complete with golf knickers with four inches of additional length. The patterned golf socks that complimented his two-tone spectator shoes seemed to highlight his white shirt and plaid tie that sat under a matching cardigan jacket. It all seemed to scream flamboyant, but the flat cap that turned slightly to the left with a pair of John Lennon sunglasses was the cherry on top. Yet strangely, it all seemed to work.

Todd came to a stop and took off his glasses. "Oh my God. This is total fab-u-lous." He looked at Nathan and then behind himself. "I did have Jeanette with me, but I lost her at a shoe sale a couple of blocks away." Before Nathan could reply in any way at all, Todd gasped as if his breath was stolen.

It sat confidently under a glass box and had a little pot light just below it that lit its magnificence. Fastened to the glass near the bottom was a beautiful golden plaque that read:

Treasure Island
A Novel by: Robert Louis Stevenson
1st Edition, May 23rd 1883

"Look at this shit," Todd said reaching out to it and then stopped. "You know, this was the first book I understood completely on my own. I mean, yes there were a few words I didn't get. Fucking pirate lingo. But I was really proud when I finished it. Been a junkie ever since."

"Go ahead," Nathan said taking a sip of his own mediocre tea.

Todd looked at him like a kid on Christmas morning and looked back and forth from the book to Nathan.

Seeing the hesitation in his face, Nathan assured him. "No alarms will go off."

Todd gently put his hands on both of the glass box. "I feel like Indiana Jones," he said and lifted it straight up. Placing the see through box gingerly on the counter Todd bent down and marveled at how well it had been preserved. "A first edition. To think someone all the way back in 1883 bought this book and took it home. Gave it to his son, or maybe just bought it for themselves and read it in the park."

Nathan smiled, but inside his mind he laughed since it was actually him who bought this exact book in London, 1883 England. Hearing that it had sold out in three other stores, he had procured the last copy from a shop on Frith Street. He remembered he was quite excited about reading about the adventures of Jim Hawkins and pirates. His excitement didn't even wane when the shopkeeper told him it was more of a book for children. To which Nathan replied, *"Sorry, a good book is just a good book no matter what age it is intended for."* That next day he returned to the shopkeeper and proposed he seek out his inner child and read it when his stock was refilled. Two weeks later walking down Frith Street the shopkeeper yelled out, *"Fifteen men on a dead man's chest."* Then they both sang out, *"Yo-Ho-ho and a bottle of rum."*

Going to touch it, Todd suddenly pulled back, as if it would somehow crumble into a pile of dust. Then against all fear, he gently grabbed onto it and held it in front of him. Opening the book cautiously, Todd slowly let his eyes soak in the words that were printed so long ago. Todd became instantly infatuated. "I must have it."

Nathan smiled and gently took the book out of Todd's hands. "I know—I know," he jokingly patronized.

"But I have money," Todd said sadly letting go. Determination soon took over. "I'll give you a thousand dollars."

"It's worth at least thirty," Nathan said placing the book back. He half expected to see Todd running out the door with the book tucked under his vest when he turned around and chuckled. The thought of giving the police a description of Todd and what he was wearing made it hard not to, at least they would be able to pick him up fairly quickly.

It didn't take long for Todd to get over the reality of it. "I would, but Martin would never understand. Oh well," he said turning his attentions away from the treasure and onto Nathan. "I popped in to see your shop. Very nice by the way," he said and gave him a thumbs up. "And to invite you to our home this evening. That is what Martin was trying to tell you before you ran out of the store yesterday."

Nathan immediately started to go flush. *"Oh,* I don't know."

"Give you a chance to see Lily. With whom I ran it by before coming here," Todd said. Then he went into gossip mode. "And if I were a little birdie, I'd tell you she became *quite excited."*

"Really?"

Todd nodded and then became matter of fact like. "Well there was a lot of on the fence, off the fence. Then hiding. Then, running into her bedroom screaming," he said with a look on his face that said maybe he shouldn't have been so detailed. *"Anyhoo,* a couple of other store owners will be there, nothing big."

"Maybe," Nathan muttered timidly.

"Fantastic," Todd said as if Nathan's answer was a yes.

The little bell over the door rang out as two women came through the door and made their way to a wall of books. The first was a stunning woman, dark skinned and elegantly dressed. Everything about her was perfect—her height, her weight, complexion, makeup and hair. It wasn't blonde so much as it was golden, highlighted by the nearly invisible strands of silver interlaced within it that only gave themselves away when they glittered off the light. Her clothes were tight and revealed a large bust that most would guess was augmented. Her backside was ridiculously curvaceous and had just enough elasticity for a forced grip in the otherwise tight component. Her beauty was so apparent that it shadowed her jewelry, which when noticed would be recognized as expensive, even by the most amateur appraiser.

The other woman was much heavier and plainer in appearance. She didn't wear any makeup or have any silver interlaced in her dark and scruffy hair. Her flannel jacket almost covered her very authentic looking 1979 *AC/DC Highway to Hell* T-shirt. Her jeans weren't stained, but worn and matched her demeanor that didn't exactly scream out approachable. The scowl on her face seemed as if it was a permanent fixture and her eyes would have confirmed it if they weren't hidden behind glasses. The type bought from a countertop display, usually seen at a checkout lane of a drug store.

An odd pairing indeed, standing off to the side, whispering and glancing every so often at Nathan, only to turn away to whisper some more.

Todd smiled and addressed Nathan quietly with a look like nothing was wrong. "Um—those two lesbians don't seem to like you. You want I should hang around?"

Nathan smiled at his concern. "They're not lesbians, they're sisters."

"Well I know one is a sister," he said taking another look. "*Damn* that bitch is hot," he cried out looking at Nathan and then realized that that wasn't what he meant. "You mean they're your sisters."

"Yes," Nathan confirmed. "Well, one sister and an adopted sister."

"*Nooo*," Todd said rolling his eyes. Except he was most likely wrong in the order. It was Maggie who was adopted and the dark-skinned stunner named Serenity that was his actual sister. It was a well-known fact that Elemental and Chakan could indeed produce offspring, it was just rare since both Monsters had a much unhidden dislike for each other. Nine times out of ten, if the baby was a girl it was an Elemental, if the baby was a boy it was a Chakan.

"Then I guess you'll be fine," Todd said putting on his glasses and straightening himself up. "Bring them along. I have a few cross-dressers that would study the gorgeous one like they were at Area 51," Todd said leaning in, "We can use the other one as a bouncer."

Nathan laughed.

Then Todd realized. "Oh shit Nathan, please don't tell your bigger sister that I said that. She looks like she wouldn't care if she was committing a hate crime."

"Don't worry, I won't."

Heading out the door, Todd reminded him. "Tonight around eight then."

Waiting until the door closed the two women made their way towards the counter.

2: Not One Older Sister, but Two. Imagine the Horror

The stunner of the two looked like she floated as she approached while the other had to turn at certain times so she didn't plow over the shelves.

Then Serenity demanded, "Come out here right now." Her eyes burned with seriousness as Nathan came around the counter looking like a small child about to be punished. "How long have you been here?" she asked, but Nathan remained silent. "I haven't seen you for how many years?" she asked again, but still Nathan remained mute. "Is this how you treat your favorite sister?"

Maggie scoffed. "Fuck off."

Nathan raised his head and gave her a sad pout. Her stern face stood fast for about two seconds and then melted into a smile. Serenity didn't wait for an invitation, nor did she believe that she needed one and began peppering Nathan with kisses.

His fight to stop her was limited since she was in fact, his big sister. "Okay," Nathan said finally holding her at bay.

Grabbing his hands she held out his arms. "Look at you, still the most handsome." Then she pulled him in and hugged him tightly. "I missed you Nathanial."

"I missed you too Serenity," he said squeezing her tighter.

Leaning back, Serenity started to laugh while wiping at her eyes when suddenly she was pushed out of the way. Maggie grabbed Nathan by the shoulders and smiled. Then wrapped her arm around his neck in a headlock. "Who's your favorite sister?" she yelled, applying more pressure with every second that passed without an answer.

Trying to hold out and wiggle free, Nathan finally said it. "You are."

Maggie laughed victoriously and applied more pressure, "I'm sorry, I didn't quite get that."

"You are!" Nathan yelled.

Letting him go Maggie watched as he checked his ears and neck. "I didn't mean to hurt you there Tinker Bell," she said rushing him and applying a bear hug. Her massive arms squeezed as Nathan gasped for air and she began swaying him back and forth like a little girl would a teddy bear. "I missed you Fuck Face."

Finally being let go he took in a long deep breath. "What is with you people," he said referring to the stronger ones practically mauling him. Then he smiled. "I really missed you too Mags."

"Got some tears in your eyes there Sally?" Maggie asked looking like she was about to punch him, a common reaction of Maggie seeing someone crying.

"Really?" Nathan asked and then answered, "I was just physically abused."

"*Aww,*" she sarcastically bubbled, "there's a number you can call, 1-800-555-S-L-A-P," she laughed and out of nowhere slapped him hard across the face. The sound echoed with a thunderous sting as Nathan side stepped awkwardly from side to side.

"OW!" he cried out. "What the fuck was that for?"

"What the fuck was that for," Maggie repeated in a low vibrating growl, a trademark common with Bruti Monsters when in use of their powers. They were known for their ridiculous strength which was usually heightened with emotion, anger being the quickest way to see their full potential. It was also a very easy emotion to bring on since patience was nonexistent in their demeanor and temper was not easily contained, nor practiced with much success. This was not just an isolated case with his adopted sister, this was a common occurrence with all Bruti in general.

Then just as the side of Nathan's face was starting to glow with a deep red handprint, the sister whom he called Mags tugged him forward and threw a right punch that Nathan easily deflected. She threw a left that Nathan again deflected, but noticed that it had a lot of power behind, strange since she looked so happy to see him only moments ago.

This is about the whisky, Nathan thought and suddenly wished that Louis and Bo were both here, so he could kill them.

As Nathan waited for the next right punch to come he was caught off guard as Maggie grabbed his hand holding her left and twisted it the opposite direction. As he used his free hand to reach for assistance the large woman kicked him in the stomach and stunned him. Maggie lunged forward and punched him in the stomach so hard that it lifted him five feet off the ground. He landed on his feet and stood up, but then bent over instantly out of breath. Looking up at his assailant and unable to breathe, he was able to muster out a whimpering, "You bitch."

As Nathan fell to his hands and knees Serenity couldn't tell if he was laughing or crying, but she could see that he was still struggling for air. "Okay Maggie, I think he has had enough."

Maggie went to say something when she was cut off.

"I agree," Nathan said still hunched over but raising his hand to second the motion.

"You shut your whisky stealing fucking mouth!" Maggie yelled.

"Maggie," Serenity called out sternly. "We both know Nathanial didn't steal your whisky."

Maggie bent over beside Nathan. "Yeah, but I'll bet he drank it."

"Well yeah, it's good whisky," Nathan laughed when suddenly he felt his legs being swept out from underneath him and a punch from Maggie aided him getting to the ground more quickly. He was now juggling between laughing and crying out in pain. "I really hope no customers come in."

"Okay Maggie, we're here for a reason," Serenity said helping her little brother up. "We need to go over some things Nathanial."

"Really," he said gingerly getting to his feet. "A quick hello and then you beat the shit out of me *and then* we have to get down to business?"

Serenity pulled out her phone and started to look for something.

Nathan leaned towards his bigger sister. "So what did you do to them?"

Maggie smiled. "Waited in the ditch, about four miles in from the highway and mowed over Louis's fucking van. Then like a trash compactor I just smashed the shit out of it with them still in it."

Nathan laughed. "They didn't run?"

Maggie shook her head. "They were too fucking afraid to get out. So by the time I was done I had wrapped the entire van around them and they were packed in there like fucking sardines. I'll tell you all about it after the commandant here is done. But it was fucking epic."

Serenity looked up and was about to start when she seemed instantly preoccupied by Nathan, or more specifically something about his appearance.

Nathan could see it on her face. "What?"

Serenity licked her fingers and stepped forward and attempted to reach Nathan's hair.

"Hello? What do you think you're doing there?" Nathan said backing up and taking a defensive stance.

"You have a tuff of hair sticking straight up, it's distracting," she said and attempted once again to get at it.

"I don't think so," Nathan said backing up some more.

"Really?" Serenity scoffed. "Now you're too big for your big sister to take care of you?"

Nathan nodded. "Something like that."

Serenity rolled her eyes and then called upon her sister. "Maggie, if you would please."

As Maggie engulfed her brother within her massive arms, Serenity licked her fingers again and began to push down Nathan's cowlick. "Don't be a baby," Serenity said adding more saliva to her hand. Eventually she was done and signaled to Maggie to let go. "Don't touch it," she warned him as Nathan was just about to rustle his hands through his hair. "We'll just have to start all over again."

Maggie chuckled and swished some spit around her mouth. "Yeah bitch, and maybe I'll help this time," she said and then opened her mouth to show him.

Nathan frowned in disgust. "You're so gross."

Serenity produced a local newspaper headline on her phone and held it up for him to see. "The killings Nathanial. Now a kid gets his heart ripped out and eaten?"

"I know," he assured them taking the phone from her and skimming through it. "I'm on it."

"Anything yet?" Serenity asked.

Nathan just shook his head.

"I told you," Maggie said and then pointed at Nathan, "it's him."

"Piss off," Nathan laughed.

Maggie continued in her sarcastic seriousness. "Hey I get it. Chakans got to eat. I'm just saying it looks like you're making a little fucking piggy of yourself."

"Nice," he said shaking his head.

"Eat some animal hearts. Not half of Chicago," Maggie said and began to chuckle.

Serenity interrupted. "The numbers are pretty low, for the moment."

Maggie rolled her eyes. "That number is what the news is actually reporting on. The media is owned by either the Order, the Immortalis Corporation or the Father," she said turning away from Nathan and pointing her thumb back at him. "Who knows how many people this fucker has eaten?"

Nathan frowned. "I know it looks like Chakan, but let's not rule out other Monsters," he said trying to balance the conversation out, not wanting to spook his family and bring them all to Chicago.

"Anguis?" Maggie inquired.

Nathan shook his head. "Too much of the body left, no necrosis around the bite marks."

Maggie looked at her sister for a translation.

She immediately explained. "Cell injury resulting in the premature death of cells in living tissue by autolysis."

"Yeah, because that clears it up," Maggie said looking at her stunned.

Nathan snorted. "Poisonous lesions in the skin."

Maggie slapped him in the back of the head. "Then fucking say that you smug bastards."

Serenity continued to cross Monsters off of the list. "Well it's not Dracos, no burns."

Nathan agreed. "They're not known to eat humans either."

"Unless they're trying to throw us off," Serenity suggested.

Nathan nodded. "Well if it's trying to throw us off, it could be any Monster. Pisces to Elementals."

"What about Suns and Moons?" Maggie asked.

Serenity shook her head. "Solibus et Lunis haven't been seen on this continent since 1871, let alone the city they were massacred in mass."

She was referring to the Chicago fire, which was the official story of what happened in 1871. But what really happened was a large group of Solibus et Lunis had nested in Chicago and other counties along the shores of Lake Michigan. A very powerful Chakan by the name of Tyre was also in the area. His hate for these Monsters was well known and proven when he and his army used fire to draw them out and purged the area of them. He was successful, but not without thousands of humans being killed and over one hundred thousand people left homeless. Nathan had no interest in history repeating itself, which is exactly what would happen if his family jumped the gun. Especially his Grandfather, who everyone else referred to as, the Father.

Maggie threw another suggestion out there, having nothing to do with their current conversation. "Can we talk about this over breakfast? I'm fucking starved."

Instead of insulting her Nathan wanted to kiss her. *Thank you Maggie you magnificent beast you*, he cheered in his head. Going for breakfast was perfect, he could be vaguer about the killings and they most certainly have to be careful of what was said if the restaurant was busy. "I will figure it out, trust me."

Maggie pointed to him. "See, baby brother will figure out who's using Chicago as their all you can eat buffet," she said and then got Nathan's attention. "And if its Suns and Moons, figure it out yourself. Solibus et Lunis creep me the fuck out."

Serenity smiled, raising her eyebrows towards her sister. "Who knows, it could even be a Bruti."

"Ha!" Maggie blurted confidently. "Bruti don't eat humans, we're not even really Monsters."

"She obviously never looked in a mirror," Nathan said, quite pleased with himself until he turned around to a dominant jab to the face.

Serenity looked disappointed. "Nathanial, you have the heightened power of all the Chakan Rings, why don't you ever see these coming?"

"Because you're family," he said clutching his nose and holding back the pain induced tears in his eyes. "And for some reason I automatically let my guard down, damn!"

"Look," Serenity said sternly and getting their attention. "Someone is eating people and Daddy wants it taken care of, before Granddaddy gets involved," she said and then signaled out Nathan directly. "Hearts are being eaten and there is only one Monster that eats human hearts."

Nathan snapped back offended. "Maybe that's what they want you to think."

"Who?" Serenity asked confused.

"I don't know," Nathan revealed, a little confused himself. "Who are you talking about?"

Maggie laughed. "It's like he went away to stupid school and graduated with fucking honors."

Serenity giggled. "We just want you to do what Nathanial does best."

Nathan stood dumbfounded.

"Holy fuck," Maggie complained and tapped him in the head. "Use that so called Knowledge Ring and figure it out you moron."

"Right," Nathan said coming up to speed. "And I will, but Chicago is a big city, guys. And I had to get the store set up and stuff on top, or this and that—" he cut himself off and went silent, trying to think of words that did not involve dating or liking someone.

His sister was content. "Okay honey," Serenity said rubbing the side of his face affectionately and then slapped it. "Close the store and we can go for breakfast," she instructed and then wondered aloud, "is there any place around here we can go for a good tea?"

The comment from Serenity about a place with good tea made him think of Sips and then fear filled his whole body. If they saw how much he liked Lily, and they would from observation or directly from Todd, an avalanche of horror would begin. It would only start with them, then it would get back to Louis and Bo. Then the most horrible thing that could happen would then actually happen, it would get back to his Mother. "No, there is a half decent place a few blocks from here," he answered her and then thought, *and in the complete opposite direction of Lily*. Nathan didn't think it was a very good idea to close the store on his first day open, but the alternative was having his sisters stay and get into a deep conversation about the killings.

"Okay," Serenity accepted. "I hope they got a full breakfast menu, I am seriously going to order three or four breakfasts. I am starving."

Maggie passed her a little angry. "Fucking bitch looks like that and eats five plates of food at each meal."

"So I have to ask," Nathan said a little hesitant as he got ready. "How is Mom?"

"Ahh, he finally asked," Maggie said to her sister.

Serenity nodded back and encouraged Maggie to continue.

The Bruti stepped towards Nathan and held her two fingers apart in a reverse peace sign. "Do you know what this is?"

Nathan was a little confused but guessed anyways. "The British version of—"

"No," Maggie halted him as she put her right elbow between the two fingers and flexed her right arm. "It's the gun rack Fuck Face."

Nathan quickly put the puzzle together. "Ah, because your arm is the gun."

"That's right bitch," she said stretching her arm out with a closed fist while making the sound effect of loading a pump action shotgun as Nathan watched with amusement. Then without warning she shot her fist forward and caught her brother directly in the center of the face.

Nathan reeled back in pain. "Will you stop doing that?"

"Don't be a fucking baby," Maggie cried through her laughter. "Don't you heal instantly with your Healing Ring."

"You know it's not instant," Nathan said sharply, referring to the two centuries of fights and beatings between brother and sister. "And it still hurts."

Loading her *gun* for the fun of it, Maggie tried not to laugh. "Right, I keep forgetting."

Serenity took Nathans cheeks in the palm of her hands and looked him over. "I would go see your mother Nathanial."

"I will."

"Fucking right you will," Maggie shot back, holstering her weapon. "Because Mom said that if you didn't get your punk ass home soon, I'm allowed to use these weapons of mass destruction to pound the shit out of you."

"The only weapon of mass destruction you have is your ass," Nathan said and then laughed while Serenity was still looking him over.

Maggie started to poke at him with her fingers. "That's right— and I'll sit on your face, Nathanial."

"Don't call me that," Nathan warned her and started to swat at her advancing pokes, which was about to erupt into a slapping match.

"Okay children," Serenity yelled breaking them up, "let's go. I'm starving."

CHAPTER XIII

1: Just to Clear His Head

NATHAN HAD FOUGHT in his head all day about going to Todd and Martin's party. He debated internally all through breakfast with his sisters, which thankfully was in a packed restaurant so the conversations of Monsters and hearts being ripped out of people was kept to a minimum. And he continued the argument all day as he sat in his bookstore, which thankfully was slow. So when it was time to close he came out in a less frequented area and ran on top of the buildings to clear his head.

That is when he heard a very loud argument, followed by the cries of a woman who'd just been hit, and upon further investigation Nathan found out that the argument was very interesting indeed.

Hidden by a blanket of darkness he dropped from the roof top to the even darker alley. Listening to them still arguing he was able to piece together that she was a hooker named Jade and he her pimp. She kept calling him baby and daddy, but he guessed that neither was his name. The pimp seemed to have a client that was willing to pay a great deal of money for a couple of hours, but she was not inclined to take the job. From what Jade was saying, a lot of girls taking these new high paying assignments weren't coming back. It wasn't like they had found their *Edward*, the man from *Pretty Woman* not the guy from that vampire series, and all of a sudden moved into mansions and happy ever afters. No, they were disappearing from the face of the earth. In fact, Jade's really close friend went on one of these too good to be true jobs, and apparently hasn't been seen since. All of her belongings and clothes were in her apartment but Jade had not seen her friend going on three weeks now.

Nathan got a little closer as Jade's voice lowered. It seems that she heard from one of her other—

The Pimp hit her again. Nathan watched as the man grabbed her by the cheeks and followed up his physical assault with a verbal one. *Look at me when I'm fucking talking to you whore.* It seemed the pimp was becoming adamant that Jade took the job, fatal or not.

Nathan growled. Maybe too loud, because they both seemed to hear it as he watched them both stop suddenly and become drawn to his direction.

Did you hear that? Nathan heard the pimp ask as Jade affirmed it by nodding cautiously slow.

Nathan leapt up into the air.

Their eyes were still looking into the dark alley where Nathan *was,* until they heard a voice call out, *Excuse me* and both turned around to find nothing but a quick breeze.

As the pimp turned back he came face to face with Nathan. "What the—"

Nathan ended the pimp's question with a back hand that sent the man into the wall of the building where he fell to the ground unconscious.

Jade backed away slowly. "Look mister," she began and started to visibly shake as Nathan ran his hand through her hair.

"I have not eaten in a very long time," he informed her, sounding like he was plucked right out of a horror novel.

Jade adopted a look that made it look like she wasn't sure what that meant, nor was she sure she wanted to, so she countered. "How's about a blow job? No charge."

Nathan smiled as his fangs plucked out of his gums and made her jump.

"Okay a fuck then," she cried.

Ignoring her Nathan lifted her arm so he could examine it. "I'm going to ask you a few questions," he said letting his thumb run over the track marks where multiple needles had entered.

"Anything, just don't kill me, I have a little girl."

"Oh, I'm sure you do," Nathan laughed putting his hand into her purse.

"No-No-No, I have her, she's not in foster care or nothing," Jade cried completely unconcerned at Nathan rummaging through her purse.

He pulled out her driver's license and smiled as his eyes glowed a bright blue. "Let me just start by saying, honesty would be very prudent in your situation—Kelly," he said while shaking her license in front of her.

Jade nodded and then the questioning began.

2: Party Etiquette 101

The party was far from a small get together as the rather large apartment was packed with guests. Todd excused himself through some people and began hovering over Lily who was in the kitchen putting the last touches on some appetizers. "How many times you going to fold them fucking tomato provolone spirals?"

Looking down she saw the filling coming out from both ends. "Oh shit," Lily said coming out of her daze and looked at Todd. "Too tight?"

"You think," he laughed nudging her with his knee. "Someone is getting antsy."

"Well you said he was coming."

Todd gave her a hug. "He will Hooker. It's still early."

Suddenly the buzzer at the front door went off.

Todd turned to Lily who looked like a deer caught in headlights. "Holy shit Lily, that is probably him," he laughed turning to the door and then back to finish, but Lily was gone. "Where the fuck did she go?" Todd asked and then saw her running towards her bedroom. "You silly bitch," he laughed as he made his way to the door. Reaching for the handle Todd noticed that it was already turning without his assistance and then suddenly the door was flying open. There stood three of his gayest friends, Lenny, Paul and John. But behind them was the man he and Lily had been waiting for. "Nathan," Todd cried, "you came."

All three men in front of Nathan poured in awkwardly.

"Well hello to you too," Lenny said sarcastically.

Todd rolled his eyes. "Please, no one cares if you show up."

Paul stepped in front of everyone to bend Todd's ear. "I thought we talked about inviting men who were not gay. As in, we would not."

"You decided that. Besides," Todd said leaning in. "*He's for Lily.*"

"Lucky bitch," Paul said moving on.

Suddenly John tried to get ahead of Lenny and stepped on his feet. "Ow whore! You can wait you know," he cried out.

"Fuck you bitch I have to take a piss," John said running past him.

Nathan made his way in and offered Todd a bottle of wine. "For the party."

Todd took the bottle and examined it. "Damn Nathan, this is years better than anything I have. Or have hidden."

Martin came over and immediately offered him his free hand. "Mr. Nathan—I mean Mr. Caesar."

Nathan took his hand. "Please, just Nathan."

"Spiral?" Martin offered since the tray was already in his hand.

Suddenly Lenny and Paul were helping themselves to the spirals.

John was the first to swallow enough of his spiral to start talking. "This might be the last party of yours I come to."

Todd stood unimpressed. "Do tell."

John was already stuffing another spiral in his mouth and passing the baton to Paul or Lenny.

Lenny took it. "There was another murder just a few blocks from here."

Martin looked doubtful. "When was this murder taking place?"

"Well, *Webster's Dictionary*," Paul directed to Martin's English. "It was early this evening, and it was all over social media."

Todd was now engrossed. "Really?"

Paul continued. "Apparently this man was a pimp."

"Oh my god," Todd cried covering his mouth for a moment. "I'm a pimp."

Lenny rolled his eyes. "This was a real pimp."

Paul nodded in agreement. "Had his heart just ripped out of him and eaten."

Martin suddenly looked doubtful. "Wait a minute. Was part of the heart found?"

"No," Paul said.

"And did they catch the man who did it?" Martin asked with a smirk. Lenny jumped in. "No."

Martin took a deep breath. "No pieces of the heart found. No killer found," he said calmly before becoming annoyed. "Then how are they knowing that the heart was eaten?"

All three men looked at each other and then John finally spoke up. "That's what it said on the Internet."

Todd looked at them as if a magic trick had just been ruined for him. "You're all idiots," he said and turned to Nathan. "Come on Nathan," he said leading him towards the kitchen where he saw Lily walking towards them. "Now look, she's just as nervous as you are."

Nathan smiled. "That noticeable huh?"

"Please," Todd started, "your mouth has been talking, but your eyes have been looking."

Nathan offered her a little wave and she smiled. I was a start and before either of them knew it, hours had passed. Lily thought that it must had been magic or maybe a dream, either way she was having the most incredible time. They were laughing and discovering things about one another with genuine eagerness, leaving each other for only the most necessary of reasons.

If this is a dream, please let me sleep a little longer, Lily thought as she just watched him talk.

"So this is a small get together," Nathan said looking around the crowded apartment that just seemed to be getting more packed.

Lily laughed. *We could go to my room,* she thought and then out of nowhere she thought of Rick, as if her having any hint of happiness triggered him to appear, just to seize and kill any thought of enjoyment. But then Nathan smiled at her and it made that thought disappear. If only she would stop thinking of how much Nathan made her not think of Rick, then she wouldn't be thinking of Rick at all.

"Does he throw a lot of them?" Nathan asked.

"God no, I mean it was a monthly thing there for a while. But Martin has it down to five a year. It was supposed to be four, but Todd argued Christmas didn't count. So now it's just five."

Nathan laughed. "Five seems reasonable."

"Yeah, and they are all memorable."

"I'll bet."

Lily started to laugh pre-emptively. "At the last one, he got my Teddy Bear from my bedroom and played, where did your uncle touch you?"

Nathan quickly raised his glass to his mouth as he successfully held in his drink.

"Yeah," Lily agreed, "and it's a huge four-foot tall Teddy. You can only imagine the horror."

Nathan was still trying not to laugh. "I'm sorry. I don't mean to laugh. But if he's planning on playing it again, a little warning please."

Lily laughed with him and then saw Todd making his way back. "Speaking of the pervert."

"Honey," Todd drunkenly called out to Lily, "I want you to tell Carl the story of –"

"I will, just shut up and walk away," Lily interrupted instantly.

Todd was confused. "But I didn't say what story."

Lily was already making her way over to Carl. "Just playing the odds," she said and then turned back to Nathan, "I'll be right back."

"I'll be waiting," Nathan said.

Todd told her what story he was actually talking about and Lily went into auto-pilot since she had told this story at Todd's request a hundred times. But in his defense, it was a really funny story, even if she was the punchline.

While she acted out the rehearsed parts with dramatic flair, the more simplistic story element, while still important, allowed her to look over at Nathan Caesar. The mysterious bookstore owner with the big oversized apartment in Florida Johnson's well-to-do building. Nathan Caesar, the man who seemed to love tea as much as she did, maybe even more. Nathan, the man now nodding to Martin who looked like he was probably drunk and playing over-protective big brother. *Shit,* she yelled within the walls of her mind. *Please don't threaten or scare this guy off.*

Right up until Martin led her right to Nathan, Lily had convinced herself that she was not ready. Rick was not gone completely from her mind, and at times she could see his shadows lurking. Or sometimes if she closed her eyes and got lost, she could feel the phantom grip of Rick grabbing hold.

But when she saw Nathan, she felt safe. Not because he could protect her, but because she actually wanted him, and was willing to face the shadows and phantom attacks. At least she thought she was.

Then as she was talking, she stalled, as if her engine sputtered and turned off.

Paul saw a man coming down the hall towards them and pointed him out to Lenny.

"I call dibs," Lenny said getting a good look.

"I pointed him out," Paul protested.

Lenny smirked. "Should've called dibs bitch."

Lily didn't realize that they were talking about the same man that caused her to stall in her story. *Can't be,* she thought to herself wondering if she had too much to drink. Giving her head a shake she focused on the new guest coming towards her and immediately backed up in a panic as horror surged into her eyes. Slipping she bumped into a bunch of glasses on the counter and they tumbled to the floor.

Paul reached for her. "Honey, you okay?"

The stranger also reached for her, from a distance. "Lily, I just want to talk," Rick said, his voice unusually timid.

Lily replied in terror and disbelief. "You can't be here." He was a footnote in her history, Rick had left her and her story ages ago but there he was, crossing the room.

Todd must have seen him too, because he yelled out from across the room, "Oh hell no."

With one look at Rick, Lily's dreams of a new life crumbled, along with her confidence. Raising her hand she saw that it was already shaky with the unsteadiness of half consciousness. He was getting closer and that all too familiar sense of dread started to drip onto her expression, starting with the pin-like pricking in the corner of her eyes. Her mind was a mess as a hundred questions screamed for answers and she did not have a single one. *He is either here to take you home, or if this is a dream he is going to wake you up.*

Taking another step closer Rick continued his appeal. "I think we should talk."

"You can't be here," Lily repeated as if her body shut down and the autopilot was turned on.

"I need you Lily," Rick pleaded still approaching.

Not only did she feel like she was going to pass out, she was being enticed by it, it would take her away and she wouldn't have to deal with it. But Lily fought it.

Seeing it in her face Rick proceeded cautiously. "If we can just go and talk for a bit," he said with a bit of careful hesitance.

Lily shook her head.

His eyes twitched and the sound of his teeth grinding screamed that what little patience he had, was about to erupt. He abruptly stepped towards her and reached for her arm. "Come on Lily, let's go home."

She couldn't go home with him. She *was* home. This was her home. Unless she was dreaming? Of course she was dreaming, why else would a hot rich man find her interesting?

BECAUSE YOU ARE DREAMING LILY!

She was going to wake up in her old apartment.

Alone.

Bruised.

>*Alone.*

>*Alone.*

Beaten.

>*Alone.*

>>*Defeated.*

>*Alone.*

All … Alone.

NOOOOOOOOOOOO!!!

Todd positioned himself in front of Lily like a shield and slapped Rick's hand away. Pointing his finger directly at his face he fiercely instructed, "Get the fuck out of *our* house!" Now pointing to the door he repeated himself and added, "Are you deaf? I said get the fuck out!"

Lily just blinked hoping that Rick would follow Todd's instructions.

Todd was loud enough that the copious amounts of conversations in their immediate area completely stopped, then the music dropped in volume significantly.

As she searched for an alternate reality she saw Martin making his way over, she also saw the confusion on Nathan's face. "*No,*" she whispered sadly.

Meanwhile Rick began his defence. "This is none of your business."

"This is my friend," Todd countered while squeezing Lily's arm to let her know he was there.

Lily was able to flee the allure of blacking out and squeezed back, starting to feel something inside of her growing.

Todd waited until she looked him in the eyes before turning back. "This is our house," he said waving his hand around to include Lily.

Martin arrived but was met with Todd's hand, it held him at bay, but Martin obviously wasn't going anywhere.

Trying to look intimidating Rick continued. "I think that should be her decision."

"Look at her," Todd said stepping out of the way and letting Rick see how frightened she was. "Just seeing you is terrifying her," he said getting back into his spot. "I made my best friend a promise. I promised her she would never have to be afraid of you again. And I will be fucked if I am going to let some piece of shit—uncouth—dingy dressing—ignorant motherfucker make a liar out of me!" Todd let out and then inhaled deeply to catch his breath as claps and cheers could be heard throughout the apartment.

"Pretty tough when you're surrounded by your queens," Rick said getting visibly angrier.

"That's right, bitch."

For a few seconds they stood toe to toe, then Rick backed off a little. "Probably would give me AIDS," he said drawing some groans of disbelief from the partygoers.

All of a sudden Lily became aware of everything that was going on around her. And she had no plans or desire to go anywhere with this man.

Rick just continued to spew his vile ignorance, a direct by-product of angry drinking, unaware that this crowd was not his usual intended audience. "You want to see how tough I am, queer?"

"Pretty tough slapping around a woman," Todd slung back at him.

"No, I can slap around fags too," Rick said getting back in Todd's face as the crowd around them started to get vocal.

Martin seemingly could not take it anymore and stepped forward. "Okay my friend, it's time for you to go," he said lightly pushing Rick's shoulder with one hand and showing him the way to the door with the other.

Rick slapped his hand away. "Fucking-touch me," he said stepping closer to Martin. "And I'm not your friend you dirty spic faggot."

Martin looked like his cool was quickly disappearing until he felt Lily grab his shoulder and calmly pull him back. He looked at her and saw she was more than coherent.

Rick was calming down himself, pleased with what was transpiring. "See," he said ready for her to join him, "come on baby, let's just go somewhere and talk."

In an instant she saw her life in the future with Rick and all it looked like was a repeat on television. He had said nothing here tonight that he had not said before, the good and the bad included. Lily didn't just assume, she knew there was nothing he could say here tonight or any other time that would make her even entertain the thought of ever going back to him. And she knew this might not be the last time that he tried, but that didn't mean her friends would be there to protect her next time. Next time she might be alone and then what would she do? If she was ever going to have a chance with Nathan and have a meaningful healthy relationship, it was time for her to stand up for herself. Lily turned to him and said firmly, "No."

Rick was stuck. "What?"

She decided to explain in a little more detail. "We're finished Rick, done. I live here now."

"But –"

"This is my family," she cut him off. "And this is where I belong," she said stepping past Todd and Martin. Now she was in front of them and standing face to face with all her fears. Standing petrified, Lily was more scared now than she had ever been, but she was determined. She had felt safe and good about herself for a while now and she was not about to give that freedom up, even if it meant she had to fight for it. "You will never lay another hand on me. And you will never threaten my family again."

"This is your family now?" Rick challenged.

"Yes. This is my family now," she confirmed.

Rick was trying to keep calm. "I'm your family. I love you."

"No you don't," Lily said shaking her head, "I know you think you do, but you don't. And I don't." Turning to Martin and trying to maintain her momentum she asked, "Would you take me to the police station?"

Martin looked like he was about to burst in joy and nodded.

Lily turned back to Rick. "I'm taking the photos Todd took the night I came here to live," she explained, feeling more empowered with each word. "And I'm going to try and have you charged. I'm also asking for a restraining order against you." As Rick went to say something Lily was not done and continued before he could even begin. "I am not going to be afraid anymore." Looking back at Todd was all she needed for an extra bit of courage. "Now like my friend here said," she started as she turned back and locked eyes with Rick, "get the *FUCK* out of our house."

Todd stepped beside Lily and threw his arm around her. "That's right bitch—the fuck out," he said pointing to the door as the entire apartment seemed to be in agreement.

Rick's face broadcasted a sharp furiousness while his lips tried to find the proper words to express his malcontent. Not being able to find them he decided to just turn around and leave. A guest had already opened the door but Rick thought it needed to be wider and slammed it into the wall. He stood in front of the elevator as a hundred eyes watched. Finally it arrived and he stepped inside. Everyone waited until the elevator doors finally closed and then cheered.

Lily turned to Todd. "I think I'm going to be sick."

He wrapped his arms around her. "I am so proud of you honey."

Martin hugged them both and tried not to cry, but his sniffling gave him away. They stepped back a little to breathe as Lily wiped the tears from her eyes. She then wiped the tears from Todd's eyes as they both laughed. Lily went to wipe Martin's eyes and he laughed when he let her.

"I'll get the pictures," Todd said and raced down the hall.

Lily looked at Martin and asked, "You don't mind, do you?"

Martin gave her another hug. "*No estés de tonta*, of course not," he said trying to control his excitement.

Lily turned to a crowd of party goers. "Sorry everyone."

Which was met with nothing but goodwill.

Todd came back with the pictures and went to hand them to Martin, but paused. "I should come too," he said looking at Lily.

Lily hugged him. "It's okay, we'll go. You stay here and keep the party going, because when I get back I definitely want a drink."

Todd finally agreed and gave the photos to Martin.

Lily walked over to Nathan who seemed to be enjoying the surrounding banter. "I'm sorry you had to see that," she said, more than a little embarrassed.

"Don't be," Nathan said politely.

"Not the way you want to let the guy you like to know about your past."

"Definitely a first. But I wouldn't worry about it."

"I totally understand if you don't want to go out on our—"

"Never crossed my mind," he said instantly.

Lily was caught a little off guard. "I just thought, now that my baggage isn't only out, but clothes are like, scattered everywhere and—"

"Lily?" he interrupted her again.

She looked at him.

"If you're okay to go out, I can't wait," he said and then took her hand.

Lily quickly nodded enthusiastically.

Martin appeared. "Ready?"

"Okay," Lily said and gave Nathan a quick wave. "See you when I get back." She turned around, meeting Martin at the hall and took him by the arm.

"Ready," she replied confidently.

"Scared?"

"Nope," she said just as confident.

Martin nodded. "My girl."

But she did not see Nathan when she got back.

3: Just to be Sure

Nathan had excused himself from the party shortly after Lily left with Martin. He thanked Todd for a wonderful and eventful evening. He caught up to them on their way to the police station, several stories above and waited. He followed them back to their apartment, just in case anyone was planning on rehashing the altercation. Fortunately there were no problems and he watched them for a little while from across the street. Then Nathan said good night to the most beautiful and bravest women he had ever met.

CHAPTER XIV

1: Silly-Silly, Boil the Kitty

IT WAS SATURDAY and like always it was painfully slow, that is until the door chimed and let the only two employees at Sips know that a customer had entered. Being the only one without a hangover since she was unable to attend last night's party due to her babysitter backing out last minute, Jeanette was the obvious candidate to leave up front. Although throughout the night she was becoming a little suspicious as to just how hungover Todd was, since she had caught him multiple times dancing and singing or just plain howling with laughter while he watched *YouTube* videos in the back.

But there she was out front, and was now watching as an incredibly sumptuous man walked in. Suddenly she wasn't so upset being left alone up front. "Hello," she offered and then looked a little harder at the gorgeous man who was now looking somewhat familiar.

Walking up to the counter he placed his arm down and turned slightly, like he was at a bar shooting a 1970's beer commercial. He offered all of his teeth with his smile and then winked. "Well hello yourself darling."

Jeanette realized that the man who *was* attractive, was also as phoney as they came and most likely just as full of himself. This didn't stop her from pondering as to why he seemed so familiar. "I'm sorry, do I know you?"

"You sure do sugar," the familiar and good looking stranger informed her. "We bumped into each other a while back, in an alley with your friend. I was trying to avoid my friend."

"Right," Jeanette said. "James Franco."

"I think I resemble a more buff James Franco," he countered.

Jeanette went to agree with him and then stood perplexed. She remembered Lily saying that he looked like a buff James Franco, but she didn't remember if Lily had said that while the stranger was there or after he had left. And now she was sure the stranger was nowhere near them when Lily said it. Or was he? Maybe it was a common comparison and he got called a buff James Franco all the time? Her face suddenly became a puzzle of second guessing.

This let the stranger continue. "I was just in the neighborhood and wondered if your local tea maker was in?"

Jeanette put her thoughts on hold and sighed. "Of course, when it rains it pours," she said referring to Lily now seemingly getting all of the attention from the men. Not that she didn't want her friend to be noticed, but a little her way would be appreciated. *Not this guy though, suddenly he radiates creepy,* she thought.

"I'm sorry?"

Shaking her head she offered the attractive stranger a sympathetic smile. "Are you looking for tea, or the tea maker?"

He leaned in and made his eyes squint. "You got me. Not much of a tea person."

"I thought so," Jeanette said letting her smile become more playful. "You're a little late to the party honey."

"How's that then?"

Jeanette being only five-foot nothing, had to jump up and steady herself on the counter to be able to lean in. "Your friend from the other night, well he's already been putting a lot of time in and I think our tea maker has grown pretty fond of him."

He nodded slowly with a look that said he knew exactly who she was talking about. "That so?"

"That is so," Jeanette affirmed as she hoped off the counter.

The stranger paused for a moment and then gave her an almost fake salesman smile. "Well good for him."

"He seems really nice," Jeanette added.

"He can be."

Jeanette was instantly curious. "What do you mean?"

"Well," the stranger started with the same tone as his salesman smile. "Between you and me, he's been known to be a bit mean to his lady friends."

Jeanette affirmed her understanding with a slow nod and alert eyes.

"But, as long as he stays away from the drink," he said and then let the statement linger in the air for dramatic effect. "All should be fine."

Jeanette suddenly started to feel uncomfortable. "Duly noted," she said, stressing to figure out if the man in front of her was a hunky stranger or a creepy douche who might not be Nathan's friend at all. Jeanette watched as he casually started to rub his chest and then nonchalantly let his hand reach inside his shirt where he continued to rub. "Are you sure I can't help you?" Jeanette asked, trying like hell not to let her eyes follow his hand crawling under his shirt. They'd slipped once already—now a second time.

The stranger seemed to take this as flirting and almost purred. "How's your *latte* skills?"

Her eyes widened. "Not that good," she said and began to laugh nervously.

He laughed with her, but it seemed very fake, like he hadn't had a lot of practice.

Suddenly Todd appeared and began laughing to just be included.

The stranger turned his hand into a gun and pointed it at Jeanette and shot her a wink with what she would describe as a small, covert kiss.

Todd watched the man leave and turned to Jeanette still smiling, hoping to be let in on the joke. "Who was that?"

"Some guy we met on the street that I thought was hot."

Todd sighed. "Oh my God Jeanette. I can see your belly with child already."

"Piss off," Jeanette said instantly. "Besides, he was interested in Lily."

"Wow, when it rains it—"

"Pours!" Jeanette yelled out. "That's what I said."

Todd was obviously perturbed at getting cut off. "Excuse me Jeanette, I was going to say—Pours Cock!"

Jeanette stood silent as Todd laughed silently to himself. "You're an ass."

"Oh shit am I funny." Todd said taking a deep breath and looking around the store. "Well, that was the first person in how long? Why don't you head home for the night darling?"

"Really?" Jeanette almost squealed. "You actually like me enough to let me go home early?"

"No," Todd answered. "I like me enough to make you get the fuck out so I can stop having these thoughts about killing your tiny spontaneous child bearing ass."

Jeanette just shook her head. "So many faults in that statement."

"Holy shit, another murderous thought," Toddy cried out.

"I didn't even do anything."

Todd rolled his eyes. "You let a customer leave without buying anything Jeanette."

"What am I supposed to do, force a fucking muffin in his pocket and demand he pay for it?"

"There you go."

Jeanette started to gather her things. "Screw you. You like me and that's why you're letting me go home."

"You shut your ass," Todd said trying not to laugh. "Don't you go and start spreading erroneous and malicious lies, you speed breeding midget."

Jeanette was already heading out the door. "I love you too."

The door shut and Todd was all alone and still looking angry. "Bitch."

2: Ambush of the Gentle and Harmonious

There had not been a customer since Jeanette left, over an hour and a half ago, which unfortunately was normal for a Saturday night. They were usually busy right up until six pm, then it would just die, every sixth day of the week. Even their older customers seemed to have something better to do on the highlight of the weekend.

Last night's party ended very late, which naturally made the morning come very soon. Todd had wasted any energy he had throughout the day on singing and dancing and was now too tired to even think of funny topics to look up on YouTube. He was now at the stage of not only regretting having let Jeanette leave early, but coming into work at all. Lily and Martin did not have to come in today, a goodwill gesture on Todd's behalf, one that would be pointed out throughout the rest of the night once he arrived home.

The sluggish feeling of someone who just wanted to spend the remaining hours of the evening on his couch would now settle for a last minute customer who would eat up these last minutes.

He quickly glanced at the register, then decided the thirteen dollars and change he made after he was left alone was not enough to warrant a detour to the bank. Then he looked at the clock. "Are you kidding?" he questioned loudly, wondering if the clock had actually slowed down in some sort of time conspiracy to keep him prisoner.

An executive decision was needed and Todd mulled it over, but obviously he was not the person to be handling these type of decisions. Finally he turned off the open sign in defiance of the remaining ten minutes. Then in his mind he saw Florida coming in the morning and giving him grief over closing early. So he turned it back on. Then thought that this was silly and turned it off. He waited at the door with his face pressed against the glass trying to look down both directions of the street.

Nothing.

Now he had nine minutes and thirty seconds to go. "Fuck it. And fuck you Florida," he said turning off the sign. Setting the alarm he turned off the lights and left. Finally he was on the other side of the door and waiting to hear the last chime of the alarm. He hated the walk home and being stagnant made it worse, especially since there was no one around to bitch about it to. Todd humored with the idea of calling a cab, but with tip, it would have eaten up all of the profit from the night.

Walking past the boutique and the thrift shop he heard a garbage can topple from inside the alley and it made him jump with a side of yelp. He didn't remember if he jumped or yelped first, just that he was frozen at the entrance, staring into the darkness, as if he was waiting for someone to turn on a light so he could see. "*Hello?*" he almost squeaked and then rolled his eyes at himself, so he decided to butch it up. "HELLO?"

Except for some white noise in the distance, the entire street was quiet.

Another bang exploded from the darkness and Todd literally jumped letting out a panicky *Ahh*. And as he stood there he couldn't believe he actually contemplated stepping into the alley to see if someone needed help, but then chuckled. "Fuck that. I watch my horror films." Finding the ability to move he began to turn when a long drawn out *Meow* sang out relief from the alley.

"As fucking if," he said dramatically putting his hand over his heart and taking a deep breath. Todd heard footsteps coming toward him and knew it was Martin come to meet him. Turning around to tell him the funny story of the cat in the alley who almost gave him a heart attack he saw that it was most definitely not Martin.

"Lights out faggot," said the voice behind the fist.

3: A Hankering for Tea

He had to hurry before Sips closed, or he would be forced to go and buy generic tea. Leaping through the window he extended his leg and pushed off the ledge, rocketing across to the other side. Effortlessly grabbing the opposite ledge he began pulling himself up onto the windowsill. Suddenly the light behind the window turned on and Nathan quickly swung to the side and plastered himself against the brick. But a scream came from inside the window anyways.

Shit! Did they see me? Nathan wondered getting ready to rocket upward.

What the hell is that? A voice yelled from street.

This was enough for Nathan to lose his balance and he quickly reached for something to grab onto. Except he didn't find anything and he fell to the sidewalk just beside the alley with a loud thud.

The same voice that caused him to lose his balance called out to him. "Mr. Nathan, are you okay?"

He picked himself up. Looking around he saw it was Mr. and Mrs. Esposito, the friendly couple that lived across the street. He had bumped into them numerous times on the street, Sips, the grocer and now as he fell five stories and landed on the sidewalk. "I'm fine," he answered as his mind scrambled to get ready to answer the next series of questions, like why was he hanging outside the window of their apartment? And why did a five-story fall not kill him, let alone not injure him?

Mr. Esposito started to help brush him off. "I heard a loud thud and turned around and saw you laying there."

They didn't see anything, he thought and waved. "I was jogging, and—"

"In those clothes?" Mrs. Esposito asked almost horrified.

She was right, he was not wearing the clothes of a jogger.

"And in such nice shoes, you'll ruin them," she continued to point out.

Mr. Esposito rolled his eyes. "Okay Bernice."

"Well they're dress shoes, he'll get blisters."

"Jesus Christ, leave the kid alone, huh," Mr. Esposito pleaded.

But she was right, he should have changed his shoes. It was one of the reasons he slipped and fell. Then it came to him. "I meant, I was going to Sips and jogging to get there before it closed. I heard a scream from the window of your apartment and stopped, then I heard Mr. Esposito yelling that he saw something and I lost my balance and fell." He quickly ran it in his head a second time. *Sounds good.*

"That was a loud thud Mr. Nathan, I thought you fell from the top of the roof or something," Mr. Esposito said about to inquire some more.

Then Mrs. Esposito slapped her husband's arm. "See what you did Frank."

"Ow," he protested and turned to her, "what did I do?"

"Your dumb voice made him trip."

Frank turned to Nathan. "Sorry kid."

Thank you Bernice, Nathan thought relieved.

Frank looked up at the window. "Our son has moved back in to the abode."

"Temporarily," Bernice added.

Frank again rolled his eyes. "He was watching the game when we left. He tends to yell and scream at the TV, I don't know where he gets it from. *Hey,* how did you know the scream came from our apartment?"

Nathan's eyes widened.

"Where does he get it from?" Bernice asked sarcastically and looked at Nathan. "This from the man who has a stroke from screaming so loud when he watches *Price is Right.*"

Frank sighed. "The people who go on that show are stupid, it just makes me so upset," he said already looking like a fresh stroke was beginning.

Thank you again Bernice, Nathan thought. He enjoyed bumping into the Esposito's, but he did want to make it to Sips before it closed. "I'm sorry, but ..."

"Right, the coffee shop," Frank said smiling, "better get a move on."

Nathan started to jog in the shops direction. "Have a wonderful night guys."

"You too," Bernice said and then yelled out, "and congratulations on your date with Lily."

Nathan waved back with an embarrassed smile. *Really Todd?*

4: Two Parts Hate & One Part Crime

Todd felt a sharp tingling feeling on the side of his face and he wasn't a hundred percent sure, but he believed he was on the ground and being moved.

How? Todd wondered.

Then he stopped.

Todd could hear talking, but the only word he could make out was *Further.* Feeling the jerky motion start again, he knew he was back on the move.

Something was not right.

Then a voice demanded someone to, *get him up.*

Todd felt both of his arms being hoisted and he tried to say something. But all he could muster was a dazed grunt. Then Todd felt the slight sting of repeatedly being slapped in the cheek, as if someone was acquiring his attention.

"Wake up you fucking homo," the slapper with the recognizable voice said.

The breath stank of cheap rye and cigarettes. *Someone punched me in the face,* he thought finally clueing in. Todd was now pretty sure the culprit who was unloading the cruel punishment of their bad breath was also the same person who punched him in the face. Now the blur was fading and clarity was dawning. "Rick," Todd was able to sputter. He also noticed he was taken deep into the alley. He tried to talk again, "Rick, I – I ..."

Rick looked at his two friends Kevin and Derek smiling, then brought his fist forward in a hook like motion and punched Todd in the stomach. The two men had to take all of Todd's weight as his legs gave out.

Immediately Todd coughed and began to choke while trying to respond, but nothing resembling actual words came out. He just wanted to curl up into a ball and hug the pain.

"You know what, homo?" Rick asked, but Todd could only try to respond to no avail. Grabbing him by his cheeks he forced Todd to look at him. "Do you know what really pisses me off, Toddy?"

Todd again tried to answer as Rick let his cheeks go and grabbed him by the hair. He pushed Todd's head down while he brought his knee up to connect directly with Todd's face. The smacking thud was so loud and explicit that everyone not directly affected by it grimaced.

Todd only heard the muffled laughter of Kevin and Derek as they dropped him to the ground and as he immediately tried to rise in some sort of heroic effort, Kevin just placed his boot on Todd's back and forced him back down. Todd just rolled to his side.

Rick was obviously getting impatient. "I asked you a question faggot," he slurred bringing his foot forward and connecting the tip of his boot with the middle of Todd's back.

Todd shot out of the fetal position and arched his back in pain on the dirty alley floor. The agony took over everything as he heard them laughing above him. He wanted to yell for help, or at least beg them to stop, but could only close his eyes and surrender to the overwhelming ache.

Thinking it was a committee Kevin made a suggestion. "I say we castrate him."

Rick grabbed Todd by the hair and yanked his head up as far as he could. "What do you think Todd old buddy, castration?" Rick smiled waiting for an answer. "At least it would stop him from shoving his cock up other men's asses."

"Then who will throw it in yours?"

The two friends, Kevin and Derek, looked around in disbelief and even Todd wondered who said such a defiant comment.

Rick's two accomplices began to laugh as Rick smiled and shook his head. "A smartass to the end. Kind of like last night," he explained to his friends before bending down to Todd's ear. "Who's the bitch now you fuck?"

Todd realized it was actually he who made the comment. *Maybe now is not the right time for such bold comments.* He lifted his head to apologize and was immediately stifled by a hard back hand across his face that sent a mouthful of blood into the air.

Shaking the sting from his hand Rick continued. "It was fucking rhetorical."

Todd spit some left over blood that seemed to straggle and decided it was not going to matter, so he threw caution to the wind. "You really are a little bitch!"

Suddenly Rick straddled Todd while grabbing his head violently and repeatedly slammed it into the ground as hard as he could.

Todd felt the gravel and cement scratch and dig at his face, making low clomping sounds that he wished would just knock him back out.

Then Rick jumped to his feet and raised his arms in victory as Kevin cheered.

Derek however had been on the hunt and found a long rusted pipe. "He's trying to get away," he said as Kevin and Rick turned and saw Todd trying to crawl back to the street. Derek made his way over while he whistled and stood beside Todd. He held the pipe like a golf club and began teeing up his shot. "Fore," Derek yelled as he brought the pipe down and caught Todd in his side.

Todd curled up again while letting out an agonizing low pitched screech.

As Rick kicked him over they saw the tears streaming down Todd's cheeks.

"Fucking Nancy's crying," Kevin said holding out his hand as Derek obliged by passing him the pipe. "I'll give him something to cry about. You ready fag-boy?"

Todd could see the pipe coming down over his head and instinctively held up his arm. It had taken some of the impact but it still caught the top of his forehead, causing the skin to split and allowed a small but steady seeping to begin.

Still they laughed.

"My turn," Rick said taking the pipe from Kevin's hand. "I will say, this is the most fun I've had on a Saturday night in a long time," he said looking at Todd holding up his hand and trying to signify he was giving up. "Oh we're not even close to being done Toddy," he informed him.

Kevin nodded approvingly. "We're gonna commit a hate crime tonight."

Rick nodded teeing up his shot. "Yes we are."

Todd's arm weighed a hundred pounds now, and he was barely able to keep it up. Not being able to see through the blood now running into his eyes, he began to sob. He knew this was not just a beat down, he was going to die tonight. "Please, I'm sorry," he cried, "I'm so sorry, please I'm—"

Rick kicked at Todd's arm. "Be a man you fucking fairy," he responded. Then he kicked Todd's other arm out from underneath him and watched as he crumbled. Now standing above him Rick eyed up the shot. "Fore," he yelled swinging wildly. Rick was drunk and his eye-hand coordination might have been off, but he was still able to catch Todd in the head.

Todd's face snapped to the right with a new busted nose and gapping cheek that allowed blood to spray. His jaw fractured immediately in multiple places, creating an internal puzzle held only by beaten flesh. The pressure in his mouth became too great and he had to open it so the large glob of thick blood could cascade out of his mouth and then off of his chin, making a dripping splattering sound on the ground.

The two friends watched silently.

Rick held his hand to his mouth in disbelief and then started to jump from foot to foot. Turning to his friends, he pointed at what they were already watching. "Holy shit do you see that?" he asked and then cheered, "Woo hoo baby!"

5: Missed It by a Beating

As Nathan got closer to Sips he was getting less optimistic. Now standing at the front door he peered in but could not see nor hear anything from inside. Giving a little rap against the glass his hope was finally exhausted, he had to concede. Smelling Todd's cologne starting to wash out of the air actually teased Nathan that he had just missed him.

Then he heard it.

"Woo hoo baby," the voice yelled in the distance.

Lifting his head, Nathan let his nose trace the air and smelled the blood seeping into it. It was coming from the same directions that Todd's Chanel Antaeus was coming from.

6: We Now Join Our Program Already in Progress

Kevin and Derek both began to cheer until Derek noticed that Todd's blood was all over him. "You asshole, I got queer blood all over me."

Kevin sympathized sarcastically. "Oh shit," he said turning to Rick. "Every time there's a full moon, he's going to turn gay."

"Fuck you," Derek said trying to wipe it off.

"Are you getting any urges to suck another man off?" Kevin asked with a condescending smile.

Rick joined in. "Hey Kevin, bend over and see if Derek sticks it up your ass," he said as Kevin started laughing.

Todd tried to prop himself up but failed. Now collapsed on the ground he wanted to stay awake because he knew when he lost consciousness, he would never open his eyes again. *Would Martin keep Sips open? Who will guide my little Mary-Anne?* Todd wondered in his head. *Poor Lily, I love you so much. I really hope she doesn't blame herself.* But Todd knew she would, her ex-boyfriend killed him. He just hoped Martin would protect her from all the other people who would blame her. "Martin," he whispered. At least he thought he did. *I Love you,* he thought with so many memories flying past him.

It was getting harder for Todd to stay awake since all he wanted to do was close his eyes and escape. With a smile of regret he laughed in his head. *I didn't even get a chance to fire Jeanette.*

Rick looked back at his friends and confessed, "This little homo has some fight left in him."

Derek nodded with anticipation but as soon as Rick turned away, he was yanked forcefully backwards. No sound was made, no yell, not even a cry for help. He just vanished.

"Finish him off brother," Kevin said, obviously not aware his friend was sucked into some kind of an abyss.

Rick raised the pipe up over his head. "Any last words Toddy?"

Kevin was caught up in the moment, seemingly reveling in it, until he caught what looked like two glowing eyes in the shadows. He turned to ask Derek if he could see it when he noticed that they were now a friend short. Panic started to overcome him as he went to ask Rick what happened to—

And just like that the second friend was gone.

Standing over Todd, Rick's eyes burned with hatred as he gripped the pipe and smiled with evil contempt. "What do you say boys, on three?"

But there was no reply.

Then Todd heard it, a growl like a tiger. *Odd for a tiger to be out this late at night,* he thought with a dash of deliriousness.

Rick must have heard it as well, because he spun around and met two glowing eyes and fangs diving towards him.

Hearing a violent struggle Todd looked up to see something that resembled his new friend Nathan and then passed out.

7: It's a Bird – It's a Plane

Todd awoke to the wind blowing in his face and what looked to be a building coming straight at him. Suddenly he felt the bizarre sensation of weightlessness as he soared past windows until he was on the rooftop. Moving forward once again he came to the edge and thought for sure he was going over and suddenly wanted to throw up.

He wanted to scream in hysterical fear but instead looked up for answers.

Nathan looked down at him. "Stay with me Todd."

Todd felt the sensation of being hurtled through the air again and it reminded him of being in the car with his dad as a kid and they would speed up when a big dip in the road was coming up.

Nathan landed on the next rooftop and took a hard left.

Todd wasn't sure how Nathan was doing what he was doing, but he was sure he wasn't going to be able to jump the massive building coming up.

"Hold on," Nathan said as he waited until his foot was on the very edge and crouched before pushing up with incredible strength that sent them rocketing into air.

Passing window after window, they inched closer to the wall of glass and steel.

Todd wanted to scream as this was now nothing like hitting a dip in the road with his father.

Grabbing them abruptly, gravity yanked downward and Todd could feel the churning in his stomach. He moaned in a state of light-headedness and was able to blurt, "Holy shit."

Nathan looked down and nodded his head towards a large building coming up.

Todd followed his nod and could tell it was Northwestern Memorial on North Saint Claire Street.

"We're almost there. You're going to be fine," Nathan said leaping with Todd in his arms through the night sky and towards the bright lights of Northwestern Memorial.

CHAPTER XV

1: Hospital Food Sucks

MARTIN CAME THROUGH the sliding doors in a panic and looking around as if he hoped to see Todd sitting there with a smile, all ready to go.

Lily came in right behind him and looked around as if hoping to find the same thing.

Making his way to the front desk where a nurse was trying to put together a file that had obviously fell, he politely interrupted. "Excuse me."

The nurse put the file down and smiled sarcastically. "Yes sir, how may I help you?" she asked, her tone matching her smile.

"Yes, I'm looking for someone. His name is Todd, Todd Jacobson."

She could tell he was concerned by the way his eyes looked ready to burst into tears and his hand was slightly trembling. Her sarcasm dissipated. "Of course dear, let me look," she said already checking the computer. "Here he is, room four-twenty."

"Okay," Martin started bringing his arms to a rest on the desk and looking like he was ready for a long debate, "we have limited insurance, but I can go get the loan when the bank opens."

Lily plunked her purse on the desk still a little out of breath and started to go through the papers in her purse, "I got his other ID, health—"

"That won't be necessary miss," said a voice from behind them.

Both Lily and Martin turned around to a smiling nurse who happened to be walking by and overheard them.

She then asked, "You're talking about Todd Jacobson right?"

Martin and Lily both nodded unsure of what was going on.

The new nurse extended her hand. "You must be Martin and Lily. I'm Jesse. I'm actually heading up."

Confused, Martin asked, "Why won't any of that be necessary?"

Jesse replied, "Well, it wasn't a robbery so he had his ID on him and the man that brought him in took care of the financials."

"Who brought him in?" Lily asked.

"I don't know his name, you would have to ask billing," Jesse said smiling, "but all of the nurses would like to know that as well."

"Billing?" Martin repeated even more confused.

The elevator chimed and the doors opened. All three of them stepped on as the Jesse hit four and continued, "A man came into the hospital carrying another man covered in blood. We took Mr. Jacobson and began prepping him immediately."

Martin looked like he was on the verge of heart attack as he struggled to swallow.

Jesse turned to Martin and told him directly with her hand on his shoulder. "He's doing fine, I promise."

Martin nodded and was able to muster a half smile.

Jesse went on. "He was a bit of a mess and he does have some rehabilitation to do, I won't lie about that."

Lily squeezed Martin's hand as the elevator *dinged* and they exited.

"Now, we have a specialist coming in the morning," Jesse said leading them down the hall. "But it's more precautionary. Once it was determined the man carrying Mr. Jacobson didn't actually assault him, he provided some personal information to our front desk and left his card information."

"His card?" Martin asked.

"His credit card," the nurse answered. "We were told it didn't matter, any tests, rehab, medicine, private room, private nurse, anything was to be charged to his card. And once a credit check was done, they shipped Mr. Jacobson to a private room." Jesse stopped and invited them to get a little closer. "Between you and me, I'm sure the hospital will find plenty of things Mr. Jacobson will *need*," she said with a disappointed smile and punched the giant OPEN button with the side of her fist. The doors swung open and they continued.

"So, we don't know who saved him?" Lily asked

Jesse grabbed a clipboard from behind a desk. "We would argue we did."

Lily stuttered embarrassingly, "Of course you guys did, I mean, the guy?"

Jesse laughed. "I'm just fucking around with you." She finished with the clipboard and returned it. "We're a little more relaxed on the midnight shift, ain't that right Patty?"

The only woman behind the desk they assumed was Patty didn't even look up from her book. She just raised her arm and twirled her index finger and dryly replied, "Woo – Woo."

Jesse waved them to follow. "In a nutshell, apparently our mystery man interrupted an assault and then brought Mr. Jacobson here. Said to be on the lookout for his life partner, Martin Ortiz, and friend, Lily Cooper." She stopped at door 422. "He's going to look bad. I'm not saying it isn't. But thankfully it's nothing that won't heal, minus a couple of scars that could make him look tougher."

Neither Martin nor Lily could help it and blurted a little laugh.

Jesse's eyes widened. "What I'm trying to say is that he looks like shit, but he'll make a full recovery."

"How's his face?" Lily asked.

"Horrible," she answered honestly.

Lily grabbed Martin by the hand. "He is going to be so pissed," she said and although Martin's eyes were tearing he was able to chuckle.

Holding her hand on the door handle she repeated, "A lot of bruising and swelling, he has stitches, but like I said."

"Looks bad, gets better," Lily said taking a deep breath and waiting for Martin who finally nodded.

Jesse opened the door and led them in.

Walking into the room Lily thought it was like walking into a VIP suite at the Waldorf, she guessed, since she had never actually stayed at the Waldorf. There were fresh flowers and beautiful paintings scattered throughout the room. A panoramic view of the city lit up the dark early morning. One of the windows was open, letting a cool inviting breeze into the room that made the white drapes flutter like little clouds.

Todd was asleep and bandaged almost entirely. Lily watched as Martin rushed to his side and pause as she watched his hand try and find a part of Todd's body that wasn't covered with gauze, a lot of which was already stained red. He only choices were some bruised skin on one side of his face and one hand. She made her way over onto the other side of the bed. "He's alive Martin."

Martin nodded, looking like he was at a crossroads and was unsure if he was going to laugh or cry. "His mouth is wired."

Jesse nodded. "Yes, it will help the jaw bone heal."

Lily covered her mouth and began to cry.

Another nurse appeared at the door and Jesse excused herself.

Lily couldn't keep it in any longer. "You know who did this," she said almost unable to look Martin in the eyes.

"We don't know anything yet," he countered.

Lily cringed violently, unable to stop her own waterfall. She gently grabbed Todd's hand and fought not to break down completely. "I am so sorry Todd," she said looking up at Martin whose face was turning a dark shade of anger. "Martin, oh my god, I really am sorry," she said unable to feel anything but guilt.

Martin kept his eyes on Todd, but reached for Lily's hand, and as he took it he pulled her into hug. "Don't you ever apologize for that, that—*Carbon!*"

The door opened and Jesse made her way back to them. "Sorry guys, but there is a Detective Sherman here and he would like to get some statements. It seems Mr. Caesar gave him a bit of information—"

"Caesar?" Martin asked surprised.

"Nathan Caesar?" Lily expanded upon.

Jesse nodded. "That was the name of the man who brought Mr. Jacobson in. He gave the detective some information, but he was hoping you two could talk to him."

"Of course," Lily said and then looked to Martin who nodded eagerly.

They quietly made their way out of the room and Todd slowly opened his eyes. "Gone," he mumbled and waited.

A gust of wind blew the drapes apart and revealed Nathan was already in the room. He made his way to Todd and stood over the bed looking at him with a mixture of relief and concern. "How are you doing?"

Todd just semi shrugged and tried to smile, letting a little drool escape his bottom lip.

Nathan walked to the other side of the hospital bed and grabbed some tissue and wiped it from his chin.

"Tanks," Todd offered unable to pronounce the *h* in his 'thanks.'

"No problem," Nathan replied noticing the way he was looking at him. He wasn't sure if it was the drugs or what he saw while he was being brought to the hospital. "How much do you remember Todd?"

"Not -uch," Todd said taking a deep breath, then through an admittance of relief he looked at Nathan.

Nathan saw it in his eyes. "But enough."

Todd nodded and went to say something.

"We'll talk later," Nathan said cutting him off. "I promise. Right now you need to rest."

It was as if Todd was just waiting for permission because when Nathan looked back at him he was already asleep. Nathan smiled and patted him gingerly on the arm that wasn't in a cast as he heard the door opening.

A nurse making her rounds walked into the room and could have sworn she saw something head towards the window. She walked further in with a look of suspicion and saw nothing but the drapes sucked out of the window and fluttering in the gusts of early morning.

2: A Man's Got to Eat

Nathan watched the nurse pull the drapes back into the room and close the window before he jumped off the ledge of the building across from the hospital. He was glad his new friend was going to be all right and started to forgive himself for not coming to the rescue sooner.

Walking down an abnormally lonely street, even for this time, he caught a hint of blood in the air. His blue eyes started to flicker as the faint scent was enough to excite him.

He stopped and listened.

Filtering out the sounds of the city, he started to walk towards the sound of awkward wrestling. He was right, the smell of internal life being exposed was coming from the same direction.

Nathan picked up his pace, always leery of watchful eyes he was aware that this was around the time the people of the night were scurrying home before the morning people were out and judging them.

The smell of blood was getting stronger, but the sounds of scuffling seemed to be over. Slowing down Nathan entered a dark alley and heard a can roll along the cold pavement floor. Hearing intermittent cries and whimpers, Nathan let his claws protract over his nails as the tips of his fangs forced themselves from his gums.

Then he came across a woman lying on her side, covered in blood. Approaching her slowly, Nathan dimmed his eyes.

She already knew he was there. "Help me."

He tried to hear if there was anyone else present. "Are you alright?"

Lifting herself slightly she shook her head. "He came out of nowhere," she said looking at the blood she seemed to be wearing. "He said he was going to eat me," she explained and began to cry harder.

"What's your name?"

"M-M-Mila," she stuttered through her tears.

"I'll call for help," Nathan said, but only pretended to dial his phone.

"He must have run off when he heard you," she said and then sniffled.

"Yes, there's been another attack," Nathan said into the phone.

"I was just going home ..." Mila said starting to break down. "He was so strong, like he was inhuman." Getting to her feet with some effort her cries intensified. "He said he was going to – eat me. He started biting," she said finally standing.

"Yes, a woman has been attacked."

"Help me," Mila cried holding out her arms.

"No," Nathan said plainly while he slipped his phone back into his pocket. "She's dead."

Her crying stopped instantly as no sign of air was escaping past her lips.

The silence that flooded into the alley was overwhelming.

Suddenly she raised her hand.

Nathan's eyes beamed.

"Wait," she screamed.

He blurred and was in front of her before another word could leave her mouth. Wrapping his hand around her throat he squeezed as she tried and failed to speak. "How fucking stupid do you think I am?" Nathan barked and then wrenched his hand from her neck with half of her throat still in it.

Her blood sprayed everywhere as she dropped to her knees, trying to stop the blood from escaping.

Nathan kicked her onto her back and followed, driving his hand straight into her chest.

Mila held one hand over her missing throat and the other tried to stop Nathan from plunging deeper with no success. Suddenly her body stuttered before going into a constant shake as she instinctively tried to scream. Her panic filled eyes watched as his hand plunged deeper and she began to turn pale from the loss of blood.

Then Nathan looked into her eyes as he clutched onto her heart and smiled as her body went from a constant shake to full out convulsion.

Footsteps.

His head turned as he heard the hurried boots approaching from behind the door of the building to the right. He saw her look to the doorway as if the multiple steps coming their way were her salvation. Nathan smiled as she extended her hand towards them, trying to call out.

But Mila could not call out, she could only wait and die.

"Solibus et Lunis!" Nathan growled and then ripped Mila's heart from her chest.

Her hands desperately reached for her heart while she silently screamed for it to come back.

Nathan was gone before the steps were identified.

They would only find Mila dead and minus her heart.

CHAPTER XVI

1: General Hospital, Todd Edition

LILY WALKED INTO the hospital room that was now full of flowers and baskets from all of their friends. She had to search a bit, but saw Martin talking to nurse Jesse. Then she saw Todd and immediately began to cry. She was happy to see him up, but they had removed some of the bandages and he actually looked worse, not that she would ever dare tell him.

Todd looked at her expression and then to Martin. "Dat why no mirror?" he asked. "Cause I hideous?"

Suddenly Lily began to laugh, she had forgotten that his mouth was wired shut and it made him sound like a cross between Elmer Fudd and Sylvester the cat.

He looked at her again. "What so f-unny Li-ly?" he asked, pronouncing Lily *Wee-wee*.

Martin looked at her. "His mouth is wired."

"I remember," she said entering the botanical garden.

Jesse nodded. "Yes, it will help the jaw bone heal."

Todd just mimicked Jesse sarcastically.

Lily walked to the end of the bed and waved. "Jeanette and Mary-Anne say –"

"No Lily," Martin interrupted, "no talking about the shop or who is covering it. It is making the machines make the bad noises."

"F–ucking J-eanette," Todd stewed but quickly changed his demeanor. "I l-ove you Li-ly."

"I love you too," she said looking to Martin and Jesse.

Jesse answered immediately, "Drugs."

"Oh," Lily acknowledged. "And how are you feeling honey?"

Todd lifted his arms like he was giving a hug. "D-rugs," he said almost smiling. "Sh-o glad y-ou came Li-ly."

"Of course I did," she smiled through her tears and gently wiggled his foot which made Todd wince in pain and she retracted her arm instantly. "Oh my God Todd, I'm sorry."

Todd started to laugh, as well as a beaten man with his mouth wired shut could.

Lily stood terrified and angry, an anger she believed she had to give a pass on, but it still showed nonetheless.

Jesse tried to give her a little comfort. "Yeah, he's been a pain in the ass any time he's been awake."

Lily looked back at Todd. "Are you serious?" she asked as Todd answered with a shrug. Then she began to laugh nervously. "What is wrong with you?"

"That's my demented man," Martin said giving him a kiss on the forehead.

Suddenly Todd got very excited and started to speak very quickly and very incoherently. Unfortunately not even Todd would remember what he said, thanks to the drugs.

Lily looked at Martin who had no idea, so both of them looked at Jesse the nurse.

"Yeah, I have no idea," Jesse admitted.

Todd huffed, slumping forward in a pout.

Jesse added, "We gave him a pad and paper, but he just drew a bunch of penises. Some had smiley faces."

Martin and Lily looked at Todd who was giggling and holding up some of the pictures. "Th-ats m-ine," he said pointing to one of the bigger phalluses that was smiling. As they stared at him he held his arms up. "D-rugged," he said in his defense.

"Drugged," Martin said gently running his hand across Todd's swollen face, "you sure are novio."

"Oh right," Lily said and brought out a gift bag. "Nathan wanted me to give this to you and he wanted me to tell you that he hopes you're feeling better."

Todd sat it beside him. "Gonna g-ive t-hat man a b-low job."

Martin shook his head. "You are not giving Mr. Nathan a blow job."

Todd shrugged. "Okay, you g-ive him b-low job."

Jesse tried to hide her laughter.

Martin continued to shake his head. "I will not be giving Mr. Nathan a blow job."

Todd looked at Lily and then pointed his finger at her with a mushed up smiley face. "Li-ly will g-ive him a b-low job," he said with a giggle.

Martin stopped shaking his head and nodded. "Yes. Lily will probably give Mr. Nathan the blow job."

Suddenly Lily slapped Martin's arm. "Hello!"

Jesse looked at her with an open mouth smile. "You're dating the hot guy that all the nurses are talking about."

Lily nodded bashfully. "Well, we're going on a date."

"Good for you girl," Jesse said and then whispered, "I am so jealous." She turned to Martin. "I have to go, but I'll be back in a bit," she said and quietly let herself out.

Martin looked over his lover's battered body and could not help but get teary-eyed again. Lily joined them at the other side of the bed and began to cry.

Todd felt the pain starting to come back and followed the nurse's instructions and pressed the button to get more drugged.

"I'm so sorry Todd," Lily said trying to hold it together.

Todd just shook his head and took her hand. "D-on't," he said. "I l-ove y-ou Hooker."

"I love you too Pimp."

Martin moved some of the flowers and sat down beside the bed. "Let's see what Mr. Nathan got you. You know, on top of paying for all this."

Todd agreed. "R-eally, someone should g-ive him a b-low job."

Lily laughed and agreed for his benefit.

Martin leaned forward and grabbed the gift bag with red and yellow 3-D balloons covered in sparkles. Removing the tissue he looked inside. "It is a book."

Todd watched as Martin pulled the book out and instantly looked like he lost his breath. "J-esus C-hrist," he said gingerly taking it from Martin. Todd could not believe that in his hands was a first edition of author Robert Louis Stevenson's first novel, *Treasure Island,* liberated from its glass prison. Opening it, he turned a few pages and laughed.

Lily saw that he was straining. "You can't read it can you."

Todd laughed and shook his head.

"A little too lax with the drugs, huh."

"F-uck y-ou Li-ly."

And they all laughed.

CHAPTER XVII

1: Don't Shed a Tyre

IN A VERY RURAL AREA of Scotland stood a castle nestled in Celtic rainforest, surrounded by dense oak and abundant flora that was carpeted in soft layers of mosses, liverworts and lichens. It was as if it was still medieval Scotland and you had entered a time warp. But upon further inspection the many buildings hidden behind the castle that had helicopter pads, observatories, laboratories and other technological constructions to name a few, gave the current century away.

Inside the castle part of the complex stood a Chakan named Tyre, who was standing over another Chakan referred to only as the German. He was laying on the ground and no longer able to defend himself as Tyre continued to slice away.

"You don't tell me what the fuck to do my son. I fucking tell you," Tyre yelled as he finally stopped his assault and stood up straight to take some much needed breaths.

An Elemental by the name of Quinn, Tyre's head of security, stepped forward to take a look at the German. "I think he's dead boss."

Breathing heavily Tyre turned around to Quinn and then back to the German and took a closer examination. "Nah, he's alright," he said stepping back.

Quinn looked again. "No, I really think he's dead."

Suddenly the German inhaled deeply and looked up.

As Quinn jumped a little Tyre laughed at him. "Told you."

"Fucking German," Quinn said catching his own breath.

The German's eyes were full of hate, and even though he was that close to death he began yelling at Tyre in a harsh and resolute tone. Not because of the injuries, but it seemed to be out of anger and contempt.

Tyre looked at Quinn. "Can you fucking believe this cunt?"

"Bloody hell," Quinn agreed.

Tyre blurred back over top of the German. "You'd think after losing that many wars they'd be a bit more humble. Coming here, to my home! And telling *me,* that Marcus Licinius Crassus demands an audience," he said and then drove his hand into the German's chest and in one continuous motion, ripped the heart out and sunk his fangs into it making a wet popping sound.

Quinn thought about the conversation that Tyre was talking about and then thought he had heard it a tad differently. "I don't believe he actually demanded per se."

Tyre dropped the heart and spit what was in his mouth to the floor, then waved his hand in an inward direction at a pair of men, one of which produced a handkerchief. He began wiping his hands of the German's blood. "Didn't have to," he said redirecting the cloth to his mouth. "It was in his little beady eyes and fucking smug German tone."

Tyre looked back at the two men. "Clean that stain, and get that fucking bawbag away from me," he instructed and then sat down at a beautiful table set for morning tea. It was complete with a fanciful tea set that included a bone china tea pot, tea cups with saucers, a sugar bowl, creamer, tea kettle, waste bowl and tray. It also had doylies, proper silverware that included sugar tongs and a lemon dish that was all laid out on a very elegant tablecloth.

Now, not only did all three men look out of place, it actually looked like it was part of an elaborated joke. If not for one participant looking absolutely infuriated.

The man looking so angry was named Percival and he was Tyre's right hand man. Percival was a powerful Chakan with one irregular Ring, the Reading Ring. His extra power was deadly, it meant that when he faced opponents, he had the keen ability to read his foes every twitch and be able to anticipate their next available moves. And since he was over 1400 years old, he was very good at it.

Quinn however was looking at the heart left on the carpet. To his belief, Chakans tended not to waste a heart since they needed it for nourishment and survival. "Seems like a waste of a heart."

"Germans are Germans," Tyre started to explain. "And Germans taste like shit. Now that's because they ferment in their *cunty* arrogance and it makes 'em horrid to eat," he finished. "Aint that right Percy?"

Except Percy was still looking at the German bleeding on the carpet as a third man joined the first two in trying to clean it. "What the fuck is that?" he inquired while pointing in the direction he was staring so angrily in.

Tyre looked back and forth. "Shit Percy, was that German a fucking friend of yours?" he asked, seriously afraid he had just killed a friend of his right hand man.

"*Fuck* the German," Percy soured. "I'm talking about my fucking carpet you prick."

Tyre looked at the carpet and then back at Percy. "So? I got fucking blood on a rug."

Percy became insulted. "That's not just any rug you uneducated cunt. It's a silk Isfahan from Central Persia, circa 1600 and *you*, just ruined it."

"Then I'll buy you a new Central Persian, Isf—Isfa," he said and stopping, as he was getting agitated. "I'll buy you a fucking new one."

Percy leaned over all matter of fact like. "The store went out of business. Four fucking centuries ago my son."

"Well fuck Percy, I didn't even ruin it. Technically, *Za German* ruined your Central Persian whatever the fuck it's called."

Percy was still stuck. "Do you know how old that carpet is?"

Tyre hemmed and hawed. "I'm guessing at the very least, four centuries," he laughed and looked at Quinn, who joined him as he poured his boss some tea.

Percy mockingly laughed with them as he took the sugar tongs and flung two cubes into his tea and began stirring with a very perturbed look on his face. It did not help that the gentlemen cleaning the recently departed German were still looking for something big enough to put the body in and it made Percy's anger glisten. "For Christ's sakes boys, the carpet is buggered. Roll the fucker up in it."

The three men immediately began rolling the body up in the very old and very expensive rug.

Tyre saw how angry his right hand and very oldest of friends was getting and smiled. "Buy a fucking new one. Like I'll just pop on down to the Tesco Superstore and maybe they'll have a sale on rugs. Regularly a million, but Tesco has got a sale, two for a hundred and fifty quid."

Quinn looked a little concerned. "Oh I don't think Tesco will have those type of rugs Percy, not even the Superstores."

Percy sat astounded. "How can you be so fucking dumb?"

"Why am I dumb Percy?" Quinn asked.

"Because you fucking plank," Percy began to yell as he started to throw sugar cubes at Quinn. "I was being fucking sarcastic you Elemental halfwit."

The cubes stopped raining on him but Quinn kept his hands up and peered over them rather than dropping his defences completely. Seeing that it was safe he began to pour his tea.

Percy watched and got angry again. "See this is why I use dumb. It is by far the best way for me to describe your level intelligence."

Still waiting for the tea to come out Quinn answered without looking up. "I think I'm rather intelligent."

"No—no you are not," Percy wanted to make clear. "Now take that teapot you keep holding up with no fucking tea coming out. It must be clogged."

"You reckon?" Quinn asked and started to investigate the spout.

Suddenly Percy's face went beat red. "No you useless ninny, it's fucking empty—Jesus Christ," he said looking to the heavens for help.

Quinn went on the defensive. "Well how was I supposed to know?"

"You're fucking with me right?" Percy said as a vein started to appear on his forehead and he began throwing sugar cubes and berating him. "You fucking know because there is nothing coming out of it."

"Okay-okay," Quinn said trying to duck the cubes while loading the tray up to go back to the kitchen. "I'll get a new pot."

Slowly calming himself, Percy looked at Tyre. "When I close my eyes at night and just about drift off to sleep, I cannot tell you the sense of security I feel, just knowing that that boy there, is the head of our security."

"Come now Percy," Tyre said sympathetically. "He's a very powerful Elemental with very rare and unique powers."

Percy shook his head. "That's what is so fucking scary."

Tyre placed his hands on the table. "What about Marcus?"

Percy took a sip of his tea and stewed on it for a moment. "Well," he started confidently. "It seems Marcus is intent on finding the young Nathanial, meaning he'll go head on with the Caesars. Meaning that'll drag the Order into the fight," he said taking a sip. "You know, Mrs. Caesar being so close to Miyamoto and the Order."

Tyre became very agitated. "I fucking loathe Miyamoto and the Order."

Percy leaned towards him with a very sinister smile. "By the time those cocksuckers are done with each other. It don't matter who fucking wins," he said giving Tyre a quick nod. "You hear what I'm saying son?"

Tyre sipped his tea and smiled. "I do."

"He's right boss," Quinn said returning with a fresh pot.

Percy laughed. "Well, if boy genius agrees," he said and then smiled sarcastically. "I'm probably fucking wrong and we should scrap the whole fucking idea."

Quinn huffed. "Even when I agree with you, you get mad at me."

"Especially when you fucking agree with me," Percy pointed out.

Tyre tried not to laugh. "What's your take Quinn?"

"Well boss, I'm thinking if we don't take a side, all of 'em will get suspicious of us just lurking about. I'm not saying we have to take the lead here, but at least interject ourselves to some degree. We don't want to be late to the dance and have no one to dance with."

Percy looked in his cup. "Someone slipped me something because Quinn actually made sense."

"I have my moments," Quinn said proudly.

Percy had already made up his mind. "Either way we should cross the pond to America. If we leave now we could go hunting in Canada. Start at Mahoney Lake, make our way to Great Bear."

"That'd be brilliant," Quinn said adding his vote.

Tyre was done mulling it over in his head. "So it's settled, call down and have the plane ready then."

CHAPTER XVIII

1: Meet Me in St. Louis

THE BAR WAS IN an old building on South Broadway and packed as the band was playing a mixture of blues and jazz. Merrick, the Raven and the Crow all sat at a table exchanging stories and pleasantries for what looked like hours now. The waitress dropped off their drinks and they continued.

The Raven shook his head. "My-my Mr. Merrick. Stuck in all of those ungodly countries must have been hell?"

"Not just hell sir," Merrick said taking raising his new drink. "But a hell where you're led around on a leash by the Order."

The Crow had already begun scowling with the mere mention of its name. "No surprise there."

"Yes," the Raven affirmed, "we prefer not to have any dealings with them. Any that we have had cannot be called upon with any positive recollection."

"That's why we prefer to stay home," she added and then turned back to watch the band play.

"It is true. The old Canada's or the odd trip to Europe. Proper Europe mind you, London and Paris. But other than that we prefer to stay within the comforts of the good old U S of A."

The waitress walked by and noticed they were almost done their drinks already. "Another round?"

"Isn't she a peach of a woman?" the Raven crooned. "Yes my dear as soon as you have the appropriate time," he said gaining a favorable and appreciative smile.

"Two please," Merrick said holding up two fingers. "One on the rocks and the other neat, please."

The waitress nodded and smiled and was on her way back to the bar.

"That rum Mr. Merrick. It has a very distinctive smell," the Raven said.

"It does. An acquired taste, but it takes me back to the rum we unloaded from the British, just before we scuttled their frigates."

"That's right," the Raven said recalling his history. "You sailed out of the Barbary Coast. You were a privateer."

Merrick decided to be honest. "We're all friends here. I was a pirate."

"I didn't want to betray any feelings of personal perception," the Raven said with a smile.

"No misconceptions, sir, I pillaged and I plundered."

"Marvelous, for how long?" he asked.

"Almost a hundred years."

"A hundred years of adventure," the Raven added.

Merrick hemmed and hawed while he thought about it. "Well, I would say a good thirty years of adventure, the rest was pretty boring."

"A true swashbuckler," the Raven said and downed the rest of his scotch.

The waitress came with a double scotch neat and two Pusser's British Navy Rums, one neat and one on the rocks. "I'll be right back with your martini dear."

The Crow nodded to the waitress and turned back into the table. "I just got it, *Meet me in St. Louis*, like the movie," she said proudly and turned to Merrick. "Do you know I almost ate Judy Garland."

"There are the heebies," Merrick whispered to himself and then looked at the Crow casually. "You don't say. I heard she was supposed to be one of the sweetest ladies in Hollywood."

"She was," the Crow answered. "I was just such a fan. And I so wanted to know what that tasted like."

"And there are jeebies," Merrick whispered to himself again before speaking up. "Well, I was a fan as well. So thank you, for not eating her."

The Crow smiled with sincerity. "You are very welcome."

"Here we go," the waitress said putting the martini on the table and noticed that the gentlemen's drinks were almost done. "And you fellows?"

"Same again if you would be so kind," the Raven said finishing his scotch.

She turned to Merrick while she gathered the glasses. "Same for you honey—one neat, one on the rocks?"

"Actually just a double of spiced rum, if you would be so kind," he said handing her his glasses.

"And you're okay?" she laughed as she looked at the Crow.

"You know, you bear a striking resemblance to Judy Garland," she told the waitress with a shiver inducing laugh that ended abruptly. "Are you on the menu?"

"Excuse me, menu?" the waitress inquired while looking at the others and thinking she heard her wrong because of the music.

"No menu necessary," the Raven assured her. "Just a joke from our current conversation. Another apple martini will be fine."

That explanation seemed to satisfy the waitress. "I'll be right back."

The Crow excused herself and headed to the bathroom giving Merrick the opportunity to talk bluntly about the business at hand. "I just want you to be clear on your job specifications—Edgar."

A tad antagonized, the Raven let his forked tongue flicker. "I do not like that name, sir."

"And you, my slithery Anguis friend. I do not like repeating myself or having my instructions ignored. So, I want you to understand right now, how serious I am," he said looking him in the eyes. "Do not take this personal, but a lot of money and man hours went down the shitter when our last employee ignored instructions."

The Raven thought for a moment. "Fair enough Mr. Merrick."

Merrick continued. "His name is Nathan."

"Nathan Caesar, of the house of Caesar, son of Julius and Cleopatra. Born with five irregularities of his Rings," the Raven said.

"Very good, and yes he is very fucking dangerous," Merrick certified.

"All Monsters have heard the tales of the all-powerful Nathanial Caesar Mr. Merrick."

"It doesn't matter. You are not to engage the target under any circumstances. You will track and report from a distance. A safe and unnoticeable distance," Merrick said trying to be absolutely clear.

"I understand."

"It is crucial that you do."

"Of course, I pride myself on always completing my objective according to my employer's instructions. And between you and me, I am a bit of a coward in the fact that I do not like to engage, unless certain of the outcome," he said with a sense of twisted pride.

"Good," Merrick said and leaned back. "Like I said, the last gentlemen under contract did not—Mikhail."

"From the Kievan Rus' era, son of Yaroslav the Wise," the Raven said. "Tell me Mr. Merrick, how did old Yaroslav take the news?"

"I do not know," Merrick said honestly. "I'm not human resources."

The Raven laughed.

"But I'm sure he'll be comforted to know that when Nathanial beat his son to death, he set him ablaze and pointed him towards his homeland," Merrick said shaking his head. "A Chakan custom I guess."

"How wonderful Chakan customs are."

"I find them strange and unnecessary," Merrick said raising his eyebrows and taking another sip.

"Come Mr. Merrick, do not Elementals usually adhere to a strict code?"

Merrick finished his drink. "Not this one."

The waitress returned with their drinks. "Sorry I took so long guys, it's getting busy tonight."

"Of course it is," the Raven said giving her an appreciative smile. "The music is absolutely fantastic."

"They are pretty hot tonight," she said looking to the stage. She turned back and took a deep breath and a quick break. "Phew, how about I just bring some drinks when I see them low and you just stop me when you're ready to call it a night?"

"A formidable plan," the Raven agreed.

And with that she was off again.

The Raven raised his glass to Merrick. "I have no desire to follow or honor any creed or code. Nor do I have any desire to go to the After anytime soon. God knows the discarded souls who will be waiting for yours truly," the Raven confessed. "What I am trying to say Mr. Merrick, is that my loyalties are bound by the job set forth and paid for."

"Good," Merrick said and raised his glass back at him. "No offence, But the Judy Garland story kind of freaked me out."

"No Mr. Merrick, no offence taken. She can be quite impulsive sometimes."

The Crow appeared back at the table. "What did I miss darling," she said sitting back down and quickly finding her new apple martini.

"Just business Lover, dotting i's and crossing t's," the Raven said leading the conversation away from boring details.

She smiled with an evil enthusiasm. "Tell us more than just the obvious about Nathan."

"Let us not my dear," the Raven interrupted. "I'm sure Mr. Merrick would probably prefer to just relax."

"Not at all, we have reason to believe that Nathanial is in Chicago, but we don't know where exactly. The only picture we have of him so far is him at the airport entering the city," Merrick said bending down and grabbing the briefcase from beside his chair and placing it on the table. Opening it, he pulled out two folders, a red one and a plain beige one. "In the red one you will find all we have on Nathanial Caesar and in the other, his family," he said seeing they both took notice of the beige one being much larger.

The Raven grabbed the beige folder and weighed it in his hand. "Yes his family, we have had the good fortune of not running into them."

"But I hear they are not a family to be trifled with," the Crow said staring at the folder like it was a dare.

"With good reason," Merrick said looking for his drink. "They have stood against almost every kind of Monster clan and organization at one time or another. And they are all still alive and well. It isn't because of their keen personality and top notch negotiating ability, I can assure you. You will find it all in there," he said while the Raven opened it. It revealed pictures of Nathan's family and extended associates. "All the Chakans have an irregular ring. I'm sure I don't have to tell you about Julius Caesar, but the Cajun is speed, the big boy there is strength. The scary Bruti is ridiculously strong, even for Bruti standards. His mother and sister are Class One Elementals. I don't even want to get into his grandfather but he's there for your reading pleasure," Merrick said looking at his empty glass. "Their family and associates extend from their Ranch to every corner of the Globe. To say that they are well connected is an understatement," he finished and caught a glimpse of the waitress. Giving her a nod, she acknowledged and headed straight to the bar. "Now, you'll be heading to Chicago immediately I'm guessing?"

"We were going to go by boat," the Crow said becoming disappointed.

"By, *boat*?" Merrick asked a little confused.

The Raven finished his drink and explained. "We were going to take the Queen up the Mississippi to Davenport. Then, cross the river to East Moline and take eighty-eight to Chicago."

The Crow saw the urgency in Merrick's eyes and decided that the Mississippi could wait. "Maybe we can drive straight to Chicago, then when this job is over we'll take the Great Lakes to Montreal."

"Fabulous idea my love," the Raven said giving her a kiss on the cheek. "Have you ever been to Montreal Mr. Merrick?"

"A couple of times," he said trying to get the last drop from his glass.

"Wonderful city," the Raven touted.

"So Mr. Merrick, I can smell the Elemental dripping off of you, may I ask what level?" the Crow inquired while enjoying another sip of her martini.

"Class One," he started.

The Crow frowned. "Of course."

Then Merrick added, "Water and Air."

The Raven raised his empty glass in spirit. "Being a pirate, Water and Air would have made you a most formable foe."

Merrick nodded instead of holding up an empty glass. "It came in handy. That and a little bit of luck I suppose. Until it ran out at Ocracoke Island in 1718. That was the end of my pirate career."

The Raven recalled his history. "That is where Captain Robert Maynard ambushed the famous Blackbeard."

Merrick laughed. "That is where Julius fucking Caesar ambushed Marcus Licinius Crassus aka, Blackbeard and yours truly, aka Black Caesar."

The Raven sat astounded in silence soaking it in until he found the words. "Absolutely wonderful."

"Not back then it wasn't," Merrick mused.

"I have heard that Marcus Crassus was Blackbeard and you Black Caesar and just took it as a hearsay fact, but Julius Caesar was Robert Maynard?" the Raven asked still flabbergasted.

Merrick wanted more rum and looked out towards the bar desperately. "Go to Wikipedia, it says, and I quote, *Very little is known about Maynard, except for when he killed Blackbeard in a fight,* end quote. An unknown captain, a couple of sloops and no more than fifty or so men take down the most notorious pirates that were actually Monsters?"

"Simply devious," the Raven said still shocked.

The Crow grabbed his hand and smiled. "You have to forgive him Mr. Merrick, he does so love his history."

"You know," the Raven said and confirmed the Crow's statement. "I always did wonder how Blackbeard and his crew of Monsters were taken down? I knew it had to be another clan or faction."

"And now you know, it was because Julius Caesar and others from the Order were sent to purge the waters of their little import export problem. Marcus was so embarrassed by the defeat that he never spoke of Blackbeard again."

"And you being Black Caesar, were you not to blow up all evidence and cargo?" the Raven asked intrigued.

"I was," Merrick confirmed. "And I did not. You could imagine my surprise when Marcus showed up and freed the man who failed him."

"I'm starting to see where his dislike for the Order stems from," the Raven laughed.

"Oh yes," Merrick continued, "shortly after that, the Immortalis Corporation was born."

The waitress appeared with more drinks and set them on the table. "Gentlemen I am so sorry it took so long."

"It did take a long time," Merrick said, looking all the more intimidating coming from an enormous man. But then he smiled. "And now that you have given me my rum, all is forgiven."

The waitress laughed and then quickly wiped down what she was able to before taking the empties with her.

The Crow became curious. "And what will *happen,* to Nathan?"

"Marcus is not only a powerful Monster, but he owns one of the world's most influential corporations on the planet. You kill the man's daughter, sick or not, you're going to pay, and my guess is slowly and painfully," Merrick said making it short and to the point.

The Raven raised his glass. "If Marcus Licinius Crassus wants him, then Marcus Licinius Crassus shall have him," he said and then cleared his throat. "Not all get to live to see another day. Not all get to see the elegance of another sunrise. Not all understand that love is not, eternal. And although you were not warned that on the day that the cold touch comes, it will be your last. And when Death whispers your demise, only then will it become all too clear. And all but too late. For there are those in the After waiting for you Nathanial Caesar. For they not only wish to see you, but they hunger to embrace you. And we will—oblige them."

The Crow raised her glass. "Quoth the Raven," she said with a dark smile. "Nevermore."

Merrick raised his glass, more optimistic than he had been in months.

CHAPTER XIX

1: Knock Knock, Guess Who's Here

SHE KEPT LOOKING at the front door and then to the time on the microwave. A knock would sound at the door at any second and it made all of Lily's excitement start to mix with her anxiety. She went to move and suddenly she wanted to throw up. "I think I'm going to be sick." Lily turned away from the hall. "Do not get sick Lily," she told herself and then turned back toward the door and began tapping her foot in a panicky rhythm. "Oh my God, what do I do?"

Martin appeared beside her. "Stop talking to yourself would be a good start."

She looked up at Martin. "When he gets here, tell him I'm sick."

Martin was already shaking his head.

Lily almost begged. "You can make him go away."

"Now you listen Lily. Mr. Nathan seems like a very nice man. You are pretty *fantástica* yourself," he said pointing his finger at her.

Suddenly Todd's voice appeared out of nowhere, distant and still sounding like a cartoon character because of the wires in his mouth. "H-oney, M-artin is ri-ght."

Lily's eyes widened. "Shit I forgot Todd in the kitchen," she said running to the counter and picking up the tablet. "Sorry Todd."

"Wh-atever," he said from the screen.

Martin bent down to the tablet. "How are you feeling *mi amor*?"

"I t-ell y-ou, th-ese dr-ugs are fan-tas-tic."

Martin smiled and touched Todd's nose on the screen. "Now tell Lily it is the true. She deserves to have the nice night out with Mr. Nathan."

Todd's head started to dip away from the screen, an obvious side effect from the drugs, but then suddenly he perked right back up again. "Y-es, wh-at he s-aid."

Lily started to calm. "You're right."

"Of course I am, I am always the right," Martin said as if it should be common knowledge. "It is the kiss you are the worried about, *si*?"

The panic all over her face was enough to convey the word *yes.*

"Now, listen my dear. You want to be calmer tonight?" he asked as she nodded. "Then you open that door, pick a right moment and then you kiss him as soon as you can."

Lily followed the instructions until the kissing part, now she just looked at him puzzled.

"He's ri-ght," Todd affirmed from the tablet.

Martin held the tablet beside his own head so Lily could see them both united. "Si, and make it a good one. This might not work for the man, but the woman, it is okay. You won't feel sick anymore, I promise."

Lily saw the logic, but didn't expect this from Martin. "Wouldn't that make me seem a little easy?"

From the screen Todd rolled his eyes. "He said a ki-ss Li-ly, not a hand j-ob at the door."

Like a horror movie a loud knock appeared from behind the front door and both Lily and Martin jumped a little. The tablet however let out a howling scream, followed by drug addled laughter. "Sweet Jesus, that scarred t-he sh-it out of me," Todd yelled out from the little speaker.

Martin waited a moment and saw that Lily was not moving any closer to the door, in fact she wasn't moving at all. He bent down and whispered, "You want I should answer the door?"

"Yes," Lily franticly hissed and bolted down the hall to her bedroom.

Martin just looked at the screen.

Todd was laughing. "Wow! T-his date is gonna be e-pic."

"Quiet, you," Martin said and lowered the tablet.

Suddenly Lily came running back down the hall and grabbed the tablet from Martin's hand. "I need him," she said and dashed back down the hall to her room.

Another knock appeared.

"I am coming," Martin chimed. Opening the door Martin saw Nathan already walking away. "Did you forget something?"

Nathan spun around and smiled awkwardly. "Martin, hello."

"Mr. Nathan."

"Sorry," Nathan responded as his face contorted stiffly and his left eye twitched.

Martin leaned into the hall. "For what are you sorry for Mr. Nathan?"

"I'm nervous," Nathan blurted out and looking as if a mountain had just slid off of his shoulders. "Really nervous, this wasn't the original shirt I picked out for this evening."

Martin smiled. "*Es que toda mi amigo*? She is nervous too."

"Really?" Nathan asked, looking like this made him feel a bit better.

"*Si*, she had to change her shirt four times because of all the sweating."

Nathan started to loosen up. "Okay, that's totally gross, but strangely it makes me feel better."

"Come on in my friend," Martin invited. As he closed the door behind them he looked down the hall to Lily's room. "I will just go see if she is ready."

"Thank you," Nathan said and stood obediently by the door.

Martin made his way down the hall and lightly tapped on the door before entering.

Inside Lily sat on her bed with the tablet in front of her and looked up as Todd's face strained to look up over the screen. "Well?" she asked.

"He is just as nervous as you are Lily," Martin said as Lily started to smile.

"Really?" she asked.

"*Si*, he was pacing back and forth when I open the door."

Todd looked up from the screen. "I t-old you Hooker."

"Oh yeah," Martin continued. "He said he had to change his shirt because he was so nervous."

"Oh my God, that is so great," Lily cried getting some confidence back. "I had to change like four times," she revealed and started to bounce ceremoniously on her bed with Todd on the tablet.

"I know," Martin admitted while joining them, "I tell him that too, and now Mr. Nathan feels *much* better."

Lily's little bounces of joy on the bed stopped immediately and her smile quickly started to deflate. "Um, what?"

Martin was still doing little jumps of joy until they finally slowed to a stop. "Um, what?" he repeated, now knowing he had said something wrong.

Todd was facing Lily. "Did he just f-ucking say w-hat I th-ink he just f-ucking said?"

"I think he did," Lily answered with her face adopting a more mortified motif.

"T-urn me the ar-ound," Todd demanded.

Lily turned the tablet to face Martin, who was now almost huddling in fear. "Why w-ould you tell Na-than th-at Lily was s-weating like a little piggy?"

"Mr. Nathan looked so nervous, I just wanted to help."

Lily began slapping Martin's arm. "By telling him that I sweated through four shirts?"

"Ay," Martin cried while raising his arms in defence. "I guess I was not doing the thinking."

"You no doing the th-inking," Todd mocked. "Who w-ants to sl-eep with a s-weaty old st-inky piggy?" Todd bellowed through the tablet and turned his head. "H-it him again."

Lily didn't even blink and began to slap Martin's arm again.

"Ay," Martin moaned as he rubbed the spot that was inflicted upon.

Todd's angry disposition changed to thought. "W-ell, he is a man and men w-ill s-leep with anyone."

Lily turned the tablet to her face. "I want a relationship, not a pig and a poke."

"Right," Todd said putting his thinking cap on. "Just to be s-ure, forget the kiss Li-ly. You better g-ive him the h-and job."

Lily huffed and handed Martin the tablet as she gave herself a once over in the mirror.

Martin put his hand on her arm. "I am so sorry, do you want me to go and talk to him."

Lily smiled and gave Martin a kiss on the cheek. Then she frowned. "Absolutely not," she said and walked out of the bedroom and headed down the hall.

2: Let the Date Begin

As she walked towards Nathan she watched as his eyes took her all in. Her confidence was beginning to elevate and it gave her the boldness to tilt her head slightly and snap it back to let her hair wave to him. Lily could feel her dress caress her curves as she swayed as seductively as she could and watched approvingly at her success as his eyes took the proper notice. So far Todd had been right on the money and she gave Nathan a deliberate shy smile while just barely biting her bottom lip. Nathan looked positively anxious. *Thank you Todd*, she thought as she came to a stop and cheered silently for pulling it off. "Why Mr. Caesar, don't you look dashing tonight."

Nathan cleared his throat. "Thank you," he got out before realizing that that was supposed to be his line. "And you look amazing too."

"Thank you."

"No I mean it, really delicious."

Delicious? Lily thought and then looked at him inquisitively.

Nathan looked like he was searching for some sort of excuse for his choice of words and then finally huffed. "I'm sorry, I have to be honest. I am totally nervous. If I say anything more or do anything that is questionable or the opposite of suave, I apologize in advance."

All of the advice given to her thus far had been right, and now seemed like the best time to try the big one. "You know, I can fix that nervous problem."

Nathan looked intrigued. "That would be great."

As Lily took a step closer she felt like she was no longer able to breathe, yet it did not stop her. *This is it,* she thought as all of her fear and anxiety swirled in her head until every sound around her became faint and distant. Lily was completely overwhelmed but as she leaned in further she had definitely passed the point of no return and decided to do it in one all-or-nothing motion.

Once her intent was made clear Nathan seemed to follow her lead. He slipped his arm behind Lily and rested his hand on the small of her back.

But he didn't have to draw her closer, Lily had begun the infusion herself and was already pressing up against him. She felt the beating of his heart and it was strong and resolute, almost like it was trying to burst free just so it could touch her.

Feeling his deep breath just in front of her, Lily took it as a sign of anticipation and grabbed his shoulder. Using his muscular frame as an anchor, she pressed herself against him even tighter and watched as his eyes filled with the fuel of eagerness.

As he brushed his lips slightly against hers, Lily could feel her body ignite like a furnace and her knees became weak. She gazed into his eyes and Nathan brushed his fingers along her cheek and she felt every hair on her neck stand to attention. Realizing that if she didn't do it now she could very well pass out, so Lily turned off all doubt, closed her eyes and kissed him.

At first, Lily was surprised at how gentle he was, since her forwardness might have invited otherwise. And as she pulled back Lily would swear his eyes were almost primitive in the way he was looking at her. As if she unlocked an evil inside of him and if she continued, he may not be able to control his more animal instincts. That thought turned her on and she kissed him harder.

This time Nathan initiated the pull back and as Lily slowly opened her eyes, she noticed that the animal was no longer staring at her with wicked resolve. Nathan was looking beyond her exterior and plunging deep into her soul, she could feel it and she almost didn't like the way that she invited it.

Finally he spoke. "Do you know I've been waiting my entire life to do that?"

Was that a line? Lily wondered and then decided she really did not care at this moment. Finally pulling back, her heart raced as he gently bit her bottom lip. It was as every bit as exciting as it was excruciatingly carnal.

Then out of nowhere, a cough rang out from behind her that made Nathan jerk. Lily felt this reflex and it felt like she was about to be thrown right through the wall. A quick last second stop on

Nathan's behalf caused Lily to avoid going through the wall, but made her clumsily turn around to see Martin standing in the hall, holding the tablet up with Todd looking onward in perverted delight.

Feeling like a teenager who just got caught by her father, Lily straightened her clothes while searching for something natural to say. "Hey Martin, Todd," was all she came up with while still adjusting her outfit.

"Jesus Li-ly," Todd yelled from the tablet. "I told yo-u to kiss him, not go de-ep sea fishing for his t-onsils."

Martin rolled his eyes and lowered the tablet, Todd was now upside down and looking down the opposite end of the hall.

"So what's going on?" Lily said still deep in the swamp of her erotic thoughts.

"Um, Lily," Martin said trying to act oblivious, "Remember that Jeanette and Mary-Anne are opening in the morning, but I told them we would be there by two."

"Great," Lily responded with a great deal of guilt still on her face.

"I also just wanted to say, I hope you two have a good time," Martin said looking at Lily as if to say *not too good of a time.*

Todd might have been looking in the opposite direction but that did not stop him from joining back into the conversation. "Looked like she w-as already h-aving a good time."

Martin turned his head and looked down. "Enough, or I will turn you off."

Lily pointed her finger at Martin as a sign of comprehension. "Two o'clock, got it."

Martin nodded. "And to remind you, I will be at the hospital most of the night, or all of the night depending what nurse is working."

Lily looked at him with the embarrassment of a daughter begging her father silently to stop.

Martin obviously took it as a cue. "I have to go," he said, but before he took a step a loud dramatic cough came from the tablet and Martin cringed.

"Ar-en't you for-getting some-thing?" Todd asked.

"*Si,*" Martin answered with a hint of reluctance. As Martin raised his head, his eyes shyly looked for Nathan's, who was desperately trying to avoid Martin's.

The tablet was brought up to face level and there Todd's face was plastered as close to the screen as he could get. "I j-ust wa-nted to say," he started and then stopped as the tears welled up. He began fanning them and cried a bit. "I can't. M-artin honey," he called out.

Martin took a deep breath. "Todd was ecstatic about the book, it was a very nice gesture," Martin said as Todd nodded and smiled on the tablet. "And he really wants you to know how much he appreciated it, thank you," he said as Todd mouthed the words *thank you.*

"No, not at all Martin," Nathan started and then looked at the tablet. "You're welcome Todd, I was happy to."

"The *Treasure Island* book?" Lily inquired.

"It was nothing," Nathan said trying to downplay it.

"No-thing!" Todd exclaimed. "Th-at b-ook was," he started and then stopped and began to cry again.

"Oh dear Lord," Martin cried himself. "It was not nothing *mi amigo*," Martin said and then turned to Lily. "It was the favorite book of *mi amor* and a first edition."

"Aww, how sweet," Lily said smiling at Nathan.

Martin shook his head trying to explain it better. "I looked it up because he kept going on and on about how much this book was worth."

"How much?" she asked intrigued.

Todd stopped crying and looked right into the screen. "Thirty-five thousand."

"What?" Lily exclaimed with a little choke.

"*Si.*"

"What the…" Lily exasperated.

Nathan tried to explain. "I saw your face," Nathan said to the Todd and then turned away from the tablet and tried to explain it to the others. "When he looked at it in the store, I wanted him to have it."

Lily looked around the hallway and mumbled, "Didn't even bring me flowers."

Not hearing her, Martin continued. "But we thank you very, very much. The hospital, the book, I don't know how we can ever repay you," he said getting emotional and embarrassed.

Nathan just shook his head and genuinely replied, "That's what friends do."

"I told Li-ly to give you an e-xtra special t-hank you," Todd said already laughing. "But j-ust remem-ber, its f-rom all of us."

Martin glared at the tablet. "Okay that's enough of you," he said turning the tablet over. "And you two have the very good night," Martin said giving them a short and quick wave, never looking so relieved to be leaving his own home.

Lily rocked back and forth. "Well that was a little awkward."

"Yeah, a little. More so for Martin I think," Nathan laughed.

"Yeah, it really was," Lily said following suit.

Suddenly the door flew open and Martin marched back into the apartment, trying not to make any eye contact. "I will not be needing this," he said holding up the tablet and then setting it down on the counter. "Again, goodnight," he said walking past them and back out the door.

Out of the corner of her eye Lily saw him, still on the tablet screen trying to look casual.

"So," Todd said on the counter, "wh-at you wanna do now?"

"Good night Todd," Lily said opening the door.

Todd pleaded. "Oh come on, at l-east put me in f-ront of the TV, I don't get *HBO* he-re."

"Good night Pimp," she said and they walked out of the apartment. She heard clomping and looked at Nathan.

"I don't think Martin wanted to take the elevator down with us," he said looking to the staircase.

"Should we wait a few minutes?"

Nathan smiled. "Unless you want to bump into him in the foyer?"

"We could go back in and wait, but Todd's in there and he'll probably ask us to kiss in front of him or something."

"Yeah, I'd rather do that in private," Nathan said.

"Me too," Lily said and couldn't believe what she heard herself say. She slowly pressed herself against him and when she finally able to feel the outline of his lips she could hear herself silently demand to taste them. Her sudden surge of sexual starvation made her feel lightheaded as his fingers whispered across her neck and then down her back. Her cravings came quick and chaotic, dissolving away at any discipline she had left. She could not feel a hint of air escape his mouth, but Lily could not show the same discipline. Hers was heavy and laboured, causing her chest to heave fully and to her advantage. This time his free hand found its way past the small of her back and firmly settled on her backside, pushing her into him. His other hand ran two of its fingers slowly down her cheek and stopped at her chin where they gently pressed to allow him to bite her bottom lip.

We have a biter, she thought as her cravings grew dirtier than she planned. She could no longer deny it, Lily wanted Nathan to penetrate her with every muscle burning on all pistons.

But then he whispered, "We should get going, reservations."

"Right," she said diplomatically, but her actions were anything but. She ran her hand up his back to the nape of his neck and then into his hair. There she clutched as much as she could and as tight as she dared. "In a minute," she whispered hoarsely and forced him forward.

Thoughts and words swirled in her head all at once causing her to feel erotically faint and Lily felt the urge to let go of that last moment of good sense. "Reservations you say?" Lily heard herself saying and wondered who the hell decided to go with good sense.

"Yes, reservations," he said, seemingly gathering his own composure. "I hope you like French."

"Um, are we talking about food?"

He laughed and led her to the elevator. "Yes, the food."

"I honestly don't know."

"We can try the other French stuff later," Nathan said holding his arm out and leading her into the elevator.

She chuckled. "Oh ... should I be scared?"

"No-no," Nathan assured her, "but you might want to stretch beforehand."

Lily stood with intrigue in her eyes. "What are we talking, Olympic-caliber stuff?"

He gazed into her eyes. "I am already having an amazing time Lily."

"Me too," she said with a smile.

CHAPTER XX

1: Reservations

THEY WALKED THROUGH THE DOOR and Lily felt as if she walked through a portal. Not to another dimension but to another tax bracket.

The Maître d' caught Nathan immediately and waved him over. *"Bienvenue, monsieur."*

Nathan led Lily to the podium and answered, *"Bonjour."*

"Bonjour," the man said and nodded with a little pretentiousness.

Nathan ignored it and replied. *"J'ai une réservation, Caesar."*

"And you called ahead *monsieur*?" the Maître d' asked while racing his finger down his list.

"Mais oui," Nathan confirmed.

"Ah, here we are. Mr. Caesar, reservation for two. *Très bien,*" he said and clapped his hands and produced the hostess. *"La meilleure table disponible,"* he said, instructing her to find the best available table. *"Amusez-vous Monsieur Caesar,"* he said genuinely. Turning to Lily, he offered the same genuine smile. *"Madame,"* he said directing her to follow the hostess.

Lily just smiled and nodded, not wanting her English to ruin the atmosphere.

Leading them across the restaurant the hostess brought them to an obvious coveted center table and held out her hand, giving Lily an automatic smile. Nathan however, got a quick once-over and then, obviously liking what she saw by the size of her flirtatious smile, the hostess walked away. But as Nathan pulled out her chair, Lily noticed his eyes had never left her and it made her feel as if she was the only one in his universe, one so blue she wanted to drown in it. "Soo," she dragged out with a hint of surprise, "French."

"*Oui*," Nathan said as if it were nothing.

"*Oui*," she copied nodding her head. "A little uppity isn't it," she stated not making eye contact and pretending to read the menu.

His tone was almost aghast, "Wait, you don't speak it?"

"No," she said and then in her best French accent and continued, "*I do not speak the French.*"

"That was the most –"

"Awesomest French accent," Lily finished.

"– horrifying French accent I have ever heard. And my brother is Cajun," he said completely ignoring Lily's vote. "But how can I expect you to speak French when you can't even speak English," he said smartly and then started to laugh.

Lily tried to respond with confidence. "Awesomest is a word."

"No," he said wincing, "it is not."

Looking around for a waiter she held up her hand and started to giggle. "I wonder if they have a dictionary here?"

Suddenly a waiter appeared at the table. "*Oui Madame?*"

Lily stopped smiling and looked at Nathan in a panic. "Oh my God, what do I do?"

The waiter was confused and looked at Nathan. "*Je ne comprends pas,*" he said slightly shrugging his shoulders.

"Shit," she exclaimed embarrassingly hunkering down and putting the menu up over her face. "Please fix this."

Nathan hunkered down to her level and put his menu over his mouth and replied in a loud whisper. "Do you still want a dictionary?"

"No!" she exclaimed immediately. Sitting back up she tried to look as sophisticated as she could while observing the foreign words in front of her.

Nathan giggled and then turned to the waiter. "*La carte des vins merci.*"

"*Bien sûr,*" the waiter said apologetically and disappeared.

She looked at him.

"I asked for the wine menu."

"Thank you. I didn't think they were that observant."

Nathan looked at her hopelessly. "When something so beautiful walks into a room it cannot help but be observed. You just witnessed the response when something so beautiful wants something," he said reaching for her hand.

Lily was caught off guard by his comment. "You're embarrassing me," Lily said extending her hand so their fingertips could touch. Looking into his eyes and feeling his finger's race along hers, Lily could not help but play their moment in the hallway over in her head. Suddenly the air was getting thick and it was early, so she urged restraint with a simple, "Please."

"Okay, but you make it hard looking like that."

"You make it hard ..." Suddenly she couldn't think of anything to finish the sentence, her mind stopped at *Hard*, and she was mortified.

Nathan looked like he was waiting for her to finish the sentence which caused Lily's face to burn a visible red shade of embarrassment.

Nathan smirked. "Wow. Who gets stuck with just – *You make it hard*."

She laughed. "I wish you did."

"Really?" he said purposely trying to embarrass her.

"I meant, I wish you were the one that got stuck – not hard," she said trying to explain as the menu was slowly raised until it covered her face again.

"Lily, nothing you could say could ruin tonight," he assured her with a chuckle.

"Oh we'll see," she wondered aloud.

"I haven't had this much fun in a long time. And, never with someone as beautiful ... Ever," Nathan said bringing a calm to her face.

"I think someone might experience fifty shades," Lily said sitting back up hoping her flirting was at par, but did not notice the waiter had returned and was standing beside her with the wine menu.

"Fifty shades?" the waiter tried to repeat with a confused smile and handed Nathan the menu.

This time Lily wanted to go right under the table. "You have got to be kidding."

"*C'est un livre*," Nathan said laughing.

"*Livre?*" the waiter inquired about the book they were talking about.

"*Cinquante nuances de Grey*," Nathan said pronouncing the book in French.

"Oh, *oui, Cinquante nuances de Grey,*" the waiter said finally understanding and giving Lily an exaggerated wink.

Lily was mortified. "Wait, is he putting down my go-to book?" Lily asked still embarrassed, but giggling.

Nathan admitted, "I believe that is why he is laughing, yes."

"How many copies did he sell of his book?" Lily asked jokingly.

The waiter did not understand what she was saying, but he turned to Lily and tried. "Très sexy, yes?"

"Oh my God," Lily said hiding her eyes under her hands.

Nathan laughed and clapped lightly. "Yes, very sexy."

The waiter seemed proud at his contribution to the conversation and waited for Nathan to make a selection.

"*Chateau Margaux,*" Nathan said ordering a wine.

"*Très bon,*" he said and left.

Nathan was trying not to laugh.

Lily just looked around the restaurant as if she had just sat down and was about to start the first conversation of the evening. "I really love what they did with the place."

The waiter returned with water for the table and informed Nathan that the *Chateau Margaux* was breathing and being chilled to a proper 45-50 degrees. He then left the water on the table and informed the table that he would return shortly to take their order.

Nathan raised his glass. "To the most fun I've had in a French restaurant, bar none."

"Why thank you," she said raising her water.

"So, what do you feel like eating?" Nathan asked while looking at the menu.

Lily did not even bother to pick hers up. "Whatever you suggest, just don't tell me what it is," she said jokingly.

"Very well," he chuckled.

"Serious," Lily said wanting to be clear. "I also know what *escargots* are, so please, no."

"I understand," he assured her.

Feeling that she had brought an elephant with her, Lily felt she should address it before the night continued. "I feel I should say something about the other night."

"You don't have to," he offered.

"How much did you see and hear?"

"Enough to understand."

Lily nodded. "I was hoping you never had to see any of that, and I'm sorry."

Nathan tried to give her a reassuring smile. "Really, you don't have to apologize."

"Thank you, but in case you couldn't put two and two together, he sometimes got rough," she explained while Nathan just nodded. "Pretty rough some nights, but I finally stood up for myself and left."

"You stood up to him pretty good the other night too," he said taking a sip of his water.

"Yeah, I did. And, please don't get upset, but I will never let anyone treat me like that again," Lily said and cringed. "And I really hope that I didn't offend you because I am really having a good time and I really-really like you Nathan," she finished with her eyes closed, then one slowly opened. "Too much?"

"I am having a great time. I really-really like you too. And I would never," Nathan said holding out his hand.

"I know," she said and took it with a squeeze. "I guess I just want to show you I'm strong. Or, really – I'm not sure what I'm trying to say," she said feeling the sting of tears and decided to change the tempo. "I'm actually surprised you picked me up tonight. I thought for sure you would've hauled it as far as you could."

Nathan smiled. "Guess I'm just a sucker for a pretty face," he said taking a sip of his water. "I won't lie, when I put it all together and saw how he was making you feel, part of me just wanted to rip him apart," he said, sounding as if his emotions were slipping.

Lily had just turned and out of the corner of her eye it looked as if Nathan's eyes were starting to glow. Almost like an old car whose battery had seen better days and took a little extra time getting the juice to the headlights. It reminded her of the time they met on the street and she thought his phone screen was really bright. But when her brain started to process it and she turned back, his eyes were normal.

"What?" Nathan asked calmly.

"Your eyes, they glowed."

"They did?" Nathan asked with a mixture of surprise and amusement.

"Really blue, as I was turning they turned—" she stopped herself and was now second guessing. "Maybe not."

"Are you okay?" Nathan asked while taking another sip.

"I'm fine." She took a deep breath and shrugged it off. "I just want you to know, that I'm not broken. I'm okay and I'm ready to have dinner with you."

Nathan nodded. "I couldn't be happier. And if we're being honest, when I saw you stand up to him at the party, it showed me without a shadow of a doubt what I already suspected."

Lily could only inquire with a look.

"That you are the most beautiful, funniest and strongest women I have ever met," he said taking her hand and resting it on his cheek. Then he gently kissed it.

Lily smiled as she became lost in his eyes. "You really got to have a talk with your friend."

"My friend?"

"The one you were looking for the night we met. He popped into the store and was talking to Jeanette."

Nathan sat up. "Did he?"

"Yeah," Lily started and sat up herself as the waiter appeared and started to pour the *Chateau Margaux*. "He warned her to tell me that you could sometimes be mean and even violent."

"Is that what he said," Nathan said as if he was trying to censor his wording. "Is that what you meant about the never letting anyone treating you like that again?"

"I'm sorry," Lily said feeling a little guilty.

"No-no, it's really okay," he said taking her hand again. "And I want you to know that I would absolutely never, ever be like that. Ever."

Lily stared into his eyes and something told her to believe anything this man told her, she just hopped it wasn't just the lust talking. "I never once got that vibe from you. In fact, I get the total opposite vibe."

Nathan raised his wine glass. "Good."

Lily raised hers. "Good."

"To better days ahead," he toasted.

Lily agreed and let her glass lightly *clang* with his and took a sip. "Oh wow, that is really good."

"I'm glad you like it."

"You know," Lily said not being able to help it and interrupted herself with another sip. "Jeanette said that he came across as jealous and a little vindictive. Creepy too. He doesn't sound like a very good friend."

"No he does not," Nathan agreed. "And I shall be having a talk with my friend in the very near future."

2: A Little Diner in Yazoo City

In a little diner in a little town, just over 700 miles south, Amber had been working since four o'clock that afternoon. And she wouldn't be leaving until six o'clock tomorrow morning. It was slow, it was always slow and usually she didn't mind, but Amber did not bring her iPad nor her phone's charger. She meant to stop back home and grab them before work but got caught up shopping and totally forgot. Now she was working the shift from hell, well until about an hour ago.

Since then, Amber had been talking with one customer in particular, an out of towner whose name she had not gotten yet. But she did know that he was a priest, since he was wearing the *on duty* badge which was the white detachable collar worn in front of his black clerical shirt and it kind of gave him away. He was an older gentleman with fading reddish brown hair and a weathered face, but he looked kind and content.

He mentioned a little history fact about Yazoo and since Amber had always loved history, a chord was struck. Besides, her only other options were Frank the cook, who was too busy getting high and two other out of towners. From the way that the other two customers were dressed, which was like they had just walked right out of a bad mob movie, along with the creepy way they watched her and how rudely they addressed her, Amber stereotypically guessed *New York* or *New Jersey*.

So she spent all her time with the priest while he was there. They had just gotten to the local legend of the Witch and without being asked, Amber had gotten him more tea. He really liked his tea.

His story went on. "She was very open about her craft, not coming out right and saying so, no. But dropping hints. Letting people in earshot hear her intentions for the evening, talked in obvious chants and that sort of thing," he said pouring the last of the hot water and evacuating every bit of tea out of the bag with the spoon.

"I can get you another bag," Amber said starting to stand up.

"No, my dear, this is fine," he said adding sugar.

"Go on," she said getting more interested in the story since it was fascinating and it kept her from thinking of the two ogres behind her.

"Well," he started again. "One spring evening on May 25th, 1884 a young fellow by the name of Joe Bob Duncan was coming down the river in his boat, when he heard a loud moaning come from the old Witch's home. Followed by what he said sounded like...sinister laughter."

"Oh my God, I have a cousin named Joe Bob," Amber said, then became a little embarrassed. "Sorry, go on."

"Right," he said with a smile. "Anyway, Joe Bob made his way to the old rickety home, which was two stories and quite large. Peering through a window, he saw two bodies lying on the floor while the Witch danced around, dropping some sort of powder on them. Singing her incantations," he said and then took a breath. "Joe Bob, unseen, went back to his boat and made his way back to town where he told the sheriff what he had just witnessed."

"Did the sheriff believe him?" Amber questioned.

"Enough that he thought he'd better make his way out to the old house and at least check it out," the Preacher said. "When they got there, there was no answer from inside. So the sheriff and the deputy busted their way in and found nothing on the floor. They checked the other rooms and still nothing." Pausing for a moment, he let the suspense grow. "Finally they made their way up the stairs, and in one of the rooms they found two bodies hanging from the ceiling, but..." He paused and leaned forward again and lowering his voice as Amber leaned forward in anticipation. "Their heads were untouched, not unlike their necks that had rope around them. But the rest of their bodies were stained red skeletons."

"Gross," was her response.

"Then they heard the crunch-crunch-crunch of leaves outside and from the window they saw the Witch running into the swamp."

"Then what happened?"

"They went back into town to organize two groups. One to confiscate the bodies in the house, and a second to hunt down the Witch. The second included a Preacher passing through town and all thought a good idea to bring along. You know, to protect them against her unholy powers."

"Did she have unholy powers?" she asked wanting a bit of a spoiler.

"Well, when they finally caught up with her, she was deep in the swamp and as fortune would have it, up to her neck in quicksand."

"I thought she fell off a bank and drowned?" Amber questioned, recalling the version she heard as a child. "That's why you don't go in the swamp at night because she hides in the water."

"I assure you my dear, she was neck deep in quicksand," he said smiling, as if he was recalling it from memory. "The look on her face was that of terror and hate, since the men who came were not there to help her, but to kill her. She cackled and screamed at them. Things I was never able to figure out. And then she singled out Joe Bob, as if she knew it was him who started the whole thing. She swore that she would return twenty years from that day and burn the town to the ground." He took a long sip of his tea and exhaled. "They watched as she slowly sank. She drowned and we finally got her out with a pitchfork and some rope. She was taken back to town and buried in the cemetery. Marked with a large stone with the initials TW, along with a large chain around her grave to stop her from ever getting out. In his proud drunken state, the Sheriff dared the Witch to try and come back. Saying that if she actually could rise from the grave and breakthrough the chains that were blessed, well then she deserved to burn down the town."

"TW, The Witch," Amber deduced.

"So it was believed, for twenty years," he said slyly.

"Why is it always twenty years, why so long?" she inquired disappointedly.

"Like all evil things my dear. Whether it be war, science, magic, curses and even revenge, they all have one common ingredient. They all need time," he finished.

Amber showed him she understood with a nod.

"And on May 25th 1904, twenty years later, a fire started in a parlor in the middle of town. Almost all accounts said the winds were stronger than usual for that time of year. And as the fire ate, building after building, the winds became more and more vicious. Some would say, determined."

"Please don't stop," Amber said wishing she had a bowl of popcorn.

"Joe Bob Duncan was twenty years older, married to a fine woman, who gave birth to two sons and a daughter. One of those boys was named William and thought to be an odd child, always playing alone or talking to imaginary people. Now when the fires started to get out of control, the whole town, including Joe Bob, pitched in to put it out." He paused for another sip of tea.

Amber waited patiently, even though she thought he was taking an awful long sip.

"And then when they could not contain the fire, they called on firefighters from all over the county to come. But even with all that help, they just couldn't battle the fire that was aided by an almost possessed wind," he said stopping for a moment to make sure Amber was still interested. When he saw she was still captivated he took another sip.

She gave him a look that made him smile.

"Finally the entire downtown burned to the ground, but the fire was eventually stopped. Joe Bob returned home where an excited William was waiting for him. He told his father that he was playing downtown in front of the Parlor as it caught on fire and that Tandy carried him to safety."

"Who is Tandy? One of his imaginary friends?" Amber asked.

"William handed his father a note and said Tandy wanted him to have it, since Tandy knew William's daddy long before William was born. Joe Bob opened the note and read it," the Preacher said and now teased her with a smile, but began again before she could protest. "The note simply said, Told you so, Tandy Warren." The Preacher let the words linger.

Amber tried to piece it all together. "But—"

"Joe Bob raced to the graveyard where he saw that the grave had actually been disturbed. The chain was missing a link, thus broken."

"Holy shit, TW is not The Witch, its Tandy Warren," Amber said and this time not apologizing for the curse.

"Holy shit indeed," the Preacher laughed.

"Is this a true story? Why haven't I heard this before? Were you a history teacher at one time?" she asked.

"Why do you ask?"

"I had a history teacher who got so into the stories that when he told them it sounded as if he was actually there. You said things like you were there."

Then the break and story time was over.

"Hey sweet ass," the one called Andy shouted while snapping his fingers, "how about some more coffee."

Amber rolled her eyes as if she had forgotten they were there.

"Are those gentlemen bothering you, my dear?" he inquired.

"Just a couple of creeps."

He tilted his head to the side to look around her. "They don't seem to be local."

"No, I never seen them before," she affirmed already starting to feel better. She looked at him curiously as she stood up. "Haven't seen you around before neither."

"No, you have not," he said immediately then looked at her adoringly. "Been a while since I've passed through Yazoo City," he said sparking more interest.

"So you have been here before," she surmised.

"Oh yes, a few times through my many, many years," the Preacher confessed.

"You're not that old," Amber said trying to make him feel better.

"You are sweet. But I really am," the Preacher said and touched her hand gently. "Don't worry about those gentlemen, I don't think they'll be around for much longer."

The touch of his hand was genuinely comforting and she could tell by the look of concern on his face that he wanted her not to be bothered by them. "God I hope so," she said covering her mouth again, "sorry."

"From your lips," he said pointing upwards.

Getting up from the booth, Amber tried to put on her best customer service face. Grabbing the coffee pot she heard a cell phone go off and glanced behind her where she saw the Preacher pull a phone out and answer it. *Odd*, she thought. She was not sure why a man of God having a phone was odd, since everyone and anyone has a phone. Then, she imagined him playing *Angry Birds* and chuckled while walking over to her two least favorite customers of the week. No month, no scratch that. The year.

The fatter of the two named Andy, dangled his empty mug from his finger. "More of some coffee honey," he said, unaware of his atrocious dialect.

Amber wanted so badly to insult him and his limited vocabulary, but since she thought his IQ was at best, an eighty-one give or take, he wouldn't even notice the affront on him. So instead she put forth her best smile. "I just put a new pot on. It'll only be a couple of minutes."

"Oh we can wait, we can wait all night long," Andy said, still dangling the mug on his finger and looking her over. Suddenly the mug twirled off of Andy's finger and smashed on the floor and by the look of the chubby man's face, it was a pleasant accident. "Looks like somebody is bending down and to clean the mess."

Even Bobby, the other gentlemen, was getting agitated by his partner's butchering of what was supposed to be his native language. "Come on man! Learn how to speak fucking English will ya?"

Andy looked insulted and confused all at once. "What the fuck am I speaking on here, Swahili?"

Bobby shook his head. "I would argue that you are the surviving evolution of another primate, a Neanderthal if you will, once thought extinct and you are in fact, not a Homo sapiens at all."

"You're fucking right I'm no Homo sapiens."

Bobby tested him. "Do you even know what Homo sapiens are Andrew?"

Andy tried to think quickly. "Of course I do. It's those killer fags."

Bobby looked like he had had enough and turned to watch the young waitress, but a look of dismay took over as Amber was already standing up. This did not stop him from ogling her while she straightened her uniform. "You have a nice set sweetheart, really firm I bet," Bobby said looking from her to his friend. "Damn girl, you could be a model—couldn't she be a model?"

Andy nodded with a look on his face like he was all alone and free to treat himself like an amusement park.

"Well, I'm not. And just so you know, I have a boyfriend fellas," she challenged, letting her hometown niceness wane.

"Shit. I got a wife and three kids," the fat ex-mug twirler said puckering his lips and sending a repulsive chill up her spine. "We won't tells if you don't,"

Amber wondered if this was his attempt at flirting.

"Let's cut to the chase baby," Bobby interjected again. "How much would it cost us to have you come back to our room with us for a little party?" he asked and then without warning grabbed at her as if he had already paid.

Stepping back and slapping his hand away. "I think it's time you left," she yelled and turned to see Frank bringing out his phone.

What she did not see was that the Preacher had finished his phone call and was already up from his seat. As he walked past the counter the Preacher straightened his arm fully, letting a no more than two inch needle slide out of his sleeve and fall to his fingers. With a quick snap of his wrist, the needle ripped through the air undetected and straight through Frank's phone.

Frank had brought it almost to his ear when a small spark snapped from the phone and shocked him enough to drop it. Picking it up he tried swiping the screen but it just stared back at him blank. "Is that a hole in my phone?" Frank asked slowly rubbing his finger over what was indeed a tiny hole.

Putting his hand on her shoulders, the Preacher directed Amber behind the counter and turned to the two men who had been harassing her all night. "My apologies for keeping you waiting gentlemen, but I was waiting for a call from Father."

3: All Good Things Must Come to a Dead

Nathan walked Lily to her building and as Lily started to walk up the steps he tugged her back towards him. Letting out a yelp, Lily fell into his arms and then laughed. Leaning in Nathan kissed her and Lily knew she would never get tired of it.

"I do want you to come up," she said with a hint of *but* in her tone.

"I understand," Nathan said trying not to sigh.

"I know you do," she said a little less certain. "It's just that it's our first date, and not that I'm old fashioned, I just want to take it somewhat slow, if that makes sense?" For a moment, Lily didn't even think that it made sense to her, but she saw Martin in her head and he was giving her a thumbs up.

Nathan gazed into her eyes. "I do understand. I have waited a lifetime for you Lily," he declared in his whisper and then chuckled, "what's another day or two?" Then he tried to kiss her again.

Pulling back Lily laughed while looking flabbergast. "A day—or two!" she exclaimed. "I may be a tramp, but I'll have you know I'm a tramp with morals."

Nathan looked at her puzzled. "I'm sorry, did you see the bill for dinner?"

Laughing, she grabbed him by his collar and guided him into her lips once again. She was turned on by the fact that he was still holding her in his arms as her feet just dangled above the ground, minus one left shoe. But she was even more turned on when his other hand firmly grasped onto her ass and pushed her into him.

Now she could see Todd in her head and he was pushing Martin out of the way and cheering. *"Give me a T-A-K-E-H-I-M-U-P-S-T-A-I-R-S. What does that spell? – SEX! SEX! SEX!"*

Nathan let her down slowly, stopping an inch from the concrete to allow her to slip the left foot back into her shoe. She would say good night and watch Nathan walk away, becoming almost as disappointed as the *Todd* in her head.

Walking into the apartment she noticed how silent it was. Not even the TV was on, which meant Martin was still at the hospital with Todd. She wished they were both here because she had so much to tell them. Hell, she would settle for just Martin right now since she was bursting at the seams with girl talk.

Having some trouble getting her left shoe off Lily wondered how the hell it fell off in the first place. Walking down the hall and past the kitchen, she went right into the living room. She grabbed the tablet on the coffee table and turned it on. The voice on the tablet welcomed her in its sexy man voice. Noticing that it wasn't as sexy as it usual was and nowhere near as sexy as Nathan's, she suddenly became appalled at herself. "Oh my God, I'm becoming one of those girls," Lily said shaking her head. She turned off the voice assist and tapped the phone icon that was beaming the number 17. She sighed and tapped the screen to start the onslaught of messages. She took the tablet and headed straight to the fridge, not because she was hungry, but because she needed something to do while the messages played. Grabbing a large carrot she closed the door and found the peeler from the drawer.

They were all messages wishing Todd well and hopes of him getting better, but then they all went into TMZ mode and spent minutes gossiping to an answering machine. Lily finished peeling her carrot and was able to start skipping them, until she came to Martin's call and turned it up.

"**Hello Lily, just checking in on you.**"

"**Hello Li-ly,**" Todd yelled in the background, his voice was muffled, but even clearer from earlier this evening. He was learning to talk quite well for someone who just recently had his jaw wired, but that wouldn't surprise anyone who knew him.

Martin continued. "**We just wanted to check in on you and we hope your date went well,**" he said and then paused while Todd talked in the background. Lily couldn't make out what he was saying. Just that Martin was getting mad. "**No, she is not. Stop it you, she is probably still out,**" he said. Then she heard Todd mumble something fairly loud, but she could not make that out either, only Martin. "**That is not why she isn't answering the phone. Why does everything have to be about the sex with you, maybe they are taking the nice evening stroll, or watching that movie she wanted to see?**" Martin lectured, now ignoring the fact that he was leaving a message all together. Todd continued to mumble and it was making Martin even more upset. "**Well she couldn't watch the movie if she was doing that now could she? No Todd, No she did not. Lily, *no tengas relaciones sexuales*. Not there Lily, Not in our home,**" Martin said and then suddenly he was calmly talking into the receiver. "**You may not use our bed *novia*, whether it is bigger or not bigger,**" he said getting stern. "**Bigger is not better.**"

"**Hel-lo!**" Todd exclaimed loudly.

Lily wished Martin was there so she could put his mind at ease, but she also couldn't stop laughing at the tablet as the carrot dangled from her fingers.

"**Just...**" Martin paused for a moment. "**Sé *una chica buena*,**" he said with the sadness of a father. This time she could hear Todd in the background yelling for her to be a bad girl. Then Martin perked right back up. "**Anyway, I'll be home sometime in the morning. We love you,**" Martin said as Todd yelled in just before he ended the call.

"**L-ove Y-ou.**"

Taking the last bite she saved the message and decided that she actually enjoyed the carrot, placing the tablet on the bar counter she headed back into the fridge.

Then a voice came from the dark corner of the living room. "So that's what you do now?" it asked in a low disappointed tone.

Lily's screamed started with her head in the fridge and followed her as she jumped back out. Instinctively she brought her hand over her mouth and stood silent, completely frozen in fear. Slowly taking her hand away from her mouth her eyes searched the living room, but all she could see was darkness.

Finally, she made out an image in the far back corner. "Who's there?" she yelled still partially frozen.

"You whoring now?" the voice asked as the figure approached her, slowly.

Lily knew the voice, but something was off. "Rick?"

4: A Preacher, 2 Gangsters, a Waitress and a Fry Cook

Inside the little diner in Yazoo city, the two men at the table sat and stared at the Preacher who stood calmly at the counter.

Then Andy finally broke the silence. "I think you're a little out of your depth perception Priest."

Bobby sighed as he usually did when Andy spoke first. "Will you please just be quiet?"

The Preacher slowly tapped his finger repeatedly on the counter. "No, Father was quite adamant about meeting you two specifically."

"Yeah well, we weren't told about meeting any priest in a diner, so fuck off," Bobby said becoming aggravated.

The Preacher smiled sympathetically. "Of course, as soon as you hand over the briefcase."

Suddenly the two men became very suspicious.

"What the fuck did you just say?" Bobby stated, obviously hearing exactly what he had said.

The Preacher leaned back and tilted his head slightly, openly gazing underneath the table at the oversized briefcase that resembled more of a small suitcase. "That briefcase there, under the table to your right. If you please," he said holding his hand out and open.

Andy pulled his gun out from under his jacket and placed it in front of him. "Again, we think you have the wrong two guys Preacher."

Seeing the gun Frank decided to keep trying to use the phone while Amber stepped back even further wishing she had brought her phone charger. Neither of them considered the ancient land line hanging on the wall in the kitchen, alone and apparently forgotten.

Meanwhile the Preacher explained. "Now you see, I have just received another job from Father while not having completed the current task at hand. It's all about time you see gentlemen, managing it, allotting it and planning it. Time is always the answer, always the deciding factor," he said and then smiled slyly. "While I sat here and drank my tea having a delightful conversation with a lovely young lady I had too much time. One phone call later and suddenly I don't have enough. Time— time— time."

"What the fuck are you talking about?" Bobby asked as he pulled his gun out of his jacket, but unlike his gambling friend, held it firmly in his hands, paranoia deeply entrenched in his eyes. "So what does time have to do with us old man?"

"Simple," the Preacher said letting his smile fade away. "Yours gentlemen, is up."

Both men sitting at the table watched as the Preacher convulsed a bit and suddenly his eyes beamed with a stunning brightness and he blurred forward. Suddenly he was standing in front of Bobby with his fangs already exposed.

"What the fuc—" he almost finished.

Because before he could, the Preacher shoved his four fingers through the flesh up in behind his chin and then wrapped his claws around the jaw. Pulling his arm back forcibly with a quick and savage jerk, the Preacher ripped Bobby's jaw away completely, which included a long strip of flesh from the front of his throat. Blood and flesh poured to the floor, sounding like someone was slowly dumping a half melted milk shake.

With no bottom jaw, Bobby was only able to scream briefly until his tongue fell out of his throat and slapped against his chest. Falling to his knees, his gargles stuttered while globs of thick blood spewed across his hands that were searching for skin and bone that were no longer there.

Seeing his friend being ripped apart caused Andy to snap back to reality and waddle to his feet. But instead of going to his friend's aid, he was placing the briefcase under his arm, grabbing his gun and looking for the quickest escape route. "Shit just got real," he said to himself and set his pudgy frame in motion. He did not get far as a chair flew through the air and landed on his head. Landing on the tile with a portly thud Andy grunted with disbelief.

Amber knew she had to stop screaming for help and then realized that the high-pitch cry for help was not coming from her at all. It was Frank screaming into his phone, a phone that did not work. But before she could yell at Frank, he had already stopped. She followed his eyes and watched as the man she thought of as a sweet middle-aged priest was standing over one dying mobster and in a blink was standing above the fat one.

Before Andy knew what was happening, the Preacher grabbed him by the neck and lifted him straight up into the air and squeezed. The obese man's face instantly started to turn so red it was heading straight towards purple. Blood dripped from his nose and ears as he tried to disrupt the grip that was choking the life out of him.

Squeezing harder, the Preacher looked like he was overjoyed as blood ran from Andy's rupturing eyes. Finally he spun around with the big man still in his clutches and walked directly to the counter. "Excuse me, my dear," he said politely as Amber got out of his way. He then slammed the large body onto the counter, causing Amber to jump and Frank to run back into the kitchen. Giving one more forcible squeeze, he created a low resonating *snap* and Andy was dead.

The Preacher wiped some blood off of his hand and then walked behind the counter. "Wait here please," he said to Amber as he headed back into the kitchen and began to whistle the melody *Twisted Nerve* by Bernard Herrmann.

Frank appeared in the order window visibly shaking while behind him, the Preacher turned on the faucet and began washing his hands. Finally, he turned off the tap and nonchalantly reappeared behind the counter. Still whistling, he retrieved the rather large briefcase and dumped Andy's corpse onto the floor. He didn't even bother with the security latches and just forced the two tiny buttons to bust through and the latches sprung open. "Would you please join us out here Frank?"

Frank did not move.

"Get out here Frank," Amber said turning her head and almost mouthing, "before he kills you."

"I am not planning on killing anyone else tonight my dear," the Preacher said hearing her lips pronounce the words. He returned to his whistling and counted the money bundles inside before setting one bundle off to the side.

Reluctantly Frank had made his way out and stood behind her.

The Preacher saw their uncertainty. "If it makes you feel better and a long story short, those men were actually bad men."

"And you're like, a good guy?" Amber asked, trying not to sound patronizing.

The Preacher thought about the question for a moment. "I'm not sure, but I am trying," he said sniffing at the air until it led him directly over top of Andy. Kneeling down his claws extended and he forced his hand into the chest. With a long wet sucking sound, he pulled out his hand and stood back up producing Andy's inactive heart.

Amber tried to keep her cool while Frank tried not to cry.

"You see, it's rotting," he said examining it. "I'd say eighteen months, two years tops and he would have had a heart attack." Dropping it on top of the body he laughed. "Most likely while eating something deep fried."

Amber and Frank both stood silent as the Preacher walked over to the other lifeless body.

"Now this one," the Preacher said as he noticed it was still twitching, "he took a bit more care of himself." Rolling the body onto its back he drove his claws into the chest and ripped out the heart that Amber would swear was still beating. "My kind can eat and drink like you, but we also need a certain amount of myocardium."

"What is that?" Amber asked, surprised at herself.

"Simply? The heart," he answered and smiled.

"Like a vampire," Frank said out of nowhere.

About to sink his teeth into it, the Preacher stopped. "In a way Frank," he said and then sunk his fangs into the heart with a loud fleshy pop. Still chewing he elaborated, "But I am not a vampire."

"You look like a vampire," Frank said quieter this time.

Amber turned to him and suggested strongly. "Will you shut the fuck up?"

"True, we have been called vampires. But I assure you that your run of the mill movie vampire, does not exist," he said examining the heart. "You see the cardiac muscle is a type of involuntary striated muscle, found in the walls and histological foundation of the heart. To be specific the Myocardium," he said bringing the heart to his nose and breathing in deeply. "The cells that constitute cardiac muscle, called cardiomyocytes or myocardiocytes contain only one unique nucleus. This is not unlike what water means to life, give it abundance and life thrives, give it a little and it starts to wilt." Forcing his fangs into the heart, he let the squishing sound of wet rubber burst with each chew.

Feeling as if she was about to throw up, Amber raised her hands and covered her mouth.

With the enthusiasm of a science teacher he continued. "We can get what we need from animals, but that one human heart, just a bite, gives us the nutrients of five whole animal hearts. Unless you prefer puppy or kitten hearts, you'd need to eat at least ten to fifteen of those," he teased with a devilish grin. "That was a joke, I have never eaten a puppy or kitten heart in my life," he said with his free hand across his chest and then took another bite like he was eating an apple.

"Does it—taste good?" Amber hesitated not sure if she wanted him to answer.

"Not really. In that regard, animal hearts are much more appetizing. Unfortunately, other parts on the human body, are much more palatable."

"Fuck me," Amber cried through her hand.

"Don't worry, my dear. Most of my kind eat out of necessity," he said looking over the body on the floor.

Taking another bite out of the heart, he grabbed the body with his free hand and placed it on the table. "Besides, there are Monsters out there far worse than my kind when it comes to human consumption, believe you me," he said and started wrapping the large tablecloth over the body. "Wonderful things these diner tablecloths," he said placing the heart in his mouth while freeing both hands to grab the newly wrapped body and exit the diner.

They could hear a trunk opening and the sound of the body being placed in it. Walking through the door and setting off the chime he tossed the last bit of heart in his mouth. Grabbing the larger body he placed it on a table and began wrapping it. Examining the girth of Andy's body he decided to take another tablecloth and disappeared outside again.

"What the fuck do we do?" Frank asked.

"I don't know, run for it?"

"Fuck that."

"You think he'll catch us?"

Frank replied honestly. "You're a faster runner than I am, he will definitely catch me."

Hearing the trunk slam shut they both jumped.

"You're an asshole," Amber said wanting to run, but from what she just witnessed she knew the Preacher would have no problem catching both of them.

He walked back into the diner wiping his mouth and picked up where he left off. "You see, there are many kinds of Monsters. I'm Chakan, and there are Elementals, Bruti, Dracos and many more. Anguis and oh my, the Astros," he said and then shook his head. "Nasty little buggers they are—Solibus et Lunis, get an infestation of them and there goes the neighborhood, literally. They would prefer to farm you like cattle. Some of them prefer to eat their humans alive and slow. Like, over the course of a week type slow."

"Why are you telling us this?" Amber interrupted.

Walking back to the briefcase he took the bundle he had set aside and held it up so they could get a good look. Ejecting a single claw and swiping it across the currency strap, he freed the money and made two piles. "Fear is a very powerful motivator my dear. And everyone fears Monsters, even if they don't believe in them." He slid the slightly larger half to Amber and the smaller one to Frank. Taking a deep breath, he tapped the top of the bundles and looked at both of them. "This if for you," he said and then singled out Frank. "It is not for drugs."

"How..." Frank stuttered staring at the bundle. "What makes you think I do drugs?"

Suddenly, without them even seeing it happen, the Preacher grabbed Frank by the arm and yanked him over the counter. Twisting Frank's hand and arm palm side up, the Preacher took his talon-like claw and slid it down Frank's long sleeved shirt over the arm. The fabric split apart cleanly with no harm to the skin, but revealed track marks. The Preacher looked at him with almost parental disappointment. "I could smell the poison running through your veins the moment you came back from your break," he said gripping the arm tighter and causing Frank to wince in pain. Suddenly his eyes started to beam as his fangs popped from his gums. "There are Demons more frightening than me young man. Do you understand?"

Frank violently shook his head and closed his eyes. "I understand. Not for drugs, I swear."

"Good," the Preacher said letting him go.

Frank grabbed the money and fell to the ground hugging it while he rocked back and forth.

"Please don't eat us," Amber said tearing fully.

"What?" Frank mumbled disappointedly, most likely at the news that he might be eaten and after just getting all of that money.

The Preacher sprouted a sympathetic smile. "My dear, I would not have gone through that whole speech and give you a bundle of money if I was going to eat you, now would I."

Amber thought about it for a moment and then shook her head in agreement.

Reaching out slowly, the Preacher took her hand. "You and Frank are going to clean this mess up and speak of nothing specific. As far as you were concerned it was an uneventful night," he explained as she began to settle down. "Two men in suits came in, ordered and ate, after they left, another man, a priest or preacher, you don't have to be sure," he explained. "That man also ordered, ate and left an hour or so after." he said sticking his thumb behind him pointing towards the exit.

Nodding, Amber confirmed that she understood. "Two men in suits came in, ordered, ate and left while a third man in a black priest-like uniform came in and left an hour or so after the first two."

"Excellent, excellent, my dear," he said looking down at Frank. "Frank like always was in the back and didn't even notice them. He just cooked the food."

"I didn't notice shit," Frank stated honestly.

Amber recalled her television, "What about descriptions?"

"As detailed as you like. They won't be finding those two ever again."

"What about the cars?"

"I will take care of that, you just clean the blood."

"How?" she asked honestly, having never cleaned a crime scene before.

"Some warm sudsy water, then bleach the pail and sink. And burn the cloths and your clothes. Meaning, get a change of clothes before you begin. I take it the evenings are quite slow?"

She nodded again and watched as he gathered his things. "You were actually here," she said finally working up the courage. "In 1884 and then twenty years later, during the fire."

"I was here in 1884 yes, but not during the fire."

"So was it?" Amber asked.

"The Witch, Tandy Warren?" He paused for a moment and then nodded. "Like I said, there are worse things than my kind."

"So she's still here," Amber said.

The Preacher smiled. "Witches are very hard to kill and they live a very long time. If you ever knowingly stumble upon one, it would be wise to play very dumb. And never drink or eat from anything they have touched. Ever," he said with full caution in his voice. "Destroy it and throw it away. They are a vicious and cruel lot." The Preacher let that linger for a moment and then finished answering her question. "But I do not believe Tandy Warren has been around these parts for quite some time."

Amber only nodded, wishing she had never asked.

The Preacher closed the briefcase and looked at the time on his phone. "Well, I should be getting on my way," he said looking around the diner and then back to Amber. "I really do hope we meet again, my dear. I did so enjoy our conversation." He then walked out of the diner whistling that tune.

Amber did not know if she could reciprocate his sentiment.

CHAPTER XXI

1: Look Who's Watching

NATHAN WALKED OUT of the building and instantly felt something was wrong, it was in the air all around him. He casually looked around and to anyone that may have been watching him, would have thought just that.

Because there was someone watching him.

Nathan took out his phone and made it seem like he was tapping and sliding his phone like anyone normally would. But he was using the front-facing camera to zoom in behind him.

And there was the distortion, on top of the building across from Lily's, it was a Monster and most likely one of the ones he had been chasing ever since he got here. He put his camera away and crossed the street. Nathan waited until he was a few blocks away and then turned into an alley and blurred, making his way back.

2: One Way or the Other

Lily watched as the figure made its way close enough so she could confirm that it was indeed Rick, but much like his voice, his face seemed to be off. Suddenly she thought that now was no time to be standing still. She quickly reached out for the tablet as Rick now raced towards her. She knew it was one or the other and she also knew she wouldn't have the time to dial, even if it was only three digits. Letting Rick get to the tablet she backed up and opened the drawer, scrambling for the longest knife in reach.

And there they were. Rick stood on one side of the breakfast bar holding the tablet while she stood on the other side holding a knife.

"I just want to talk Lily," he said turning it off.

"I don't," she said raising the knife.

Rick confidently laid the tablet on the nook. "You won't hurt me."

"Oh I wouldn't be so sure," Lily said with a nervous smile. She could feel the apprehension growing inside, causing her to lean to her left and then to her right, over and over. Then, she noticed his face and realized why he looked so different and his voice was off. Rick looked as if he had been in a fight, and lost. The man she was terrified of was now standing in front of her, beaten and battered. He was not the unstoppable monster she feared all this time. He was just as capable of being every much the victim as she was. It made him look weak and pathetic. And although he was bigger and stronger than her, she did not seem to be as scared as she was a second ago. Smiling she nodded at his bruised and lumpy face. "Did you go and get yourself in an abusive relationship too?" she asked, almost regretting it the moment the words left her mouth. Her new sense of empowerment was a rollercoaster.

Rick chuckled mockingly. "That's funny Lily, no. This is the result of your new boyfriend blindsiding me."

"Like you blindsided Todd," Lily countered. Lily knew Nathan interrupted the assault, but she just assumed they ran away.

"That faggot embarrassed me," Rick said staring at the knife in Lily's hand and trying to calculate her intentions.

"The cops are looking for you Rick. Why are you here?"

"For you Lily—for us. I have to get you away from him," he said while making his way slowly around the breakfast bar.

Lily bit her lip and shook her head trying to hold back the tears. "You beat the shit out of me Rick," she reminded him.

"I didn't mean it," he said shamefully.

"What time, the first or the fiftieth?" she asked as if reminding herself.

"You know I have a problem."

"That doesn't make it okay," she cried.

"I'm getting better."

"How Rick, by almost beating my friend to death?"

"I had a setback, I—"

"I can't!" Lily yelled cutting him off as she watched Rick's face turn from ashamed to rage in a blink of an eye.

"Hey!" he yelled back while pointing his finger, "I said I was getting better." Now he was pointing the finger at himself. "I said I had a setback."

"And what happens when you have another setback Rick? Do you put someone else in the hospital? Maybe kill them? Maybe you kill me?"

He lowered his arm. "I would never…I just want another chance."

"Then turn yourself in and get help," Lily pleaded.

"I need you Lily, I have to leave. We – have to leave," Rick pleaded back, taking another step around the bar.

"I will go with you and I will help you, whatever way I can," she said wiping away the tears.

"And we can be together?" he asked as more of a threat then a question and then before she could answer he offered her a solution. "Then let's just go."

Lily laughed through her tears, "Go where?"

"Anywhere away from him. He's not human."

"You're not human, you're the monster."

"I'm not the monster here Lily," he tried to explain.

"Really, then how do you think we ended up here?"

He was quiet for a moment and then went to say something.

Lily interrupted. "You're not listening Rick," she said taking a deep breath and looking for the courage. It was slight, but it was there in a whisper when she exhaled. "We're over."

"Because of that… *thing* you're fucking?"

Lily snapped back, "That is none of your business."

Suddenly Rick took the tablet and began slamming it repeatedly across the edge of the breakfast bar.

Lily hoped that it was enough of a distraction and ran towards the hall. Suddenly she felt sleepy as the door at the end of the hall went up and out of view. It felt as if she was suspended in midair and then she confirmed the feeling as she looked straight ahead of her, but she was facing the floor.

Then it went dark.

3: Under the Moon the Nipple Clamps Shine Brightest

Without making a sound Nathan walked up behind to the figure standing on the rooftop across from Lily's apartment. Nathan peered over the shoulder of the unsuspecting Monster and could see that her balcony drapes were closed. Refocusing on the current problem he also noticed a table beside where the Solibus Monster was standing and it looked as if he had been watching Lily's apartment for some time. It was littered with lubricant bottles, an ashtray, cigarettes, tissue boxes and more lubricant.

This caught Nathan off guard. "What the…"

Startled the Monster turned around as his pants slid completely down to his ankles. Now standing in front of Nathan was a Sun Monster holding his hardened prick in one hand and he seemed to be twisting his nipples with the other, quite vigorously from the dark redness of them.

Suddenly Nathan didn't want to act upon his first reaction, in fact he didn't want to touch the Solibus at all. "Could you," he said and motioned for him to pull up his pants.

The Monster just looked at him with the appropriate amount of shock and annoyance. Then he looked past Nathan and made a clicking noise.

Nathan just shook his head. "Yeah, your Moons aren't coming to help."

The half-naked man stood for a moment with his hand still on penis. "You should not be here. James Franco is in the middle of something."

"Yeah I know, but…" Nathan started and then trailed off with a chuckle. He had forgotten that Solibus are named after ancient Egyptian Gods and since there are only a handful of names to choose from, they tend to take other names when coming of age. They have totally embraced the growing phony plastic celebrity lifestyle of Hollywood and the media. Being so egotistical about their looks and self-obsessed myth that they not only buy into the over-hyped world of beauty and celebrity, that they take the names of famous celebrities that are plastered all over the media. But the first name is not enough, the full name of the famous person must be used so that the full reference to the *beautiful* person is known. Some even changed their name when the actors or actresses grow old or lose their high standing in the media. Their Lunis or Moon children, who are also their protectors, are nowhere near what is considered attractive. For most Moons, *homely* would even be a stretch and thus given simple generic names. Nathan shook the chuckle away. "I'm probably going to regret this but why James Franco?"

"She called me a buff James Franco."

"So you changed your name to James Franco."

"Yes," James Franco admitted. "He's really famous, and good looking. Most of his movies are good. He modeled. I mean, the man did a stint on General Hospital for God's sakes."

"So why are you watching her?"

James Franco looked back at the balcony and then back to Nathan. "How do you know I wasn't waiting for the gay guys?"

Blurring towards him, Nathan wrapped his hand around the half-naked man's neck and lifted while his eyes turned on like a lamp in a dark room. "Wait. I remember you," Nathan said examining the man's face and letting his fangs spring from his gums with a loud click. "From the alley," he growled and lifted the Solibus higher into the air.

James Franco grabbed on to Nathan's hand and covered it with lube, strawberry flavor.

Nathan shuddered in revulsion. "That is so fucking gross!"

James Franco exhaled with difficulty. "I beg your pardon Chakan scum. I am a Solibus God. A true Sun. You are nothing but a—"

His sentence ended abruptly as Nathan tossed him into the side of the roof entrance where Mr. Franco let out a loud yelp and fell to the ground.

Nathan went to continue the assault when his eyes were directly confronted by the still fully erect penis that seem to glisten from the light overhead hitting the lubricant. "Okay, I swear dude, either pull your pants up, or that is going to the first thing I rip from your body."

"You should be honored by my Godly cock," he said starting to pull his pants up.

Nathan couldn't help but laugh. "You really are a weird fucking bunch. I guess I didn't give your friend enough time to remind me before I ripped her heart out," he said trying, and successfully getting the Sun Monsters attention. "Just off Division Street."

The Solibus' face became severe. "You killed Mila Kunis!" James Franco accused with courtroom gumption. "You will pay with your life."

Nathan just stood abashed. "Seriously? Mila Kunis? Jesus this is getting really hard to be serious about," he said gruffly with a mouthful of fangs. "But now I need you to answer a few questions. Why are you here, did someone send you?"

As soon as Nathan took another step closer the Monster started talking. "I met her in the alley that night you were chasing me."

"I know, she told me you went to Sips," Nathan growled.

James Franco smiled nervously. "Oh, she told you about that did she?"

"How you told her friend *that I could be mean and sometimes become violent?*" Nathan said bending down as the Solibus raised his hands, seemingly to protect his face. "I've had my fair share of dealings with Monsters. Even with your kind. But you're the first Monster that actually tried to cockblock me."

"Can't blame James Franco from trying," James Franco said with a *feeling sorry for himself* shrug.

Nathan took another step closer and growled.

James Franco raised his hands to the defensive position. "Okay-okay. She just does something for me."

"Wait," Nathan said calming a little. "Your kind only mate internally, incest like?"

James Franco shrugged. "We're trying new things?" he answered in the form of a question.

Nathan looked at the table with all the lube and nipple clamps. "Yeah, I can see that."

4: Dazed & Confused, with a Side of Splitting Headache

Lily felt dazed and as she opened her eyes she wondered why she was lying on the ground.

This was way too familiar, Rick must have put her here.

It felt like he'd hit her.

Seeing pieces of technology scattered around her, she then realized that he had thrown what was left of the tablet and caught her in the back of the head. At least that's what the pain in the back of her head was telling her.

Hearing him getting closer she frantically searched for the knife.

But she was already being flipped onto her back.

As he reached for her, Lily found the knife and swung it wildly.

He moved back fast enough for it to miss his eye, but not quick enough to avoid it completely. Grabbing his already spilling cheek in pain, he lurched backwards in agony.

Scrambling to her feet, she turned around and staggered towards the hall. Rick lunged forward with his right leg extended and caught her on the left butt cheek. It was with enough thrust that it sent her tripping forward where she slammed into the corner of the wall with her shoulder.

Sliding awkwardly to the floor, Lily rolled over holding her shoulder and started pushing herself towards the front door, but Rick was soon on top of her. He grabbed her by the hair and she screamed as he lifted her upwards. He struggled to hold her still when suddenly Lily thrust her hand forward and clamped down on Rick's face as hard as she possibly could. Dragging her fingernails across his flesh she hooked his lower eyelid and caused it to split.

Rick howled in pain and used his hand full of Lily's hair as leverage to spin her around towards the living room. Letting her go, Lily unwillingly ran with the momentum and crashed onto the coffee table. Magazines and Martin's mother's fruit bowl, which held everything but what it was supposed to, went flying before Lily herself slid off and landed on the floor.

Delicately, Rick dabbed the cut under his eye with his finger, wincing in pain. "You fucking bitch!"

Lily was already on her knees and shaking terribly. "What's the matter?" she stalled. Spitting the blood that was forming in her mouth Lily reminded herself that giving up was not an option, no matter how badly she wanted to. So as Lily stood up, she grabbed the glass bowl that was on the floor and held it behind her.

"I'm going to kill you," Rick said calmly and then suddenly darted towards her with his hands aiming for her neck.

Lily thought that he could not have made it any easier and swung. The glass bowl soared through the air until it connected directly into the side of his head, making a loud thump that sent Rick wobbling three steps to the side.

He caught his balance, now he was either hesitant or confused as to how to fall over.

Lily limped ahead and swung the bowl again.

This time, Rick caught her wrist and shot forward with his fist. Catching her in the face Lily wobbled backwards having no problem falling over and landed in between the coffee table and the couch. Letting out a harrowing cry she grabbed for the drapes as the pain lit up her back instantly as she tried to pull herself up. Unfortunately the rods were nowhere strong enough to sustain her weight and started to bend until the whole set up was pulled off the windows to the balcony.

Lily then decided to try and just straighten herself out to relieve the agonizing discomfort when all of a sudden the table was thrown to the side. It gave her a bit of relief that was short-lived as Rick grabbed her legs and pulled her away from the couch. Straddling her, he pinned her arms under his knees. The pain was unbearable, but she was still forced to endure it as his knees kept digging in.

Looking up she saw the damage she caused to his face and it made her laugh.

"What's so fucking funny?" Rick raged furiously.

"You're pathetic!" she screamed back.

He punched her in the face again, and the blood from her nose quickly painted her lips. "I love you Lily," he said shaking her head.

Lily started to cry but stopped, and just stared.

Rick cautiously let go of her head and smiled.

She felt the stare of domination on her like she had so many times before. And then unexpectedly, she spit the blood pooling in her mouth all over his face. Her mouth was left wide open and exposing her crimson stained teeth, as she looked almost as surprised as Rick.

The blankness in his eyes held steady as he wrapped his hands around her neck and started to squeeze.

5: Sometimes It Just Doesn't Work Out

James Franco hissed from the ground as his dirty red eyes exploded with hate and fear. His good looks seemed to disappear and now reflected his current mood. The corners of his mouth stretched and raced towards his ears as his gums seemed to pulsate. His mouth was now home to large yellowish and black teeth that were a wide range of shapes. Some were regular while others were sharp and pointed, but others were just jagged or broken. The greyish white around his eyes crinkled as his mouth widened and he let a wailing of a cry escape.

Nathan squeezed his neck tighter "Where's your nest?"

James Franco reeled in pain and said nothing.

Nathan lifted him and then slammed him right back down. "How many of you are here in the city?"

The Solibus laughed in agony, but still said nothing.

Nathan picked the Solibus monster up again, and again he slammed him even harder. "Are you working for anyone?" Nathan knew that this was unlikely since Solibus regard other Monsters as lesser and their larger than life ego would make it hard to broker otherwise. But he could not rule out anything when it came to Marcus. "Start speaking. Everyone knows Solibus aren't as powerful at night and it's a long time till sunrise."

"I need her," James Franco said with saliva crashing against its teeth like waves on rocks.

Nathan loosened his grip. "Why are you stalking Lily?"

James Franco suddenly smiled with revelation. "Her name is Lily. I love this Lily," he choked.

"You are about to be dead," Nathan said trying to attain the Sun Monster's attention.

James Franco turned to Nathan. "If you kill me, my brother, the great Channing Tatum will avenge me."

Nathan rolled his eyes. "Now I just feel absolutely ridiculous for even having this conversation," Nathan said and squeezed harder. "Start answering me, or I promise—I will kill you."

"I really should have eaten her days ago," James Franco spit in defiance.

Nathan jolted him forward, letting his blue eyes beam and teeth snarl. "Enough! Your species is a joke. You nest in groups because you are weak, feeding on the defenceless. You scurry away and hide in the darkness like cockroaches. Now, why are you watching Lily? Where is your nest? And who are you working for?"

Suddenly James Franco became very calm, turning his head slightly to look at Nathan unnervingly. "Yes. But we will come out of the darkness. We will feed upon them and when the humans are gone, we will feed upon your kind."

Nathan laughed. "There is not enough Solibus et Lunis on the planet, let alone in Chicago," he said knowing a nest would be nothing more than an annoying inconvenience, a hive on the other hand would prove to be problem.

Then the Solibus began to laugh as if he knew something that would shock him. "Forget it," Nathan said extending his claws and drove them into James Franco's shoulder.

The Sun Monster's eyes widened as a low squeal like moan exited his mouth. "Okay-okay-okay," James Franco surrendered. "They wanted us start mating outside of our gene pool, to build our ranks," he said looking at Nathan's disturbed facial reaction. "I know, I thought it was gross at first too."

"Who's us?"

"All of us, Suns and Moons."

"Keep talking," Nathan instructed still keeping his fangs and claws ready.

"Only two Suns can make another Sun and the pregnancy takes a decade. A Sun and a Moon can only make another Moon but they're born in two years," he said and then let his mouth curl that created a hideous smile. "And when our Moons mate with humans..."

Nathan was now intrigued. "Go on."

"It took. We give them an accelerant. It speeds up the birthing process by twenty times."

Nathan thought quickly. "That's just a month."

"Oh yes. And on top of that, they give birth to a minimum of five Half Moons. Half the power of a moon and half the intelligence,

I mean if you can imagine that," he said and then sighed in relief as Nathan withdrew his claws. "The human host never survives of course. And the Half Moons are the weakest of our lineage but like I said, they fill our ranks. We just have to collect the females to mate them."

"The hookers," Nathan concluded. "What about you, Suns mating with humans?"

James Franco scoffed. "A human sperm cannot penetrate a Sun's egg. And our sperm can penetrate theirs, but the child becomes too powerful too quick and starts to eat from the inside out to escape. Once the human host dies, the child dies within seconds."

"What about the homeless?"

James Franco looked at Nathan a little dumfounded. "We need to feed them."

"How many Solibus et Lunis are involved?"

James Franco started to laugh. "All of us you silly *Chakan*. They're bringing us all here by the boat loads. "

"Who is?"

"The—"

Nathan heard the click almost half a mile away and could hear the bullet screaming towards him. He could only move his head out of the way and when he did, he followed the bullet as it flew past him. Nathan turned back, staring right through the now large hole in James Franco's head and could see someone or something already packing up their gun. Nathan growled and dropped the dead Solibus, ready to blur, but then heard it come from behind him.

He spun around to see the drapes across the sliding door and windows being pulled down, and then watched as Rick threw a coffee table out of the way and dragged Lily away from the couch.

Nathan turned back trying to squint to see what type of Monster it might be that shot the Sun Monster, but he couldn't make them out.

Nathan began to panic as he looked at Lily now being punched in the face and then back to the Monster sharpshooter almost done packing. Then he saw Lily spit in Rick's face and the look of intent it had provoked in his eyes. "He's going to kill her."

He really did like her, so the city of Chicago would have to wait as he leapt to the ledge of the building and hurled himself towards Lily's balcony.

6: Dying is Looking into a Rear View Mirror and Seeing All of Your Regret

Lily knew she was going to die, and she began to panic. Her body thrashed beneath him, but his size anchored her to the floor. Feeling the lack of air as his grip tightened, she was no longer able to spasm. She arched her back one more time, as hard as she could while the heat from all the blood rushing to her face started to help wash away her ability to see.

Her back fell and pressed against the floor again as she became pissed that this asshole was the last thing she was going to see. She wanted to see Todd and Martin one last time and tell them how much she loved and appreciated them. She wanted to wish Jeanette so much luck with her five children and tell her to stop sleeping with men just to get them to like her, because there was so much about her to like. She wanted to tell Mary-Anne to stay in school and most of all, don't sleep with men just to get them to like her like Jeanette. She wished she had a chance with Nathan, something she felt she deserved—earned even. Nathan would have been a chance you only get once in a lifetime, which now seemed especially cruel since it seemed that hers was about to come to an abrupt end.

The pressure around her neck loosened and she saw Rick getting off of her.

Then it went black.

7: You Were Warned

Rick was not getting off of Lily as she was passing out, Nathan had grabbed him and then wrenched Rick off of her. And before Rick could comprehend what was going on he was sent flying over the breakfast bar and into the kitchen fridge. He crashed into the top freezer portion and instinctively grabbed at the door handle while trying to stop himself from falling. It did not work and he landed on his back hard, instantly winded.

Nathan kneeled down and put his hand on Lily's neck, he found her pulse and smiled briefly with relief. Closing his mouth to hide his fangs he kissed her gently on the forehead and heard Rick moan. The sound put him back into a fiery rage as he marched into the kitchen and looked down to see that Rick had made it to his knees.

Rick looked up confused, a confusion that quickly turned into fear as he realized he was looking at the same creature that almost took his life in the alley way. "You!" he gasped in horror.

Not wanting to wait anymore, Nathan wrapped his hand around Rick's neck. "I warned you," he growled while lifting him into the air like he was nothing more than an over stuffed toy, "I told you to leave."

"I—love—her," Rick sputtered as the pressure around his neck increased.

"Enough to die?"

Rick's face started to go bright red as air quickly became something of a limited quantity. "You can't kill me," Rick coughed.

"I can't?" Nathan mocked letting him go.

Rick was so weakened his legs could not support the fall, and they buckled.

Watching Rick collapse to the floor made Nathan grin.

Rolling to his stomach Rick took a deep and forced breath. "You'll be a murderer," he said starting to raise himself up.

"Oh Richard, if only you knew," Nathan revealed casually with a chuckle. Placing his foot on Rick's upper back he forced his body against the floor and continued to apply monstrous pressure.

"They'll catch you," he cried losing his breath while being forcefully compressed against the floor.

"Haven't been caught yet," Nathan said applying enough pressure to cause Rick's chest to start collapsing.

Rick wheezed while trying to get out from under the crushing strength of Nathan's foot, but he only struggled with no success. "I can't breathe!" he exclaimed going from red to blue expeditiously.

"That's the fucking point Rick. I'd say you're a minute or two from a full cardiac arrest." Nathan paused for a moment and decided to enjoy the fact that Rick could no longer speak, only squirm as his arms flailed and hands reached out to nothing. Then, it hit him. "Maybe we should make this look like a suicide," Nathan said inspired.

Before Rick could finish his breath he was lifted off of the floor by his shirt and then being carried like a suitcase across the room. Suddenly he was on the balcony and then dangling in the air over the safety of the railing by the back of his shirt. Rick let his legs and arms hang lifeless out of fear that the fabric of his shirt might not be able to hold all his weight.

Nathan turned his hand that was holding Rick's shirt slightly and Rick slowly rotated around to come face to face with Nathan.

Rick went to say something, only to be stifled by a deep growl that left Nathan's fangs exposed and saliva dripping from them. Rick closed his eyes and continued to help aid his life by trying very hard not to move.

Nathan yelled, "Open your eyes."

And when Rick did, Nathan dropped him.

Just as Rick was almost to the point of freefalling to the concrete below, Nathan shot his arm out and caught him by the neck.

Rick's hand clutched to Nathan's hands for dear life as his feet kicked repeatedly in search for something solid to appear underneath them. But there Rick dangled over the balcony, only feeling the fleeting emptiness under his feet and the grip of a Monster's hand around his neck. "Please!" Rick begged.

"Let you go?" Nathan said loosening his grip and letting him dangle a little more liberally. "Sure."

"No!" Rick screamed in a whisper.

"Maybe I should just eat you," Nathan said letting his eyes sharpen.

"What?" Rick blurted out and hoping he had heard him wrong.

Tightening his grip, Nathan pulled him over the railing and back into the apartment. He slammed Rick into the wall and widened his mouth to reveal the long razor like fangs protruding from the top and bottom gums.

Rick tried to scream.

Nathan shot forward and let his fangs dive deep into Rick's flesh. He pulled back, bringing a fresh bubbling hunk of meat with him.

Rick closed his eyes while grinding his teeth and making his entire body tense up to assist in working through the excruciating pain as he exhaled a long hollowing hiss. Then he opened his eyes just as his own flesh was being spit into his face, causing him to shudder and spit out a piece that had found its way into his mouth.

Nathan loosened his grip, allowing Rick to take a deep breath, but then tightened it and leaned into his ear. "Whether I eat you. Stab you. Or make it look like a suicide. You are not going to hurt Lily, ever again," Nathan said pointing to her without looking.

As Rick's eyes lit up, Nathan followed them to find Lily now awake and sitting up from the floor, staring in confusion at the puzzling violence in front of her.

She looked like she was processing the image slowly, but as she did her eyes widened expediently with the reality that she was looking at an actual living breathing nightmare.

Letting Rick go Nathan turned to her and cried out, "Lily!" He raced to her side and bent down, only to watch her eyes flutter before she passed out and let her head fall into his hands. Nathan held her closely and brushed the hair from her face, mindful of the all the new contusions. "I'm so sorry Lily," he said lightly kissing her forehead and laying her back onto the floor. He looked at her fragile face and frowned. "I should've been here sooner," he said apologetically. "I should've known," he hissed getting angrier as he spun around and rose to his feet, his eyes glowing and in a perfect pitch of anger. "I should've taken care of you in the alley, permanently!" Nathan snarled while closing in on Rick, who was trying to make his getaway by crawling towards the hall leading to the front door. Nathan, who was in no rush, joyfully inhaled the fear pouring into the room and finally caught up in time to see Rick turn around and see Nathan's claws extending slowly.

Rick returned to original plan and tried to scurry away as fast as he could.

It was not fast enough.

Suddenly Nathan's claws wrapped around Rick's ankle and as much as Rick tried, he could not stop himself from being dragged back down the hall. "No—No—Nooo."

CHAPTER XXII

1: 265

THE DARK BLUE COMPACT flew down Interstate 55 as the Crow sat behind the wheel, enjoying the ragtime jazz playing on the radio. The Raven sat in the passenger seat letting his head lean on the window, staring out and watching the night clouds rushing past them.

Noticing his less than excited mood, she turned down the radio. "I take it the job pays well?"

"Yes lover, very well indeed," the Raven said not taking his eyes off of the night sky.

"I am very excited about going to Chicago," she said glancing over at him.

"I know you are," he said, distant and still staring outside.

"What is wrong, my love?"

The Raven slowly turned his head. "It's this job, my depraved Angel of Death."

"What about it?"

He sighed, knowing the closer to Chicago they got, the more excited she would get. "The instructions for this job call for a lie low approach."

"How low?" she inquired.

"Complete and utterly."

"I see," was her response.

Expecting a little more protest, he explained in greater detail. "This is Marcus Licinius Crassus my love. You do know what this means if we are successful?"

"I have an idea," she said plainly.

"Then you know we must do this job perfectly. That means no night life, no chases, no fighting and absolutely no killing unless the job calls for it."

"And if we are attacked?" the Crow asked as if trying to find a silver lining.

"Then we will flee into the night and lick each other's wounds," the Raven said poetically.

The Crow rolled her eyes. "Like dogs."

"Yes my love," he said and then changed the tempo. "The money is enormous my pet. More than we have made in the last two decades."

Suddenly she started to perk. "Well, at least I can look forward to Montreal when we're done."

"Forget Montreal" he scoffed. "We will travel by boat to England. Then when we are bored, we will cross to France, to Paris. We will spend a mountain of money, for the most frivolous of luxuries," he said sliding towards her and started to undo her pants.

"What are you doing?" she asked surprised.

"All this talk about money has made me quite horny my love."

The car swerved and the Crow pulled the car straight as a car in the next lane honked its horn. "Should I pull over you *fucking* sex crazed lunatic?"

"That won't be necessary," he said pulling out his sickle and running it down her legs.

The Crow yelped in pain as the razor sharp blade split her pants fabric along with some of her skin. "Not very surgical Lover."

Finally he made it all the way down to her ankles and then ripped her pants off cleanly in one swift yank.

The Crow yelled in pain. "The friction burnt."

"And now I am going to make your pussy burn with desire until you are begging me to fuck you," he said letting his snake like tongue flicker frantically as he dropped his head and buried his tongue inside of her.

The dark blue compact began swerving all over Interstate 55 as it passed and almost clipped the familiar green highway sign. This one read: **Chicago 265 miles.**

2: 41 000 Feet Above Glasgow

A private jet soared through the sky above the city of Glasgow. Inside Tyre and Percy sat and drank, while Quinn just sat in his seat petrified. Three more men that were accompanying them sat near the back playing cards.

Percy took a large gulp and finished his rum. "So who we going to fuck over eh? Marcus or Miya – Mia – Miyamo-mo," he said laughing and reaching for the bottle. "The fucking Jap fellow."

"I say we fuck 'em all," Tyre said holding out his empty glass.

Percy filled it and smiled. "Yeah, fuck 'em," he laughed holding up his rum as they both raced to finish.

Hitting an air pocket the jet dropped they both watched as Quinn's eyes morphed in and out of their Elemental state.

Percy looked sad and worried as he turned to Tyre. "I forgot that the Elemental Puss has a fear of flying," he said and then started to laugh again.

Quinn gripped the arms of his chair so tight that he was indenting them with his claws. "Fuck off Percy. You knew that I don't like to fly."

Percy took another shot. "Well how the fuck did you think we were going to get across the Atlantic? In a fucking canoe?"

They hit yet another air pocket and watched as Quinn's eyes kept morphing back and forth while his claws extracted and retracted with every little bump.

"I don't get it," Percy slurred, "most of you Elementals soar through the sky like little fucking birdies."

"Actually it's more like riding the air," Quinn corrected. "And I don't."

Tyre leaned over and examined the sickly looking Elemental. "Christ Quinn," he said examining him. "You don't look so good."

Quinn's eyes yellowed and then changed as soon as the red finished its circle. His ears tightened to a point and then gave way back to its more human normalness. His lips pulled back in an evil smile to make room for rows of sharp pointy teeth, only to retreat and let his lips relax.

Percy joined the examination. "He looks like a fucking mental patient."

Tyre grabbed the rum and smiled at Quinn. "We're just fucking with ya," he said handing Percy his glass and pouring another for himself.

"Don't worry Quinn," Percy said slapping his leg and giving Tyre a wink. "Five more hours to go."

Quinn looked mortified. "Oh yeah, that's fucking lovely, thanks."

Tyre took a swig and was already laughing. "Then we fuel up in St. Johns and its back up into the air."

"Maybe I'll just take a cab from there," he said trying to stop from morphing, unsuccessfully.

Percy leaned in beside Quinn. "If you think about it eh, it's five-five and a half hours. We've been up here for a bit, but it's a three and a half hour time difference, so really, it's like ..." Percy trailed off while blowing his lips as he tried to do the math in his drunken state. "Shit, I think we should've landed twenty minutes ago." He held up his glass and turned to the three men behind them. "Brilliant, we're here," he bellowed taking another drink.

"What the hell are you talking about?" Quinn asked confused.

Percy put his arm around Quinn's shoulders. "I'm talking about you being so fucking stupid," he said giving him a big kiss on the cheek.

Tyre stared at his rum and became somewhat serious for a moment. "So after we fill up in St. Johns, we're going to get the man in the well. And I want Renny packed up and shipped to meet us there."

"The man in the well?" Percy asked surprised. "Why the fuck do you want to go and do that then?" Percy shook his head slowly. "Auntie is going to be right fucking upset she is."

"You just let me worry about that," Tyre said smiling again.

Percy poured them another drink. "And just so you know my son, I am totally fucking against prying that cunt from the well," he said raising his shot glass. "There, I've said my piece on the subject and that's the last you'll hear from me on the matter."

Tyre just rolled his eyes and took another drink and rolled his arm in a motion that said Percy was not done.

And he was right, Percy obviously did not say his whole piece. "I'm just fucking saying. Whatever sanity that bastard had, I'm sure he lost it from being locked in that well for centuries. But, you are the fucking boss and that is that."

"Thank you," Tyre said looking at Quinn and raised his eyebrows as if to say it wasn't over.

Percy went to take a shot and then stopped. "It's just that we were both so fucking betrayed by that cunt. To align himself with the Order and try to kill us like that, over and over," he said shaking his head and then snapping out of it. "Well, it's not like me to dwell on the past. So that's the last you'll hear on the subject from old Percival here."

Tyre leaned over to Quinn who was still morphing in and out, but at least distracted. "Wait until he sobers up. He won't fucking shut up about it."

Percy held the bottle upside down over his shot glass, which was only half full or to Percy, half empty. "Well that bottle did not last very long," he said turning to the three men playing cards at a small table. "Pass us another boys," he instructed and caught the bottle they tossed his way. "And why Renny? My ass has puckered close so tight just thinking of him," he said and stood up and bent over while opening the new bottle of rum. "Go ahead. I dare you to get a finger up there, not gonna happen my son."

"I like Renny," was Tyre's answer.

Percy frowned as he sat back down. "Not only is he a goddamn lunatic, but he's a disgusting perverted little deviant fucking weirdo."

Quinn was able to control himself briefly. "I have to agree with Percy Boss. Never met the man in the well and that's all but your business. But I have heard enough stories about Renny to be officially creeped out."

Tyre nodded and continued. "It'll be all right. I'll protect you."

Quinn looked a little concerned. "What does that mean then?"

Percy took a gulp of his rum and held up his finger. "But I am warning you, if he even looks like he wants to hump my leg, I'm putting him down."

Tyre laughed and took a drink. "If I'm to be honest, I think I miss his lunacy."

Percy slapped the table. "The fucking looney toon and the cunt in the well it is then," he said raising his glass, "Renny, bringer of death, Renny the rapist, Renny—"

"Rapist?" Quinn asked a bit perturbed and turned to Tyre. "Is that what you meant by protecting me?"

"Oh yes my son," Percy said turning to Quinn, "but don't worry, he only likes handsome young looking lads."

"I'm a handsome young looking lad," Quinn protested.

"I know you are," Percy informed him. "I meant that I don't have to worry because I'm fucking old and ugly," he giggled.

"Fucking lovely. Trip just gets fucking better and better doesn't it," Quinn said morphing again as they hit another air pocket.

"And remember," Percy said whispering loudly into his ear, "he's got an irregular Ring. A fucking Reader Ring like me. So whatever you think you can do to fight him off, he's already calculated it."

"Okay, fuck off now Percy," he said getting uncomfortable.

"Do you know he is also called the Mad Tickler?"

"Serious Percy, I don't want to hear it."

Percy could hardly speak because he was laughing so hard. "He likes to tickle his victims and hear them laugh before—before he violates their bum."

Tyre finally came to his rescue. "Don't worry Quinn, I won't let him do anything to your bum."

"Yeah, old Tyre here will protect you," Percy said offering Quinn a drink of his rum by putting it just under the Elemental's nose. They watched as Quinn turned away like the smell was going to make him sick and it made them laugh even harder as Percy roared, "What a fucking puss."

3: 25 Miles Outside of Yazoo City

Twenty-five miles outside of Yazoo City, a car pulled into a gas station and set off the bells. Almost instantaneously a young attendant came out to greet the Preacher who was getting out of the car.

Already turning on the pump and beginning to take off the fuel cap the young man asked, "How much can I get you sir?"

"Fill it up if you would, please," the Preacher answered.

"You got it," he said sticking the nozzle in.

The Preacher looked up and took a deep breath. "Beautiful night is it not?"

"Sure is. Would be better if I didn't have to work though."

He laughed. "Indeed."

"Where you heading?" the kid asked making small talk.

"Chicago."

"Never been," the young man admitted.

"Wonderful city."

"Business or pleasure?" the kid asked checking the meter.

"Business I'm afraid. When serving the Father, it is always business," the Preacher said looking back to the sky.

"At least you get to travel."

"Yes, Father has me going all over the world," he said reaching into his pockets and realizing he had no money on him. Walking behind his car and opening the trunk he grabbed a couple of bills out of the briefcase that was laying on top of the two dead mobsters. Then he heard the slightest shift of movement on the concrete. He didn't even have to raise his head to know the young man had followed him back and had seen inside the trunk. The kid was quick and if the Preacher had not been a Monster, he might not have noticed. But he was, and he did.

The young attendant was obviously trying to act as natural as possible. "And I guess your, or the clergy just gives you, um— assignments?" he asked patting the back of his jeans.

The Preacher sighed. The boy's speech was already broken with mistakes and he surmised that he was patting his back pocket to see if he had brought his knife to work. The Preacher also knew by the way the young man's eyes blinked and looked from the pump to the garage that he was debating. Most likely on whether or not to give an excuse to go back and call the police now or finish the transaction and call when the Preacher had left. "Something like that," the Preacher answered a little agitated. If only he had remembered to take some of the cash out for pit stops just like this. Taking a few more bills, as to not make the same mistake twice he closed the trunk.

The nozzle violently clicked and came to an abrupt stop. The young attendant shut the pump off and checked the total.

He obviously decided that he would call the police when he went in to make change.

The attendant took a deep breath and began to turn around. "Okay, that'll be—"

The Preacher was already standing in front of him with his hand around his neck. His eyes glowed so inhumanly bright from the overhead lights that the kid stood hypnotized, briefly.

The young man tried to say something, but a loud crackle, like celery being twisted ended the sentence before it even began. The attendant just dropped to the ground and lied lifeless on the cold concrete.

"And here I said that I didn't plan on murdering anyone else this evening. I am truly sorry, my boy," the Preacher said apologetically.

Grabbing the young man by the ankle, he dragged him around to the back of the car. Opening the trunk he picked the boy up off the ground as one might a bag of groceries and then dropped him inside with the others. He raised his eyebrows and paused for a moment. "It is a long drive I suppose," he said and then tore into the boy's chest. Blood sprayed across the trunk, painting the metal and staining the upholstery. "Suppose I should have gotten the extra insurance," he chuckled to himself and slammed the trunk shut.

Opening the door he slid in and started the car while looking out beyond the highway. "The modest Rose puts forth a thorn. The humble sheep a threatening horn. While the Lily white shall in love delight. Nor a thorn nor a threat stain her beauty bright," he said poetically. "Dear Mr. William Blake," he continued quietly to himself and bit into the heart. He pulled his head back with a fight, making it look as if he was eating a piece of human taffy, until it finally snapped. "Who is this Lily in Chicago?" the Preacher asked with his mouth full.

The car pulled out of the station and headed down the black stretch of road. And as the red lights glared back at the empty gas station, "Blue on Blue" by Bobby Vinton played on the radio in the abandoned shop.

Finally, the red taillights disappeared into the distant night, getting that much closer to their destination, Chicago.

CHAPTER XXIII

1: Was It a Dream?

LILY SLOWLY OPENED HER EYES and recognized those all too familiar pings in her head. The pain started to flood into her body, Rick obviously didn't kill her and she noticed that she was still in her apartment. "Thank God," she said grateful that she didn't wake up in the hospital, or worse, chained up in a basement. Then, she noticed the apartment did not look disturbed at all. "What the hell," she said standing up from the couch a little too fast. She had to catch her balance and it made her wobble for a moment as she let her body catch up. Lily slowly looked around and took stock. The coffee table was right where it was supposed to be, along with her magazines. Martin's mother's fruit bowl was full of keys and other junk that it had collected over time. Then she remembered and rushed to the end of the kitchen by the hallway where she had cut him.

No sign of blood.

She walked back to the couch and moved the coffee table. She knew she bled on the floor, but it was perfectly clean. If she did not actually feel the bruises and cuts, she would swear she had dreamt the entire thing.

"I cleaned up," Nathan said calmly from behind her.

Spinning around she saw Nathan holding a bag that looked like it had clothes in it. Glancing down, Lily noticed she had different clothes on. She turned back to Nathan with a look that demanded an explanation.

He evidently read it clearly. "I cleaned your cuts and got you out of your blood-stained clothes," he said holding up the bag that did indeed contain her blood stained clothes.

Marching over to him Lily ripped the bag out of his hand. "You changed me?" she asked infuriated.

"Just the outer clothes, I didn't peek, or do anything perverted, I swear," Nathan said raising his right hand as if he was being sworn in by a court of law.

"Where's Rick?" she demanded.

"Gone," Nathan said quietly.

Suddenly she started to get a little nervous. "Did you eat him?"

Nathan gave her a look as if he was clueless as to what she meant. "What?"

But his eyes gave him away, Lily saw that he knew exactly what she was talking about. "You changed."

"I don't know what you're—"

"Don't," she interrupted him with her hand raised and body as stiff as a stop sign.

Nathan went to say something and then paused. "Yes. I changed."

"Show me," she said diving right in.

"Show you?" Nathan asked surprised.

Lily walked up to him and took a very deep and apprehensive breath. "Show me."

"I don't want to scare you Lily."

"I'm not going to be afraid anymore."

Nathan nodded.

Lily heard a few pops and crackles that made her twitch and step back as she watched Nathan's clothes get tighter on him as his body grew slightly bigger. Then she watched as claws slid out from under his fingernails while fangs emerged from his gums and overlapped his regular teeth. His eyes beamed and seemed to use the glare off of the lights until they glowed all on their own.

He stepped towards her holding out his hand.

Lily screamed and instinctively threw a right hook across Nathan's face, making a loud painful smacking sound. Unfortunately for her, it was not painful for the receiver. Lily however staggered backwards and shook her hand feverishly as it felt like someone had just dropped a cinder block on it. And although it didn't help, she blew on it frantically as she alternated lifting her legs very high and very slowly in an awkward circular march.

"I'm sorry," Nathan said, his fangs slightly interrupting his speech. Reaching out and wanting to comfort her, he forgot he still looked the part that ignited her terror.

Turning towards the apology Lily quickly screamed again. Obviously not thinking it through Lily threw a left hook across the other side of his face causing her hand to throb instantly. "Fuck me," she yelled doing a 360 and skipping faster and more frantic then before.

Nathan looked dumbfounded and helpless. "You said you weren't afraid."

Lily stopped blowing on her hand and looked at him. "Of a man— not afraid of any man. You just grew claws and sprouted goddamn fangs."

"Can I change back?" Nathan hoped.

"Did you eat him?" she asked returning to the blowing on her hands thing.

Nathan rolled his eyes. "I don't really eat people. Not like you think," he said looking as if he wasn't sure if he used the right words.

She looked at him stunned. "That was not really an answer that instills comfort Nathan." But Lily was easily pulled into distraction and became very curious. "Are you a vampire?"

"*No*," Nathan replied as if he was being insulted.

"Werewolf?"

"Nope," he said raising his eyebrows, obviously knowing where this was going.

She stepped a little closer, forgetting the pain she was in and started to study him. "Alien."

"I'm not a Hollywood monster," Nathan said and took a step towards her.

Lily squealed as she stumbled backwards and fell on her ass, atop of the coffee table. "Don't eat me," she said turning away and raising her hands while using her fingers to make a cross.

Nathan just shook his head and leaned down in front of her. "Again, I don't eat people, and I am not a vampire," he said flicking her fingers apart as Lily yelped.

She slowly turned her head back around and opened her eyes. She looked at the Monster in front of her and suddenly started to see the man it was.

Nathan knelt cautiously and then slowly brought his hands closer until they caressed Lily's cheeks. "*Rick* was a monster. *He* was going to kill you."

"But did—"

"I swear to God Lily, if you ask me if I ate him again."

Lily sat quietly for a moment and then smiled. "What? You'll eat me?"

Nathan started to laugh in his Monstrous state and Lily could not believe how normal it seemed. The man she fell for was kneeling right in front of her, he just had fangs and claws. The last man she dated was a monster who actually attacked her on a regular basis and just tried to kill her. She thought if this Monster wanted to beat on her or eat her he would have done it already. Then she realized this was the same Monster who not only saved her tonight, but from the bus as well. He saved Todd from being beaten to death. Not to mention paid for every hospital bill with no expectation of being paid back, all in the name of friendship.

Nathan gave her a warming smile. "Before you woke up and attacked me, I was about to take you to the hospital, you know, at the very least you have a concussion. Even though I'm pretty sure the good people at Northwestern Memorial are going to start getting suspicious of me."

Lily stopped and her eyes lit up just before she slapped him in the arm.

"Ow," Nathan embellished. "What was that for?"

"Earlier tonight. That was your eyes glowing."

"They don't really glow, not like you think. You see they attract the light and capture it. Like a solar panel," he said sarcastically going into teacher mode.

She slapped him on the arm again.

He laughed. "Yeah that totally was my eyes," he admitted as they both laughed.

Reaching out she let her hand observe every monstrous inch of his face with the most unintimidating curiosity. Lily brushed her fingers along his cheek and looked at his hand as he raised it for her. She took her one hand and placed it on his wrist and then led her fingers to the tips of his claws. Looking at his eyes, she became almost hypnotized. "What are you?"

"I'm just me."

Closing her eyes Lily let Nathan kiss her gently. She could feel the pressure and outline of his fangs and then thought of how hot it seemed. Then, she started to laugh at how perverted that seemed.

Nathan pulled back. "What's so funny?"

"Nothing," she said letting the laughter subside to a grin and then leaned into his ear. "My boyfriend is a monster."

Nathan leaned into hers. "My girlfriend is a dork."

Lily had a thousand questions to ask as she threw her arms around him, but for now she just wanted to kiss him...and he wanted the same.

TO BE CONTINUED IN

**MY BOYFRIEND IS A
MONSTER
2**

MORE GREAT READS
FROM BOOKTROPE

Saving London by **Taylor Dawn** (Urban Fantasy) After devastating news, London maps out her last year of life on a journey to complete a bucket list. What she didn't expect was for a mysterious stranger to show up who isn't quite human.

Sally Singletary's Curiosity by **J.M. Cataffo** (Urban Fantasy) Can a teen sleuth find a way to stop a plot that may have far-reaching consequences for all of mankind, or will Sally Singletary's Curiosity lead to the end of humanity?

The Elemental by **Lisa Veldkamp** (Paranormal Fantasy) Time is running out and only the elemental can save the world.

Through Love and Hate by **Jennifer Felton** (Paranormal Fantasy) What would you sacrifice to save someone you love?

Gravedigger by **Michael-Israel Jarvis** (Fantasy) Gravedigger subverts the expectations of that oldest of foes in fantasy, the dead that walk, in a fast-paced adventure through a world of culture, intrigue, magic and blood.

Would you like to read more books like these?
Subscribe to **runawaygoodness.com**, get a free ebook for signing up, and never pay full price for an ebook again.

CPSIA information can be obtained at www.ICGtesting.com
Printed in the USA
LVOW07s1016290116

472236LV00005B/224/P